LOVE'S SECRET FIRE

RENA KOONTZ

ISBN: 978-1-7322709-3-0

ISBN: 1-7322709-3-7

www.renakoontz.com

First published in 2012 by Crimson Romance

ALSO BY RENA KOONTZ

Other Heels & Handcuffs Novels

The Devil She Knew

Thief Of The Heart

More From This Author

Crystal Clear Love

Broken Justice, Blind Love

Off The Grid For Love

ACKNOWLEDGMENTS

I thank:
My husband, Jed, for traveling this road to publication with me.
My friend, Gina, for convincing me this is what I was meant
to do.
My friend, Shirley, for her vision to see what I miss.
My RWA group, NEORWA, for their support and motivation.
My Crimson Romance editors, Jennifer and Julie.
Police, fire and law enforcement personnel everywhere.

For Jed

1

Valerie Daniels maneuvered the green beans on her plate with her fork, creating the letter "D."

"D" for dull. How much more of this boring man could she stand? If only she'd stuck to her guns and met him for lunch instead of an early dinner, she'd be long over her misery by now.

His lips were moving, but she'd tuned him out thirty minutes ago. He looked at her like he expected a response. She forced a smile. "Pardon me?"

"I asked what it would take to make you famous. Wouldn't you like to be an anchor on the national nightly news?"

"Maybe someday. I have to earn my way into a position like that. This is only my second news job and it's technically part-time. I have to pay my dues first and, as they say, earn my stripes."

"But all you need is one big story to send you to the top, right?"

"It really doesn't work that way." She repositioned the green beans into the letter "L." Loser.

Richard Fredtoni had spent most of the evening talking about himself and how, as the new financial officer for the county, he could salvage the financially strapped district. She'd asked him for details, pressed for specifics. But he circumvented each question with a lot of hot air. She'd studied the county budget and knew its weaknesses. He spoke as if he'd not reviewed a single line-item. If he had a plan, it didn't have any teeth.

She hadn't been able to coax him to reveal what the county was paying for his so-called expertise, either. Now that would make a good news story. But instead, he droned on like a bee trapped between the glass and window screen and the interview she'd hoped to record in her notebook had dissolved into doodles.

"You've hardly touched your dinner." Spoken in a monotone. "Aren't you hungry?"

"Not really. It was very good though." In truth, Chez Cher's was her favorite seafood restaurant and the salmon had been expertly seasoned. Well worth the hour drive. She loved the main dining room's seashore motif with its small, round, intimate tables, and the subtle sounds of waves crashing that piped softly through the acoustical system.

If she closed her eyes, she could almost smell the ocean. With the right dining partner, the restaurant was the perfect prelude for a romantic evening. But Richard sure didn't fit the bill. Would he notice if she covered her ears to muffle the whine of his words?

"How about another drink?"

Valerie shook her head. She'd made sure to sip only one glass of white wine. A tiny voice nagged her that something about him was out-of-sync, and she usually listened to that voice. She'd felt it in his initial weak, clammy handshake weeks ago. She'd seen it in his smile that was dangerously close to a leer. And he was perspiring, despite the room's comfortable temperature. She didn't trust him.

Why the heck had she agreed to go out with him? Her boring —make that nonexistent—social life must have seemed exceptionally bad this morning when she agreed to this meeting. That's all it was, a meeting between two professionals. It fell way short of a date.

"Would you like some dessert?"

"No, thank you."

Richard signaled for the check and she said a silent prayer of thanks. As she reached for her purse, he offered to walk her to her car.

Sitting alone at the bar, Adam Michaels watched the couple. He'd recognized Valerie Daniels the minute she walked into the restaurant. A group from her radio station had toured the agency last year and he'd noticed her then. Striking good looks, runner's legs, and a killer smile that weakened his knees.

He'd tried flirting with her, but she blew him off by saying she'd call him. She never did. He became an avid listener to her morning radio show after that, despite being a devout country music fan.

Valerie rarely disclosed details about her personal life on the air. On the few occasions she mentioned a fun-filled weekend or wonderful dinner, he'd wondered about the man she likely spent it with. Her demeanor tonight, though, told him she wouldn't be talking about this dinner date unless it was begrudgingly.

Observing body language was second nature to him, even when he wasn't on duty or working undercover, and hers spoke volumes. She checked her watch every two or three minutes. She followed every new diner with her eyes, paying more attention to them than the man across from her. And whatever was on her plate had to be mush by now. She'd shoved it around enough with her silverware. Whoever this guy was, he'd struck out.

As Valerie and Mr. Loser walked out of the restaurant, Adam checked the time himself. He should probably hit the road, too. It hadn't been that great a night for him either. Ending his latest relationship had been ugly, despite the public place he'd chosen to give her the news.

Asking that woman out had been a big mistake. He appreciated a woman who depended on him, but this one had been downright suffocating. He needed a clear head for the five o'clock meeting tomorrow morning with the brass.

Christ, who held meetings at five in the morning? It was a good thing they summoned his partner as well or he'd be worried his ass was in trouble again. Neither of them had a clue about the topic of the mandatory, top-secret session. He finished his beer, paid his tab and walked outside, turning up his jacket collar against the chilly night air.

For a restaurant as popular as this one, the poorly lit parking lot surprised him. He stepped carefully into a gravel area set apart from the main lot and designated for overflow cars, aware of crunching pebbles beneath his boots.

Several parking spots ahead, he noticed two outlines in the shadows. Were they making out in the parking lot? Not the most romantic spot, but his track record with women proved he didn't know much about romance. He'd walk by as quietly as the stones beneath his feet would allow.

Then he heard the scream.

Richard waited while Valerie dug into her purse for her keys. She touched the unlock button on the keyless remote, forced a smile, and turned toward him. "Thank you for a nice evening."

He caressed her cheek. "Are we going back to your place or mine?"

Valerie jerked her face away from his hand. What the hell? "I'll call you." No smile of any kind, this time.

"I don't think so."

He grabbed her shoulder and forced his body against hers. "I didn't just spend one-hundred dollars on you to get a goodnight kiss at the car."

The air rushed from her lungs when he shoved her against the door. He made a clumsy grab at her breast, yanking at her clothes, and leaned in to kiss her. Her neck muscles strained as she forced her head backward to avoid his lips. Stale beer breath assaulted her nose.

"Let me go," she hissed. Using the car for leverage, she balled her fists and slammed them into his mushy stomach. His sour breath expelled in a whoosh but he pressed harder against her. She was at least six inches shorter and, suddenly, small and vulnerable.

With two hands, he captured her arms and dragged them to the top of the car roof, lifting her breasts into his chest. Cool air kissed exposed skin as her shirt tugged free from her waistband. She struggled against his clamped fingers, feeling her watchband cut into her wrist.

He leaned forward again to kiss her and she pressed backward, exposing her neck to his mouth. Nausea rose in her throat when his tongue spread warm slobber on her skin. His knee wedged between her legs as he leaned his full weight against her. His erection dug into her thigh.

Oh God. She couldn't breathe. She squinted and scanned the parking lot. Not a soul in sight. She was alone. There was no one who could help. The door handle dug into her lower back. Pain surged the length of her spine as his hot mouth kissed her ear. Surely he wouldn't...

"This isn't the way I wanted it, but you must like it rough." The words weren't spoken, they were growled, low and slow, like a crazed dog. Valerie tightened her leg muscles and arched her back to drive him off, but there was no budging him. Sweat soaked through her blouse as she struggled and screamed.

"Let me go. Get off me you, moron."

Richard sank his teeth into her shoulder. And then pain, sharp, quick, biting pain. She screamed again.

Adam bolted toward the scream and witnessed the scuffle. He grabbed the bastard by the shoulders, yanked him backward and threw him, hard, against the car parked in the next space. Glancing quickly at the woman, he didn't recognize her. Her head was low between her arms as she clung to the car.

Her shirt was ripped and with each heave of her chest, her left breast exposed itself in the dim light. A pitiful croak escaped her. The sound infuriated him. He despised men who preyed on women. He refocused on the asswipe trying to catch his breath against the other car. Two quick shots to the face, the last jab directly against his mouth. He deserved it.

"The lady said no, pal." Trained in self-defense, he anticipated a reaction. With clenched fists and bent knees, he stepped in front of the woman, ready for the lunge. The night air cut into his lungs. The man steadied himself on the car and raised one arm, panting when he spoke.

"You're interfering with private business. My wife and I like to playact. Everything's fine."

Adam couldn't see his face clearly but sweat pooled on the man's upper lip. A husband wouldn't be that worked up. Why wasn't the wife saying something?

"Is that right ma'am?" Adam posed the question over his shoulder, never taking his eyes off the attacker. She breathed in air in gulps, still trying to catch her breath. A trembling hand touched him between the shoulders.

"No. Please don't leave," she croaked. "He was trying to rape me."

The fool lunged at Adam and that was all the invitation he needed. He sank his right fist into the left side of the asshole's face, scraping his knuckles on his teeth. The blow knocked him back against the car and down to the ground. He reached to grab Adam's leg, but Adam kicked his arm away, dropped down on one knee and punched him in the face a second time.

"Stay down if you know what's good for you." He prayed the lowlife wouldn't heed the warning. He wanted more of this creep. The man exhaled, laid his head on the cement and closed his eyes. Adam flexed his right hand, noticing blood on his already stiffening knuckles. When was the last time he'd been in a fight? He couldn't remember, but this was kind of exhilarating.

The loser didn't look like he was going to move so Adam stepped to his left to help the woman. Only then did he recognize Valerie Daniels, trembling and struggling to regain her composure. Her face was streaked with tears and makeup. A huge blotch of blood spotted her neck. Did the bastard bite her?

If she was in shock, she'd react violently if he touched her. Once again, he anticipated the response. He slowly raised his hand toward her shoulder and she immediately screamed and flailed at his arm.

"Don't touch me."

"It's all right, ma'am." He deliberately kept his voice level. "I'm not going to hurt you. I was just going to cover you up."

Her eyes followed Adam's. She gasped when she discovered her breast hanging out of her ripped blouse. Her hand shook as she yanked at the fabric to cover herself.

"Do you want to press charges, ma'am?"

"No."

She said it too quickly and too loud. It was a panicked response. She raised wild looking eyes to him.

"No, please. No police."

"I'm sort of the police, ma'am. I could be your witness."

∽

Valerie shook her head emphatically. Oh God. There couldn't be an official report. The competing news stations would have a field day if they knew she had dinner with a county consultant and it had gone bad. This was just a business meeting, but what if Richard twisted the evening into a date that she'd proposed? Or worse.

It was unethical to date someone she worked with, whether at the station or in the regular course of business. She'd be fired, her dreams of becoming a successful newswoman dashed.

Her stomach turned when she looked at Richard. "I don't want to report this to the police. He won't come near me again. If-if he does, I won't hesitate to call the authorities."

She looked at her Good Samaritan and pleaded. "Please. I-I don't want anyone to know this happened."

On the ground, Richard's coat buttons scraped the pavement when he moved. She gasped but her rescuer stepped in front of her again, his fists clenched.

Richard held out his hands and mumbled "no more." He eased up onto one knee and used the car to rise to his feet.

Wiping blood from his mouth and nose he glared at her. "This was a mistake, Valerie. A big mistake." He stumbled away swearing at a foursome in the parking lot who walked into his path. A scowl creased his face when the man who'd saved her turned. "Do you want me to take you to the hospital?"

He towered over her by more than a foot. But his height didn't pose the threat that Richard's had. She relaxed against the car. "No. I just want to go home."

"You really should report this, ma'am."

Her teeth clenched. She was trying desperately to hold it together, and he wasn't helping. Tears threatened to spill and that would be her undoing. She took a deep, fortifying breath.

"No, please." Had he heard her? It was barely a whisper. "No police."

He stared at her as if debating whether to argue the point. Then his shoulders relaxed. "Where are your keys?"

"I-I don't know. I must've dropped them."

He knelt on the ground, running his hands over pebbles and dirt. In the dark, he couldn't find them. "I have a flashlight in my car. Wait here, I'll get it."

She nodded, refusing to look at him, her embarrassment was so intense. Thank God it was dark.

She saw him running back toward her when she drove out of the parking lot, her knuckles white as she clutched the steering wheel and sped home. She willed her eyes not to water until she'd driven into her garage and turned off the engine. Then she dropped her head to the steering wheel and cried.

Jesus. She was almost raped. She eased out of the car on shaking legs and walked through the garage door into the kitchen. Tossing her purse on the counter, she kicked off her heels and went into the adjacent half-bath. A blotch of crusted blood and the start of purple discoloring marked the spot where Richard bit her. It throbbed in time with the pounding in her head.

Trembling, she fingered her broken bra strap and assessed the ripped sleeve of her blouse. It was ruined. She leaned against the sink, taking deep breaths, counting out loud. She'd read once that was a way to force your body out of a trauma. "One."

"Two." Don't pass out.

"Three. Four." She dropped her head back and winced as the broken skin tightened.

"Five. Six." She swayed on the way to the kitchen, using the wall, the chair back and the counter for support to reach the freezer. She removed the bottle of vodka, popped the stopper and filled a shot glass with the thick, chilled liquid. She threw it back in a single swallow.

The heat of the alcohol sliding down her throat steadied her nerves. Closing her eyes immediately brought the feel of Richard's hands and mouth on her, and she shuddered. She ran to the master bathroom for a long, hot shower, letting the beating water work the tension from her muscles.

Gingerly, she stepped from the shower on legs that still quivered. Despite the alcohol and the soothing hot water, her hand shook while she smeared an antiseptic ointment on her neck. The healing salve pinched and burned.

She wrapped herself in the fat folds of her oversized cotton bathrobe and strode barefoot to the kitchen for another jigger of vodka. Without it, she wouldn't be able to sleep.

After crawling into bed, she propped the pillows against the headboard and leaned back, staring at the opposite wall. The whole evening was like a bad dream. Her trembling resumed simply reliving the events in her mind. If only she could tell someone who would help her sort everything out. But it was better if no one knew.

She didn't even dare tell her brother. Like most twins, they shared a bond closer than the average brother and sister. Vince was nine minutes older and her protector from her first memories. He would surely go after Richard if he found out what happened. His temper rivaled hers.

She swallowed the second vodka and placed the empty glass on the nightstand. Tugging the bed sheet and blanket up to her neck, she sank deeper into the pillows and closed her eyes. She wanted to forget tonight had ever happened.

She conceded a moment's pang over the man who helped her. She hadn't even thanked him. But when she'd moved her foot and her keys scraped the cement beside her shoe, her only thought was to get the hell out of there. It was lucky he didn't recognize her. Thank goodness she would never see him again.

gent Adam Michaels looked at the five printed fire reports spread in front of him. It had to be more than a coincidence, the boss was saying to the half-dozen agents sitting around the conference table.

"It's a stretch but there is a detectable pattern. Each fire gets a little bigger than the previous one, like a stripper peeling off her clothes slowly to entice the audience. The guy gets a little hornier each time."

Manuel Sanchez, the assistant director in charge of the agency, fanned out his copies of the yellow pages and pointed to the first. "The first one was this wooden playground set after hours at a local elementary school. Small and not much value. Then the ticket booth at the football field that mysteriously exploded after the football game. A little bigger and some stragglers to witness it."

He pointed to the third sheet. "Here, he gets a little bolder. Two car fires, one parked in a detached garage that destroyed the car and the structure. Fortunately, the occupants weren't home but we have to ask, did he know that? Then, this abandoned house last week and earlier today a second abandoned house.

Bigger buildings. Bigger balls. How did he know those structures were empty?"

The question was rhetorical but around the table, heads nodded. Sanchez continued. "We don't have details yet for the fire this morning, but that brings the number to six. All suspicious and all within the last two months. I think we have an arsonist playing a deadly game. So does the Benton Falls public safety director. He's asking for our help."

Adam's boss leaned forward. "What's your proposal for us?"

Sanchez looked at Adam. "We want to place Michaels in there undercover as a fire investigator. He's familiar with procedures because he was a volunteer fireman with his hometown fire department. He has incendiary training, and he's worked arson cases before. He can pose as Gina Gordi's boyfriend."

Adam shot a quick glance to his partner, Gina, and winked as she rolled her eyes and studied duplicate copies of the reports. Sanchez went on.

"We want Agent Michaels to chum-up with the men in the Benton Falls fire department. We suspect it's one of them. Gordi is already set up undercover on the Sanchillio racketeering case in the bar that is five blocks away from the fire station, and we know some of the firemen frequent there.

"Gordi's primary focus should remain the Sanchillio family. Michaels will work the arsons. Dropping him in the bar with Gordi provides a backup for her, even though the Sanchillios will know he has a badge. Who knows, maybe they'll try to add him to their payroll. That would be a bonus to our case."

The boss jumped from his seat, his palms coming down hard on the table. "Are you crazy? Gordi is in there undercover. You can't send someone flashing a badge in there unless you want to preside over both their funerals. And Michaels is too local for this assignment. We should bring someone in from out of state for something like this."

Sanchez held up his hands to interrupt the challenge. "There isn't time. The City of Benton Falls is a hundred miles away from headquarters. Agent Michaels, have you heard of it before?"

He hadn't heard of the Pennsylvania town until Gina drew her assignment there two months earlier. His boss wasn't ready to concede.

"So his geography is bad. That's not a reason—"

Sanchez stepped on his words. "This isn't open for debate. Not even the fire chief will know Michaels' true identity. As far as he is concerned, the state is sending an inspector to be a pain in everyone's ass while he noses around."

Turning to Adam he added, "Michaels, given your history with this agency, I know that won't be a problem for you."

Sanchez leveled a cold stare on the semi-circle of agents. "Orders from higher up are to move fast and to focus on the firehouse. Statistics show it's often a fireman setting arson fires to get his rocks off."

Adam's boss attempted to protest again, but Sanchez cut him off. "I told you we don't have a choice. It seems the Benton Falls public safety director and our director are boyhood friends. This is a directive right from his desk with instructions to implement it immediately. The assignment is on."

He passed Adam an oversized white envelope that held a fire inspector's badge and credentials with Adam's picture, a printout detailing Adam's exaggerated fire career, and other items he'd need for his new persona as Inspector Adam Mitchell. Sanchez stood, indicating that the meeting was over.

They'd orchestrated this rendezvous in the conference room of an insurance office thirty miles from Benton Falls because it was safer than bringing Gina into the office. You never knew who was watching.

"Show up at the fire station tomorrow morning," Sanchez told Adam. "You'll be working shifts with the men, so take your toothbrush. When you're not on the job, you'll be with Gordi."

He directed the partners to leave by the front door while the rest would leave at varied intervals to avoid suspicion. "Check in as usual, Gina."

She nodded and winked at Adam. "Well, honey, let's get this show started."

Adam picked up his cowboy hat, grabbed her hand, and they walked out of the building. Besides work, they spent much of their free time together and people often mistook them for a couple, which is what they wanted today. His six-and-a-half-foot frame complemented her five-feet-seven-inch stature, which appeared taller in the three-inch heels she regularly wore. Today, as always, she looked like a model.

Adam squeezed Gina's hand. "If they only knew you'd be the last woman I'd hook up with."

Gina chuckled. "Yeah well, don't think you'd even get the chance."

She'd been his partner for more than five years and his best friend for most of that time. Together, they were one of the most successful investigative teams in the agency. Two more years of breaking big cases and they each would be able to name the city where they transferred and select the squad they wanted to work on permanently. Few agents found themselves in that position.

Gina already knew she wanted to move back to her hometown, Pittsburgh, and work white collar crime. He wasn't sure where he wanted to end up. He was an only child and, in some ways, Gina was the sister he never had. Even though he was twenty-eight, four years older than her, most times she filled the role of older sibling.

While he was still sowing his wild oats, she was plotting a steady life course. Gina was engaged to a man whom Adam liked a lot. He likewise trusted his beloved's safety with Adam at her back. Because of the success of their partnership, Adam thought he, too, might settle in Pittsburgh. They had good sports teams. It would be a far cry from Louisiana, the place he still considered home. But there wasn't anything or anyone for him to go home to in Louisiana.

Working together undercover seemed almost normal. Twice they'd posed as husband and wife. They were as close as a man and woman could be without intimacy. Thankfully, they stopped just short of crossing that line one night after too much tequila, which cemented their friendship.

"How'd you scrape your hand?" she asked when they were outside.

"I rescued a damsel in distress. It's a long story. I'll tell you later."

"How do you want to play this? Want to come to the bar tonight and show your face or start tomorrow in an official capacity?"

"Tomorrow will be soon enough." He kissed her on the cheek, in case the other buildings had eyes. They started their cars and drove their separate ways.

Adam strolled into the Benton Falls fire station shortly before eight the next morning dressed in his navy blue suit, white dress shirt, a multi-colored blue tie and black leather western boots. He was a country boy at heart who longed for his jeans and Stetson. But undercover meant concessions and he had to look governmental.

A bell, similar to the one that let students know their school day is over, alerted the men in the living quarters upstairs that someone was downstairs.

He heard footfalls on the stairs and walked in the direction of the sound, passing two bright red ladder trucks and a red and white fire rescue vehicle backed into their bays. Ah, those days of waxing fenders and polishing chrome. Back then, it'd been a privilege rather than a chore.

A young man in a dark blue fireman's uniform greeted him. "Can I help you?"

Adam extended his hand. "Fire Inspector Adam Mitchell. Is your chief here?"

"Bud. Bud Eagle." He shook Adam's hand. "The chief's not here at the moment, but we expect him shortly. Can I help you?"

Adam shrugged. "I guess I'm signing on for a while." He produced his undercover credentials as he looked around. "The higher ups sent me to make sure this department is in compliance with state regs. It's routine. I have to observe operations for a specific time period, review the books, stuff like that. You guys been busy?"

"Yeah, actually. We've run several calls lately. Lot of nuisance fires, I call 'em. Had one early this morning. That's why the chief isn't here yet. He's still at the scene. Garbage dumpster adjacent to a double-wide mobile home that served as an outbuilding at the elementary school. We lost the whole thing."

Adam arched his eyebrows. "Whoa. You lost the whole school?"

"No, no, the equipment house or portable classroom or whatever it was. I'm not sure. But the whole building went up in flames pretty much before we got there."

"Was school in session?"

Eagle shook his head. "Kids were just arriving. They saw an eyeful. Kind of an exciting start to their day, I'd say."

"Do you think the school was the target?"

Eagle shrugged and seemed to write it off as a mundane fire call. He didn't know the details, but his own theory was that the local thugs were bored and set the thing on fire.

Adam considered the idea as a possibility. "That happen often?"

"Thugs gettin' their jollies? Not often enough, if you ask me." He grinned, showing teeth speckled with chewing tobacco. "I mean I hate to see a place burn down, but it's job security, if you know what I mean." He laughed at his own joke, amusing Adam.

"Does the chief have an office? I'll wait in there for him."

"You wanna come upstairs? The coffee's hot. We just finished breakfast, but we could probably scare up something for you if you're hungry."

He spoke as he started toward the door leading upstairs.

Adam followed him up a winding cement stairwell to the second floor where the men made their home away from home.

The smell of fresh coffee permeated the room. The area was divided into quadrants by the furnishings. Adam walked from the stairwell into the living area, which had three reclining chairs grouped around a television with a couple of end tables beside them and an oblong coffee table positioned in the center. A large round area rug covered the floor. Magazines, newspapers, videos, and CDs were piled high on the coffee table in an organized clutter.

To his right was a thick brass pole that went through a three-foot wide round hole in the floor to the first level. Bud introduced Adam to Chester and Jimmy, the other men on duty, and handed him a steaming mug of coffee.

From the kitchen table where he sat, he viewed the back room. Bunk beds lined the walls, each neatly made with a dark blue cotton bedspread stretched tight, military style.

"How long you going to be here?" Chester asked.

Adam leaned back in his chair. "I'm supposed to spend two to three weeks at each site. But I'd like to drag this inspection out a little longer if I can. My girlfriend runs the bar down the street. I'll have a lot more time to spend with her if I have to resolve issues here, if you know what I mean."

He chuckled for effect. "You boys will be glad to give me some issues to work on, won't you?"

Bud's laugh turned into a snort. "We can come up with something." The other men smiled and nodded in agreement.

"Any of you ever go there? To the bar? It's called Shots in the Dark." Jimmy and Bud nodded.

"I'll mention you to Gina. Tell her who you are. She gives discounts to firemen and law enforcement for food and booze. Just don't go in dressed in your uniform and drinking on the job. That's the kind of issue I don't need."

That made the men laugh. Everyone turned at the sound of footsteps as the chief walked in, his face grimy and an odor of smoke clinging to him. Bud handed him a mug of coffee as the chief eyed the visitor.

"You got some credentials?" he asked after Adam rose and introduced himself. Adam handed him the leather-bound case with his badge and photo ID. Chief Rocco Cozza grilled him about his background. After studying all night, the answers came easily.

Cozza sighed and returned Adam's identity to him. "I didn't think inspections started until the fall. You're here early and unexpected. How long has it been since you rode a ladder truck?"

"Been a while," he conceded, wondering if the fire truck replica he rode last year on a merry-go-round with his then-girl-friend qualified. The chief pointed his finger at Adam. "That fire bell sounds, you stay off the truck, you hear? As far as I'm concerned, you're a liability, and I don't need any more problems right now. You ride with the rescue squad or you follow in your own vehicle. My men don't have time to save your ass."

Adam spread his hands out, palms up. "I'll try to stay out of everybody's way, chief. I have a job to do just like you. I'm not the enemy."

The chief took a deep breath and shook his head. "Sorry. I'm not a fan of surprise inspectors wearing designer suits and cowboy boots. Country's not my thing. Not your fault."

He ran his hand through a full head of salt-and-pepper hair. "We've had some unsolved fires lately. Nothing big. But nerves are starting to fray, including mine."

He placed his coffee mug on the table. "Where do you have to start your inspection?"

Adam wasn't sure. "How about the books?" Did fire depart-ments still keep paper logs or was everything tracked electroni-cally these days?

The chief nodded and motioned for Adam to follow him to his office. Adam handed his empty coffee mug to Bud, nodded to the others, and walked downstairs.

From the dossier the agency had provided, he knew Rocco Cozza was fifty-years old and had been the Benton Falls fire chief for eighteen years. He'd been considering retirement. A recent news article quoted him longing for the old days when he thought fighting fires was easier. He'd explained that houses were smaller, their contents weren't as toxic, and there were fewer administrative headaches because there was less paperwork. These latest fires couldn't have helped his attitude.

The chief turned to Adam with a ring of more than a dozen keys. "We're in transition to computerization. Supposed to be fully digital by next year. That'll be one more annoyance for me. The system isn't refined yet so I still back up everything with paper reports. Call me old-fashioned but I don't trust computers."

He inclined his head toward a corner desk with a laptop, router, printer and mass of wires. "You can try your luck on that. Otherwise, here are the keys to the file cabinets in the office. I don't know what you need, so you can look at anything you want. Everything is filed alphabetically, so it's easy to find. No keywords to search."

Adam couldn't help the smile that creased his face.

"I have no secrets, Agent Mitchell. This is a clean department. We follow all the rules to the best of our abilities."

"Thank you, chief. I'm not here to cause any problems."

"I hope not, son. I have all the problems I can handle right now."

Adam raised an eyebrow. Did Cozza already suspect a connection between the fires? The men stared at each other until the phone rang in the radio room next door. Caller ID showed it was the Benton Falls police dispatcher.

The chief answered, grabbed a marker, and wrote an address

on the whiteboard mounted to the wall beside the phone bank. "Tone us out," he snapped before hanging up.

He hit a black knob on the wall and a shrill bell began ringing in groups of twos. The chief switched on the intercom and barked into a microphone, sending his voice echoing into every corner of the fire station. "Car fire. Seventh Street and Superior. Let's go boys."

Cozza turned to Adam. "You want to observe this one?"

Adam shook his head.

"Then man the phones until back-up gets here." He was already climbing aboard the squad truck when Jimmy, Chester, and Bud slid down the brass pole from the second floor. Each grabbed their jacket and helmet from a hook on the wall and ran to their respective spots.

The men always had their turnout gear ready. At first glance, it appeared as if their clothes had been left in a heap on the floor, like teenagers shedding school garb. But their pants were neatly turned over their steel-toed boots beside the fire trucks, one at each door, or in Jimmy's case, beside the driver's side of the rescue squad. That way each man stepped into his boots, pulled up the pants and slid the suspender straps over his shoulders.

They slipped on their jackets and locked their helmets in place with a chinstrap as they climbed into the fire trucks, all in one fluid movement.

Firefighters were typically expected to don all of their equipment in one minute or less. Chester, Jimmy, Bud, and the chief were ready to go in forty-five seconds. A well-tuned and impressive team, Adam noted. They jumped on the pumper and were out of the bay in one minute with the lights flashing and the siren blowing.

Adam respected firemen. He'd wanted to be one once. His job was dangerous at times, but these men laid their lives on the line every time they went out on a call. It hadn't seemed dangerous when he was a young volunteer. Back then, he'd embraced the rush. Now, older and wiser, he didn't think he could do it for a living.

The firehouse phone rang. He punched the blinking red light under the words Line 1. "Fire station."

A woman screamed into his ear. "There's a car on fire on my street. You better come quick."

"Yes ma'am, we know. We're on our way,"

"Well hurry, dammit." She hung up.

The same doorbell that sounded when Adam walked into the station alerted him that someone had come in. He walked out to see two men dressed identically in the same dark blue fire uniforms running in the door and toward the office. They stopped when they saw him.

Adam reached into his jacket pocket to retrieve his credentials as he repeated his name and title. They nodded and quickly gave their names. Dave Oswalk went directly to the radio room to establish contact with the chief, and the other man ran to the second pumper truck. Neither gave Adam a second glance.

He walked into the chief's office, closed the door, and touched the keyboard to awaken the computer. Without a password, it was useless. Oh well. At the moment, he wasn't sure what he was looking for. He opened the drawer marked personnel and began sifting through the folders. While he scrutinized the personnel files, the men returned from the car fire, wiped down the trucks, re-rolled the hoses and cleaned every inch of the instrument panels. A second call came in later in the day for fuel spilled on the road after a two-car accident. Adam noted that other than at mealtime, the men stayed downstairs around the trucks, checking equipment, cleaning, or otherwise keeping busy. It appeared to be a routine day on duty.

By three o'clock, he'd had enough. He massaged his temples to ease the throbbing, rubbed his eyes to coax them to relax, and silently told his growling stomach it had made its point. As a courtesy, he let the chief know he was leaving and would return tomorrow. He decided to ease his way into spending a night there. Those bunks didn't look too comfortable.

As he said goodbye to the men, he offered to buy them beers at Shots in the Dark later. Just mentioning the beverage made his mouth water. He couldn't wait to drink a cold one.

He drove the five blocks to the bar and found Gina at a table reviewing the books with the bar manager. Her first order of business when she'd begun her assignment had been to keep the manager and staff intact, since she didn't know jack about running a bar or serving food. She'd given everyone a hefty raise to ensure their loyalty. None of the employees knew her real identity.

Gina whistled at the sight of Adam dressed in his suit and tie and he felt heat creep across his cheeks. She stood for a hug.

"I gotta tell you, hon, your two-hundred-and-forty-five pounds of hard muscle is looking pretty hot right now." She raised her face to his for a quick kiss, then introduced him to her manager and suggested they finish the books another time. She signaled for the bartender to bring Adam a beer.

He tossed his suit coat on an empty chair, yanked off his tie, unbuttoned his shirt collar, and slid out a chair.

"You look tired and cranky." He grunted in response and reached for the frosted mug before it touched the table. Taking a long draw, eyeing Gina over the rim of the glass, his eyes roamed from her face to her pale blue cotton shirt and her cleavage. He grinned.

"You look voluptuous."

When she was at the bar, she wore low-cut tops with push-up bras and short skirts that looked still shorter with her stiletto heels. Two of the Sanchillio brothers were enthralled with her and had become daily patrons, which was good for her case. She laughed.

"How'd it go today?" He reached for his jacket and removed his pocket notebook to share his notes.

Bud Eagle and his job security remark placed him on the short list of possible suspects along with three new hires listed as Vince Daniels, Jeff Framer, and C.J. Kwin. The men were all hired two months earlier, around the same time the arsons began. He also told Gina he offered discounts to the men, to which she whined as if she truly did own the bar. But she agreed it was probably a good idea.

Coins clanked into the jukebox change catcher, and Trace Adkins' voice filled the room. Gina looked at the wall clock. Happy hour was starting. A cheese steak sandwich silenced his growling stomach and a second beer eased the tension in his shoulders and back. Laughing men and women hoping to end their day on a bright note filled the room, occupying every barstool. Gina and two bartenders worked hard to keep everyone's glasses filled.

Shortly after six o'clock, Bud and Jimmy wandered in and sat at the far end of the bar. Adam motioned to the bartender to put their first round of drinks on his tab. The firefighters held up their glasses in acknowledgement to him.

Fifteen minutes later, two more men whom he didn't recognize joined them and he pointed them out to Gina as firefighters who could eat and drink at a discount. Adam mentally debated if he should walk to the end of the bar and chat with the men or keep a newcomer's distance. He was looking in their direction when Valerie Daniels rushed in and his stomach somersaulted. He'd tuned in to her radio show this morning, but she wasn't on the air. The disc jockeys said only that she was off today.

Valerie scanned the room, then headed toward the corner where the firemen stood. They all appeared to know her and smiled when she joined them. Adam watched her kiss one of the men on the cheek and slide her arm into his. Both of them had short dark hair, dark brown eyes and olive-tinted skin. Valerie sometimes discussed having a twin brother and after seeing the close resemblance between the two, he'd bet that's who it was.

He reached for his notebook and flipped through the pages. There it was. Vince Daniels. One of the new hires. It had to be him. Vince was about a foot taller than Valerie, probably about six-three. They shared the same striking white smile. Valerie wore a sleeveless coral top with a high collar that clasped at the back of her neck. There was a keyhole-shaped piece cut out of the back revealing flawless skin and toned shoulders. The high collar conveniently covered the bruise he was certain marred her neck. He was unsure what he wanted to do. Sneak out the back and avoid a meeting all together or casually join the group to see if she recognized him? Bud made up his mind for him.

"Hey, Adam. Thanks for the drinks. Why don't you come over and meet a couple of the other men and our local star?"

"I'd be happy to." Adam grabbed his mug and sauntered toward the group. Valerie's eyes widened as he approached.

Bud began making introductions. "This is Vince and C.J., both on our unit, and this is the famous Valerie Daniels."

Adam shook hands with C.J. and turned as Valerie stepped forward and quickly offered her hand. "It's nice to meet you." Her hand trembled in his and her eyes stayed wide, almost pleading. She caught her bottom lip between her teeth and looked to hang on whatever his next words would be.

He held her hand a little longer than necessary. "My pleasure. I missed you on the air this morning."

"Another fan," Bud chirped, holding his arms up in touch-down style and snorting a laugh.

She yanked her hand from his. "I-I was off today."

"My sister never learns." Vince stepped forward and extended his hand, introducing himself again. "She insists on ordering salmon, and this is the second time she's gotten sick when it wasn't cooked right."

Adam kept his focus on Valerie. "Sorry to hear that. I can't resist a good salmon dish either, even though sometimes I barely make it out of the parking lot."

Valerie blinked, looked away, and touched the neckline of her top, tugging on the edge to coax it higher. She reminded Vince that she had to get up at an ungodly hour and if they were going to grab a bite to eat together they should do it soon. She tugged on his arm, practically dragging him to a nearby booth but away from the group.

She eyed her brother over her menu and debated telling him what had happened. As long as she could remember, it had always been just the two of them. Their mother was an abusive alcoholic and their father gave up trying to make a happy home for them when they were in grade school. Now that Vince and Valerie were on their own, their dad was gone. Neither of them knew where he was.

Their mother was in and out of rehab in another city and rarely contacted them unless it was to ask for money.

So it was as it had always been, "The Daniels Duo," as Vince dubbed them in third grade the night they realized neither parent was coming home and there was no dinner. That night, they locked their right-hand pinkie fingers, and Vince promised to always take care of Valerie. She'd promised the same and then made peanut butter and jelly sandwiches.

She chanced a peek at the group of men at the bar. Thankfully, Adam had his back to her. She strived to make her question sound casual "Why's a policeman working in the fire station?"

Her brother scanned the menu. "He's not a policeman. Bud

said he's a state inspector, here for a routine annual inspection I guess."

That confused her. She was certain Mr. Good Samaritan said last night he was the police or something like that. But she couldn't pursue it without telling her brother what had happened. And she wouldn't do that.

4

Valerie stared at the e-mail on her computer screen, squinting despite the enlarged font. The neon green capital letters offended her eyes. Seven large words filled the screen, causing her stomach to jump.

THE FIRE WAS SET. DO YOUR HOMEWORK

She scanned the top of the electronic message, mentally processing the information on the bar that identified the sender. It read "Favfan." Whoever it was, he subscribed to the same Internet service provider that millions across the country used. No clue there. Grasping the computer mouse, she maneuvered the cursor over the reply box, her forefinger pausing momentarily before she tapped the left button. The result surprised her and she stared wide-eyed as an error message expanded through the middle of the screen, like a movie presented in letterbox format. Five exclamation points that increased in size followed the red word "ERROR." She scrutinized the upper and lower toolbars on the screen. Everything seemed in order. An encrypted message? She'd never seen one before.

This was one of dozens of e-mails she received each day at WARJ radio station, where she worked as the morning show producer and part-time news reporter. Usually, her inbox contents ran the gamut from hate mail, usually notes that cursed her comments and wished ill health for her and her family members, to humorous, mostly from young teens professing their love in poems and sappy prose, to suggestions from listeners for off-the-wall program ideas.

All of the on-air personalities regularly received correspondence. Some of her coworkers never responded to the communications, but Valerie replied to each one if for no other reason than it was the polite thing to do. Often, she typed only "Thanks," then clicked the send button and the delete key.

Favfan's e-mail wouldn't let her. The message puzzled her. She shared the workspace with the music coordinator for the afternoon show. She refused to call their compartment an office. A windowless cubbyhole with two desks jammed into a space meant to accommodate one was hardly an office. He had to stand for her to reach her chair.

She touched his shoulder. "Hey, look at this for a sec, will ya?"

He leaned over and read the screen. "Huh. What's it mean?"

"I don't know."

"What fires have you reported lately?" She closed her eyes and pinched the bridge of her nose trying to recall any major fires in the last few weeks. Part of her job involved chasing police and fire news, but she kept tabs on so many departments that sometimes they all ran together.

"There was that small fire at the playground a few weeks ago, but no one thought that was out of the ordinary. And there was that dumpster fire. But that was ruled a summer accident. They thought maybe a smoldering cigarette butt caused it, or charcoal ashes that hadn't completely cooled when they were tossed in the dumpster. Nothing comes to mind beyond that."

He shrugged. "It's probably just some prank. Delete it and forget about it." He returned his attention to his own computer monitor.

But she couldn't simply blow it off. Not with Vince working as a fireman now. She refocused on the screen. The message didn't make sense, but there was no time to dwell on it. She tapped the print button to generate a paper copy of the cryptic communication, closed it, and logged onto her daily phone file.

She had an hour before her first newscast. Her day started at five o'clock in the morning and ended around one, although she often spent her evenings on her laptop in front of the TV surfing the Internet for breaking news and contacting interesting guests on the West Coast who'd make interesting interviews on the morning talk show. She sacrificed her evening hours to reach them during their office hours and they would, in turn, rise before dawn for the show.

As the talk show producer, her role was to keep the interview timeslots booked. The bosses said Valerie had a knack for finding fascinating experts, quirky surveys or news items that easily generated phone calls from listeners. Maximum audience interaction was the goal. A list she discovered identifying the top ten singers someone declared should never record again had kept the phones ringing for days last week.

As part of her news duties, she scanned the morning newspaper and, per usual, she was on top of the day's breaking news. She always monitored the reports running on other news outlets to ensure she'd missed nothing major. Shortly before her first newscast she'd call the bigger city police and fire departments to ask about any major activity overnight. After the broadcast she'd make more phone rounds, dialing fifty-three different departments over her eight-hour shift.

She'd been doing this job for about a year and that's how long it had taken to break the ice with most of the police dispatchers and firefighters who answered the phones. At first, it didn't matter if there had been a murder or a ten-alarm blaze the night before. They would tell her there was no news and hang up before she uttered her name. Caller ID likely preceded her voice. News people were the enemy in their minds. She had, on her own time, scheduled visits to the different police stations to meet the folks she bothered by phone every morning. Linking a face to a voice sometimes helped. Other times the cakes and cookies she brought worked better. Either way, most of them were friendly to her now and some—not all—would let her know if something newsworthy had happened and where she should look. It made her job a little easier

The station's ratings were at the top of the market, in part because of the cutting-edge news team, and the bosses strived to promote that with the advertisers. There were several billboards and newspaper promos in circulation right now. She doodled on one in this morning's paper.

Damn those ugly billboards. They made her straight white teeth look enormous and her big brown eyes look like saucers. At least her pixie haircut came out okay in the photo. Today's guest was a pet psychic who would arrive in fifteen minutes. Time to start making her phone rounds. She'd memorized most of the phone numbers by now. The calls didn't generate anything. She already knew about the shooting in New Castle. The city averaged one a night. Overnight, a semi had overturned on the main highway leading into town. That promised to be a rush-hour nightmare for commuters. A small car fire in Koppel roused that fire department out early, but that hardly seemed newsworthy. She dialed Benton Falls, the next number on her call list.

"Fire district four-two. Daniels," the phone answered.

She hadn't expected to hear her brother's voice. "I didn't think you were on duty until Thursday."

"Hey, Sis. A call came in early this morning. I haven't made it home yet."

"Anything newsworthy?"

"Probably not for you. It was an abandoned house on Columbo Street."

"Anybody hurt or any homeless people living in it?"

Vince chuckled. "Nope. Sorry. Just a plain old empty building that burned."

Could that be the fire that Favfan referred to? It didn't seem likely. "Well, I'll make a note and if I need to I'll call back and talk to the chief, okay?"

Her brother laughed again. "In other words, if you don't find something sexier and you still have time to fill, you'll use our fire. Boy, if the public only knew that the news they hear is determined by the amount of time you have to fill."

"Yeah, yeah. I've heard it all before. Go home and get some sleep. I'll talk to you later. Love you."

She hung up smiling and made a star in her notebook next to the Benton Falls fire notes. As it turned out, she didn't need the fire for her news broadcast. A local businessman had been caught with his pants down in the backseat of the mayor's car with the mayor's wife.

5

Bud Eagle snapped off the radio the next morning, clasped his hands and stretched his arms over his head. "That's it. I'm calling it a day."

C.J. Kwin chuckled as he spit-polished Truck Two's rear fender. "You could have done that two hours ago. I can't believe you stayed here just to listen to your little girlfriend."

"I didn't want to miss the show, and the radio is broken in my car. What do you care what I do?"

"I just think you should get a life, is all. You know, it's a little sick, your obsession with her."

"At least it's a woman that turns me on and not a fuckin' fire truck."

Adam looked up from the manila folder he was reading just as Bud stood and flashed Kwin the finger. Kwin hurled the rag to the floor and jumped up from his knees. "You little jerk. I'll kick your ass."

Vince and a part-timer were on their feet to separate the two before Adam could reach the pair. "Boys, boys," Vince said, backing Kwin away from Bud. "We're all family, remember."

Bud flashed the finger one more time. "I'm going home. You

deal with the pervert." The words incensed Kwin again but Vince restrained him.

"Relax, C.J. You know he's only trying to get a rise out of you. Keep your cool." Kwin took a deep breath, looked toward the doorway where Adam watched, then turned his back on him. "You ought to warn your sister about him." He shrugged off Vince's grip and stormed outside. Adam raised his eyebrows when Vince glanced his way, then returned to the office, handing the file to arson specialist Rick Martellan.

Rick was bent over a legal pad scribbling notes. "Everything okay out there?"

Adam shrugged. "Interesting mix of men in this department." He eyed a small but growing pile of reports. "What's this?"

Although he had incendiary expertise, Adam's gut told him he needed someone with finer instincts, and he trusted Rick after working with him on two prior arson cases. He'd called Rick just before midnight, briefed him, and asked for a second set of eyes to review the logs. They'd reported to the fire station at seven-thirty this morning to find the men rolling hoses, filling breathing tanks, and hosing down the fire trucks.

A call had come in just before four a.m., but by the time the firemen arrived, the flames were out of control. When Adam inquired, the chief claimed the abandoned building exploded in the middle of the night, knocking pictures off the walls in five homes on the block and scaring neighbors into running outside to witness a spectacular scene.

Rick stopped his scribbling on the yellow tablet and eyed the pile. "If I'm right, it's our firebug's budding repertoire. These are the last three fires, not counting the one today. I want to inspect these sites, Adam. Your gut was right. Something's very wrong."

~

Having worked through the night, the chief had already gone

home for the day so Adam and Rick left the station without anyone questioning them. They found yellow police tape encircling the abandon building's property line and billows of smoke still rising from the pile of rubble. Rick edged close to the burnt pile of debris, closed his eyes, and inhaled. He squatted, ran his forefinger through a dark stain on the concrete floor, and sniffed.

"Could be butane. Or maybe some kind of kerosene mix." His eyes watered from the fumes. "Not sure yet how it was ignited, but it was likely right here." He pointed to a crisp burn mark indented in the floor. "Something detonated. I wish I'd seen this baby in action."

He stood, swatting soot from his jeans. "I want to see the other sites, even the small ones. And let's add our numbers to the call-out list so we don't find out about the next fire after the fact. This is serious, Adam. Each successful burn boosts his confidence. We have to step out in front of this because it's just a matter of time before he hurts someone."

They spent the rest of the day sifting through ashes and inspecting charred I-beams. Rick drew a diagram of each site on his trusty legal pad and made notes in the margins. At four-thirty Adam called it a day. He had a meeting with his best friend, Dolan, who wanted to introduce him to a new girlfriend. Dolan had it bad for this woman and used words like committed and marriage when he talked about her.

Under normal circumstances, Adam avoided contact with his personal friends while undercover but the date for this get-together was set weeks before he assumed the fire inspector's identity. Adam wasn't worried about Dolan revealing his true identity. They started out at the agency together, before Dolan took his career in another direction. Dolan knew Adam often went undercover. He never used his last name and never specifically discussed Adam's job.

Two years earlier Adam was undercover as an airport baggage inspector when Dolan and a woman came through on their way to the Bahamas. Dolan did a double take but knew immediately not to acknowledge him. As he inspected Dolan's bag he asked where he was heading and what hotel he was staying in. It sounded casual but professional. Adam made sure a bottle of wine was chilling in their room when Dolan and his date arrived. There was nothing to be concerned about tonight. He wanted a beer and a sandwich and he'd call it a night. This new woman was likely no different from the others.

Valerie stared at the newest e-mail while absentmindedly rubbing the clear tape that sealed the worn edge of her gray metal desk. If it weren't for the block with today's date displayed, it would look like a repeat of the one she opened yesterday. Neon green letters glared at her.

THE FIRE WAS SET. DO YOUR HOMEWORK

Her eyes searched the screen for clues. The e-mail landed at four thirty-two in the morning. Once again, the sender was Favfan. She clicked the reply button and another bright red error message exploded on her screen, just like the first. She printed her second paper copy.

Whoever Favfan was, he had her attention.

As near as she could determine, the notes weren't connected to any major blazes. There had only been nuisance calls reported last week. Flipping through the back pages of her notebook, she listed every fire incident. Maybe if she studied a list, the messages might make sense. Should she show her boss these notes? He'd react in typical knee-jerk fashion and want a story and, right now, what was the story? That some crazy person was sending her anonymous e-mails? Or she'd attracted a firebug who wanted publicity?

Both ideas made the hairs on the back of her neck twist. It might not be wise to tell her boss but she sure as hell thought

Vince should know. Maybe as the analytical one, he'd see something she was missing. The firemen worked twenty-four hours on and forty-eight hours off duty. Vince clocked in at six o'clock that night, but Valerie had already committed to meet her best friend, Sue, at a restaurant called Chips. Sue was in love with "the perfect man" and it was time for her best friend to meet him. For the last two months, Sue had talked endlessly about Dolan, mainly how he was Mr. Right. Valerie didn't think such a being existed but she had to admit, Sue made him sound like Prince Charming. For her friend's sake, she hoped so.

In Valerie's book, Mr. Right had to meet a long list of criteria: strong but sensitive, intelligent, fun-loving, neat about his appearance and a non-smoker. He'd need to be tuned in to current events with opinions about politics, the economy, and life in general. Confident enough to let her have her own career yet jealous enough to want her all to himself. And drop-dead gorgeous wouldn't be so bad either. Maybe Vince was right. He often teased that she'd never let her guard down long enough to make a commitment even if she did find Mr. Right.

Hopefully, Sue was a little less particular. She was picking Valerie up at five-thirty so they would arrive at the restaurant on time for their six o'clock meet-up.

Valerie glanced at her watch. If her afternoon didn't morph into a nightmare, maybe she could squeeze in a call to Vince before he reported to work and share with him the anonymous notes. She'd prefer to have the conversation with him while he was at home, rather than at the station. The emergency line was recorded but she often wondered if the other phone lines were monitored as well. After all the city fathers always wanted to know what was going on.

But murder and mayhem were the order of the day. Two people were shot and killed in a domestic dispute and a third was critically wounded. A friendly card game had gotten out of control and erupted into a major brawl, and a group of teens had a field day running through three different residential neighbor-hoods with cans of white paint defacing houses and businesses with graffiti.

Valerie didn't make it through the entire police checklist and never called Benton Falls to see if they'd responded to any fires.

Valerie and Sue chose a high table to the side of the main bar and climbed onto the chairs facing the doors. Sue's nervous chatter clued Valerie into just how big this evening was for her friend.

"Relax, Sue. If you think that much of him, I'm sure I'll love him, too." The double doors opened and Valerie saw the pair first. "I don't believe it."

But Sue didn't hear her. She jumped off her seat and headed toward the man who walked in the restaurant's double doors with Adam Mitchell. That man was smiling and moving quickly toward Sue. Valerie watched from the table, ignoring the fast pace her heart raced. Jesus, she couldn't avoid this guy.

She narrowed her eyes to study him. She hadn't realized Adam Mitchell was so tall. He towered over Sue and Dolan. Dark hair, neatly trimmed mustache and goatee, and ocean blue eyes. She remembered those from meeting him in the bar.

He had a small waist compared to his broad shoulders and his black jeans fit him snug enough to make her appreciate them. She shook her head at the western getup though. A black T-shirt with a Harley Davidson motorcycle emblazoned on the front, a wide leather belt with a round buckle sporting the initial "A" in the middle, and black alligator boots. And, of course, a black cowboy hat. Country didn't do it for her. She wished she could run out the back door and avoid this meeting all together. But it was too late. Sue was already motioning toward the table and dragging Dolan to meet her.

Adam studied Sue while Dolan introduced them. He had to agree that she was stunning with her blond, nearly white, hair falling softly around her face and touching her shoulders. The word hourglass described her figure but the most striking thing about her was her smile. It was wide and bright and contagious. You just had to smile right back. He did.

Sue shook his hand. "I've been so nervous to meet you. Dolan has told me so much about you, I feel like I know you, but my friend asked me what your last name is and I don't think Dolan ever told me. So I guess I have a lot to learn."

That smile was infectious. He liked her already. "It's a pleasure to meet you. I could hardly wait." It was when Sue clutched Dolan's hand and directed him toward a table that Adam spotted Valerie sitting, waiting, glaring at him.

His breath caught in his throat momentarily. Then he broke into a wide smile. Son of a gun. He followed Sue and Dolan to the table.

He detected excitement in Sue's introductions. "Finally, you two meet. Dolan, this is Valerie, my best friend in the whole world. Val, Dolan. And this is Dolan's friend, Adam."

Dolan shook Valerie's hand, saying he listened to her radio show all the time. But Valerie's eyes never left his face, prompting a Cheshire cat grin he couldn't contain.

"Nice to see you again, Ms. Daniels." Adam touched the brim of his hat and then removed it. Valerie's chin tilted upward. "You, too, Mr. Mitchell."

Dolan's head snapped up at the exchange and Adam quickly winked. "You didn't tell me we'd be dining with beauty and fame tonight, my friend. We should have talked in the car."

Sue's mouth dropped open in surprise. "Do you two know each other?"

Adam cleared his throat. "Ah, well, lately it seems our paths keep crossing."

Sue's forehead wrinkled. "Really? Where? Through Val's radio show?"

"No," Valerie said, refusing to look at him. "Mr. Mitchell is a fire inspector. He's conducting a routine inspection at Vince's fire station."

Sue slid onto the chair opposite Valerie and patted the seat by her for Dolan. Adam's only choice was the seat beside Valerie. Dolan stared at him and he winked again. Dolan understood the message and redirected the conversation.

"I know all about him. Valerie, tell me about you. And tell me some secrets about this woman that I'm head over heels in love with."

He leaned over and embraced Sue, planting a kiss on the top of her head. The waitress arrived for their drink orders as the first chords of a song filtered through the bar's speakers. Sue clapped her hands and sweet-talked Dolan to the dance floor, leaving them at the table.

Valerie clenched her teeth and hissed, "One of us should leave."

His cheeks were starting to hurt, he was smiling so broadly. "Why's that?"

"Because. This is an uncomfortable situation. It's only going to ruin their evening."

He liked the spark in her eyes and felt something, somewhere down deep, stir. Clearing his throat, he exaggerated his Southern drawl, "I'm not at all uncomfortable, Ms. Daniels. Of course, ya'll probably never expected to see me again. You sure drove away fast enough the other night. And yet, you can't seem to stay away from me."

∽

Sitting so close, Valerie detected a hint of his cologne, not fruity like her co-worker but subtle and definitely masculine. He smelled delicious. She clenched her jaw tighter and refused to look at him, causing him to let out a low chuckle that sent a warm rush down her spine. He really was good looking.

"This evening isn't about us, sweetheart. It's about them." He nodded toward Dolan and Sue. "I realize you like to run off on people but if you are truly her best friend, you won't ruin it for her."

She spun around to level her best don't-mess-with-me stare on him. "Listen, Tex..." But Dolan and Sue's return silenced her retort. Sue canted her head, looked from her friend to Adam and back to Valerie.

"Is everything okay? Val, you're wearing your mean face."

She consciously tried to soften her facial muscles. Sue and Dolan resumed their seats and Sue folded her hand into his. "You two better learn to like each other."

It was too much for her to disguise. "Sorry, girlfriend, you know I don't do country."

Sue waved off her words and giggled. "Well you might have to learn. If Dolan and I get married, you're our best man and maid of honor. You'll have to dance together."

She turned liquid eyes toward Dolan and Valerie's stomach knotted.

Dolan looked aghast. "What do you mean if?"

Valerie rolled her eyes, feigning disgust. The thought of dancing with Adam created disturbing thoughts. Thoughts that surprised her and sparked a moment of anticipation.

Next to her Adam threw back his head and laughed at the look on her face. "Hope you know how to two-step, sweetheart." Everyone thought that was funny, except her.

She couldn't take a whole evening of him. Listening to his baritone words flowing over her like warm honey. He seemed quite the conversationalist, chatting with Sue about her job, her childhood, and how she met Dolan. Sue laughed often at his jokes. She avoided looking at him but when she did, she noticed long, thick eyelashes over dark, bedroom eyes. She swallowed hard and tried not to imagine them in her bedroom. When their sandwiches arrived, she announced that she'd have to eat and run. She had to be at work earlier than usual the next day, she lied.

But Adam also said he needed to make it an early night.

"Where do you live, Adam?" Sue asked.

"I'm staying at an extended stay, just outside of Benton Falls."

Sue's face brightened. "Oh that works out perfectly. Valerie lives in Benton Falls. I picked her up tonight so we're in one car, but if you're going back that way maybe you can give her a ride home. Would you mind?"

What? No. "There's no need to do that. I'll call a cab. I planned to."

Adam displayed that stupidly wide grin again. "Don't be silly. I'd be happy to offer you a ride."

Much to her dismay, that ended the discussion. Sue was already teasing Dolan about whether they should go back to her place or his after dinner.

Valerie couldn't remember seeing her friend so giddy. A twinge of jealousy stabbed her heart. Would she ever feel that way about someone? At this point in her life, she doubted it.

Passion, the kind of heat that burns in your soul and makes it impossible to live without your partner, had never burned its way into Valerie's heart. She blamed her career choice for turning her too cynical to believe such heat between two people existed. She discovered too many domestic disputes through her daily police calls to think happy-ever-after lasted.

But seeing Sue's eyes light up when Dolan smiled at her, seeing them eat off each other's plates and whisper secrets that ended in suggestive giggles made her wonder.

After their plates were clean, Adam asked what time she wanted to leave. She was ready to get that part of the evening behind her at least.

Dolan clapped Adam on the shoulder. "Thanks for coming, buddy. Call me when you can. Keep your head down."

"You know it." He kissed Sue on the cheek and turned to her. "Ready?"

She nodded and he placed his hand on the small of her back to guide her out of the bar. She stiffened her spine as straight as a two-by-four. He opened the passenger door of his black SUV and helped her inside. Easing into the driver's seat, he stowed his hat in the back seat, and started the car.

"You want to ride in silence or would you like to talk?"

She jumped at his words. "Silence will be fine."

He snickered. "I was just wondering if you are okay, and if you've seen or heard from your parking lot friend since last week."

Valerie twisted to look at him. "I'm fine. And no, I haven't heard from him. I don't think I will."

"Nothing out of the ordinary?"

Geez, why did he care? "A couple of hang-ups from numbers I didn't recognize. Probably solicitors."

"Always the same number? Or different ones?"

She wasn't going to discuss her personal life with him. "I don't remember."

"You might want to pay better attention. And I hope you keep your eyes open and are cognizant of your surroundings. He didn't sound like he would just go away quietly."

She didn't want to be reminded of the whole night and who was he to be giving her advice anyway? She remained quiet.

He snapped on the radio and a country music song filled the car. Her exasperated sigh drew a chuckle from him.

The silence stretched on until she was forced to recite directions to her condo, part of a planned unit development. "These look nice. How many bedrooms?"

Each unit was two floors with a built-in garage. One of the things she liked was the varied colored siding on the buildings, which avoided a cookie-cutter appearance and gave each condo individuality. Some windows displayed shutters and some units had balconies, which also helped customize them. Adam stopped his SUV across the street from her two-bedroom unit, placing them in the perfect spot to notice a shadow pass by the bay window in the dining room. "Your roommate is home."

Her heart thudded and she clutched her hand to her throat, swallowing hard. She could barely find her voice. "I don't have a roommate."

Adam quickly looked back toward the window but the shadow had disappeared. He turned off the ignition and leaned over her legs to unlock the glove box. He retrieved a handgun and slid it from its holster, dropping the leather holder on the floor between his legs.

"Lock the doors and stay here." He approached the house in a crouched position, pressing the gun along his thigh. He sneaked under the bay window to the side and peeked in. Then he moved to the front door and tried to open it, but it was locked. He crouched again and disappeared behind the building.

Her heart pulsed in her ears while her mind raced. What if the intruder was still there? What should she do? What if something happened to Adam? She scanned the street, twisted to see out the back window then looked from side to side. How long had it been since he disappeared behind the house? Should she get out of the car? She looked around again and released a sigh when he came walking toward her from the opposite side of the building. "It appears your back window was pried open. The screen is on the ground. Give me your keys."

She grabbed her purse and jumped out of the car. "I'm

coming with you." She couldn't sit in that car alone another minute.

"Stay behind me." They walked up to the front door and he inserted the key. He let the door swing wide but kept his back against the wall and both hands on his gun, which he pointed downward. He slowly edged around the open portal, raising his gun to eye level, and looked around before moving inside. Valerie waited twenty-seconds and then followed him. The intruder was gone. She gasped at the condition of her home. Her oval glass-topped coffee table and two end tables were overturned, the pictures on the walls were crooked, and papers and magazines usually stacked beneath the TV were strewn on the floor. A similar scene of disarray repeated itself in the dining room where chairs were overturned and the items that had been on the table lay scattered on the floor. In the kitchen, every cabinet door was opened and the refrigerator door was ajar.

Adam followed her into the bedroom. The queen-sized covers were in a heap on the floor beside the bed, the contents of her dresser drawers emptied into piles on the mattress, the drawers dumped upside down on top of them. The Tiffany lamp on her nightstand was overturned, its shade leaning against the wall.

"Oh my God. Someone broke into my home." Tears threatened to fall. She turned toward Adam, who slowly surveyed the room with narrowed eyes, as if memorizing the details. He took her elbow and drew her out of the bedroom.

"Don't touch anything. Come back out here and look around again. Tell me what you see." He led Valerie back to the living room. Pillows from an L-shaped beige overstuffed couch lay on the floor. A small television sat safely on an oak stand with Valerie's laptop leaning against one wooden leg. Newspaper pages were strewn across the carpet. She regarded the mess with a clogged throat and ran her hand through her hair. She couldn't control the quiver in her voice.

"I see my home in a shamble."

Adam gently squeezed her elbow. "I know. But look again. Nothing is broken. Things are overturned but not in a frenzied manner. The dining room chairs look like they were placed on their sides. The couch pillows are just dragged off. The pictures are simply crooked. Your laptop is out of the way. Somebody was in here, but they didn't want to ruin anything you have. They just made a mess."

She looked at each object he pointed out. He was right. "But who would do something like that?"

"Somebody's trying to get your attention. Who has a beef with you?"

She shook her head, unable to think clearly amid this confusion. "No one."

"How about your parking lot friend?"

Her stomach clenched. She hadn't seen or heard from Richard since that night. She wasn't certain he still held his consultant's job. "I don't think so. I don't know where he is."

"Who else has a key to this place?"

"Only my brother and Sue."

"Well this time, Ms. Daniels, you're calling the police. This needs to go on an official report."

She started to protest but Adam already had his cell phone in his hand. "Let me handle it, okay? I can be discreet."

He walked out onto the front porch, leaving Valerie standing in the middle of the mess that used to be her living room. He called his agency and asked the nighttime switchboard operator to patch him through to the Benton Falls police dispatcher, avoiding a direct connection. He recited Valerie's address off the brass-plated digits nailed beside the front door. He requested the police not to use their lights or sirens. When he returned, Valerie wasn't in the room.

"Valerie?" Using her name for the first time caused him to smile. It felt nice on his lips.

"In here." Her voice came from the kitchen, where he found her pouring vodka into a shot glass. Her hand trembled when she tossed back the drink. She set the glass down and refilled it, but he took it before she touched it. "One is enough." He drank the shot. "You don't want the police to think you're drunk."

She shot him an angry look but a knock on the front door deterred the biting tirade he expected her to unleash. She opened the door to let two uniformed police officers inside. One of the officers whistled when he looked around at the mess. "I suspect you aren't simply a bad housekeeper?"

Valerie offered a weak smile at his joke. Adam leaned on the doorjamb in the archway between the kitchen and the main room while Valerie answered the necessary questions for the police report. When the officers asked his interest, he said he had merely given Valerie a ride home and waited out of courtesy until the police arrived. He removed three business cards from his wallet and wrote the name of his hotel and cell number on the backs of each. He handed one to each officer and placed one on the small table beside the couch. He nodded to Valerie and left.

6

"Well?" Sue asked when Valerie answered the phone the next afternoon.

"Well what?" She'd barely slept after the police left her apartment and, after going into work at four this morning, she wasn't sharp.

"What did you think of him?"

"I don't like cowboys." There was a pause before Sue laughed. "Not Adam, you silly. Dolan. Although I did think Adam was really handsome. And did you notice the great body?"

She didn't want to discuss Adam's toned physique. Lord, she didn't even want to think about Adam Mitchell, not now. Not after he'd invaded her dreams when she finally had managed to doze off.

"What I noticed is that you never stopped grinning the whole night. I can practically hear you smiling through the phone. Does your face hurt?"

Sue giggled. "It has for weeks."

"Dolan seemed really nice. I liked the way he treated you and I liked that you are so happy. I'm excited for you, hon. I'd say I'm as happy as you but I don't think there's another human being able to achieve that level."

She'd never heard Sue laugh so often. "Me neither. Thanks, Val. You're a good friend."

She saw a natural opening. "Speaking of friends, what do you know about Dolan's friend? Other than some humorous stories about old girlfriends, we didn't learn very much about him. Is it just me or does he seem kind of mysterious?"

"Adam? I didn't think so. They worked together when they were younger. Dolan never said where exactly. Dolan says he would do anything for Adam and vice versa. I thought he was really nice. I can't believe you met him before. You never said when or where."

"I forget exactly. It was through the radio station, I think. Did Dolan say if Adam was a police officer before he became a fire inspector? Or maybe he was in the military?"

"He didn't say. Why?"

Valerie couldn't dismiss the mental movie of Adam concealing a gun and creeping across her front lawn exactly like she'd seen hundreds of times in cop shows. And even though the details of the parking lot night were muddled, she thought for sure he'd said he was the police. She'd been around enough cops to recognize one. Vince owned guns but he didn't handle one like that. Something didn't add up.

"He just seemed so secretive, that's all. He asked you a lot of questions last night but there was very little said about him."

Sue cleared her throat. "I'm surprised you're asking so many questions now. You didn't seem like you were that interested but we can always get together again if you are. Dolan said he's single and I think you two would make a great pair."

"Don't start. Let's focus on your love life for now."

She didn't tell her friend about the break-in at her condo. There was no point in ruining Sue's good mood. After they hung up Valerie opened her laptop. Adam had been right. Whoever was in her apartment didn't steal anything. The intruder simply made a mess.

She signed on with the station's user ID and password and began accessing driving records, voter registrations, and even dog license databases. Her nails clicked the keys in a musical jingle.

She searched criminal and civil court actions and ran a person locator search through a service the station purchased. Beyond a driver's license, there wasn't a record of Adam Mitchell anywhere in the state. No property owned, not even a car loan. She ran similar searches in Texas, guessing that could account for the Southern drawl that sometimes sneaked into his speech. Nothing.

She retrieved his business card from the end table where he'd left it the night before. The state logo and office address were printed on the front of the card, along with a phone number. Valerie dialed the number and Adam's recorded voice said the caller had reached the state fire inspector's office and should leave a message unless it was an emergency. She hung up.

She turned the card over and dialed the handwritten cell number that he'd scrawled on the back. Again she listened to Adam's recorded voice and hung up before the message beep. Her screen asked if she wanted to save the new phone number to her list of contacts.

She stared at the question, feeling her skin tingle a little, then pressed yes and typed Adam's first name. She wasn't convinced that Mitchell was his last name, so she left it blank. The man existed. She knew that for certain. But why couldn't she find any record of him?

Valerie caught her breath. Could he...she shook the thought from her head. There was no way he could be Favfan.

7

Adam met Rick the next morning for breakfast before they reported to the fire station. The arson specialist wanted to review the work schedules for the last two months in case one fireman was on duty when all of the fires occurred. He also wanted to go over the background checks on each man. He laughed when Adam asked if solving the arsons could be that easy. "No, but it's a place to start. What do we know about the newest hires?"

Adam had done his homework. Jeff Framer had been hurt on his first call and was off for four weeks. In that time two arsons had occurred, so they agreed he could be eliminated. Vince Daniels and C.J. Kwin were either on duty or had been among the first responders to all the other fires. Chief Cozza had told Adam it was because the new men had to pay their dues. They were asked to substitute when someone was on vacation, called in sick, or reported off for whatever reason. It gave them more experience, the chief said. When Framer was off for a month, Daniels and Kwin logged a bundle of extra hours.

Adam asked the chief that afternoon to assess the new men as part of the personnel evaluations. Cozza leaned back in his chair. "Is this part of your routine state inspection, son?"

Adam looked across the chief's cluttered desk at the veteran firefighter. Cozza's face was weathered and his shoulders slumped from the daily responsibilities he carried. "You've got a problem, chief. Maybe a new set of eyes can help you see a solution."

Cozza stared at him for a full minute, his eyes rarely blinking. Finally, he nodded his head slowly as if in the preceding silence there had been a secret communication between them.

"Daniels has the heart to step into the line of fire in any situation. He has the head to keep himself and the other men safe while he does it. Right now, he is young, like a puppy eager to learn and please. Maybe a touch excitable but that will diminish with time.

"Kwin is apprehensive and it makes him pause before he advances on a fire. Maybe that's smart but I'm never sure if he'll move forward and charge in or take one step backward and retreat. I'm not sure he's right for this job simply because he doesn't know the answer to that question himself."

"Which one would you want on your six?"

"Daniels. Every time."

Adam made several notes before requesting permission to log nighttime shifts with each unit. The bottom bunk on the left wall was a spare, the chief said. Adam was welcome to use it on whatever schedule he wanted.

Adam checked the posted schedule. Vince Daniels came out the next night. "Guess I'll tell my girl she'll be sleeping alone tomorrow night."

Adam strolled into the fire station at five-thirty the next night with a backpack. The men had never seen him in anything but his three-piece suits and his casual country attire generated catcalls and whistles, making him laugh.

He tipped his hat to Vince, Chester and Bud. "Ladies."

Chester laughed. "Glad to have you, cowboy. Hope you can handle my Texas chili."

The same team regularly worked their shifts together and had assigned in-house jobs. Adam learned that Vince was studying to earn his paramedic certification and had been taking a test the first day Adam arrived at the firehouse. On this crew, Chester was the chief cook, and Bud was the laundry man. Vince was in charge of housekeeping and any other menial jobs his two senior officers didn't feel like doing. He didn't seem to mind.

The men enjoyed supper and played cards to pass the time. Only two calls came in that required the squad truck, which was essentially an ambulance. Vince went on both runs, one time with Chester and once with Bud.

Adam remembered his days as a volunteer. Firemen were like brothers. They each had their families and homes, but when they were on duty, they lived together as their own family. They shared ups and downs, solved each other's problems, and knew each other's secrets. In a life crisis, the men would turn to each other first. He'd expected to hate every minute of spending the night here, but he relaxed as he shared their time. There was a genuine warmth here, something he didn't have in his own life. A feeling of belonging, maybe.

Chester was the senior man on duty and the father figure. Married twenty-six years and a grandfather, he was the one Vince and Bud looked up to. His knowledge about firefighting and the city's history was extensive, and he easily recalled former fire practices and past fires. Vince and Bud hung on his every word when he started telling stories.

Compared to Vince, Bud seemed to operate in first gear. He was a little slow to get the jokes, a little behind on the conversation, and quite gullible, which made him the brunt of some good-natured jibes. He professed to have a girlfriend, but neither Chester nor Vince had ever met her. It was apparent to Adam that Bud had a major crush on Valerie and fantasized about her. He worked her name into the conversation often. Vince seemed unimpressed with his quasi-famous sister and always laughed at Bud's remarks. He said it was difficult to see Valerie as anything beyond a little girl with a runny nose or a flat-chested teenager with acne and braces.

She wasn't flat-chested anymore. Adam dismissed the thought as quickly as it popped into his head.

"Are you two close like most twins?"

"Yeah. All those stories you hear about twins are true. When I broke my arm as a kid, Valerie broke hers. We needed our tonsils out at the same time and shared chicken pox. Sometimes we finish each other's sentences.

"If there is a day when I'm out of sorts, you can bet she has a bad day, too. Dating one of us is like dating both of us. Whoever our life partners turn out to be, they'll have to accept that they marry both of us. And they will have to meet with our approval."

"Are either one of you close to getting married?" He held his breath, waiting for the answer. Why did it matter?

Vince chuckled. "Nah. I'm not sure my sister will ever set her profession aside long enough for a relationship. She's pretty career driven right now. And I think she has the bar set really high for what she expects from a partner. It will take one hell of a man to break through her armor.

"I'm having too much fun playing the field. I don't even want to start thinking about a serious relationship. So it will be just us for a while. Unless Bud's dreams come true, and Valerie falls for him."

Bud laughed, snorted, and shrugged his shoulders. "A man can dream."

Eleven o'clock was lights out. He climbed into the unyielding cot and doubted he'd be able to sleep. Shoved against the wall, the single bunk was really cramped. The mattress felt like an ironing board covered by a sandpaper blanket. Chester began snoring almost immediately, and Bud muttered his way into oblivion.

The shrill scream of the fire alarm cut through Adam's brain at four-fourteen a.m. A structure behind a housing complex was on fire, the police dispatcher's voice barked through the loud speaker. Fourteen twenty-eight Rippey Street, she recited over and over.

All four men bolted from their beds. Adam ran down the steps and grabbed the helmet and overcoat the chief had issued him. Chester, Vince, and Bud slid down the fire pole but Adam was fast enough to be at the pumper truck's passenger door when Chester jumped into the driver's seat. Vince leaped on the back and they sped out of the station.

They passed Kwin running into the fire station on their way out. He and Bud would wait on the second truck for additional manpower. Adam's heart hammered in his chest. Stay with the radio when they found the fire, Chester yelled, and he nodded acknowledgement. An orange glow lit the sky ahead of them and clouds of black smoke billowed above the buildings in the distance. As they approached, the acrid smell of burning wood stung Adam's nostrils.

Chester rounded the corner, threw the truck into park, and ejected from the driver's seat before the vehicle came to a full stop. He grabbed a hose and started toward the blaze while Vince adjusted the valves and geared up the pressure for the water attack. Adam stood outside his opened passenger door. The heat from the fire warmed his face and neck. His eyes smarted. A slight wind blowing east allowed the flames to lick the apartment building next to the structure. The tenants stood huddled outside crying and pointing for the firemen to save their homes. Adam watched roof shingles pop off from the intense heat and the aluminum siding started to melt and sag.

Bud arrived with the second pumper truck and more firemen. Adam heard Chester on the portable radio calling for more help. In seconds, the truck radio sounded the fire signals for mutual aid from neighboring fire departments.

The scene was controlled chaos. The iridescent yellow stripes across the backs of the fire coats bounced and blurred in Adam's vision as he watched men position themselves and advance on the flames. When he built a fire in his living room fireplace, he loved the sight of embers soaring up the chimney after he tossed another log on the flames. This was that picture magnified one thousand times with embers as huge as quarters. A loud cracking, buckling sound drew his attention to the rear of the apartment building as a wall gave way, followed by screams of panic from the residents who watched part of their home crumble. Then a high-pitched wail of horror came across the radio waves.

"Chester's down. Chester's down," a muffled voice screamed from inside a facemask. He couldn't identify the voice but he spotted two men running in the direction where the collapse had occurred. He reached inside the truck and keyed the microphone.

"Man down! Man down! Northeast corner." His words echoed back to him from the other vehicles. He jabbed the radio button linking the fire truck to the police station. "We've got a man down. We need an ambulance at the Rippey Street fire. Fast!"

"Ten-four. Already on its way."

He refocused on the building as two Benton Falls firemen emerged from the dust and smoke, struggling to drag a body with them. He broke out into a run, heading toward them as he snapped the catches on the front of his coat and flipped his face shield down. They hadn't yet cleared the edge of the flames when he reached them, just as the taller one of the pair collapsed on top of the man they were trying to rescue.

The smoke was too thick to make out their faces. It didn't

matter. He grabbed the one standing to get his attention and yelled through the visor, pointing to the fireman who had just fallen and was on his knees trying to stand. "You take him."

Adam turned to the unconscious form on the ground, hunched down, and unsnapped the breathing apparatus strapped to Chester. Without it, he'd be much lighter. He yanked his right arm to drag Chester into an upright position. From there he threw him over his shoulder into the standard firemen's carry and stood.

It took a few seconds for him to establish his balance and he wobbled before steadying himself. Once he had his footing, he rushed away from the heat and the smoke with Chester draped over his shoulder like a dish towel.

An ambulance screeched to a halt behind the pumper truck and two paramedics ran toward Adam with outstretched arms. The trio half-dragged, half-carried Chester to the ambulance. He wasn't breathing.

Adam turned to see the two firemen he'd left behind trying to make their way out of the black and ash. Both were disoriented and staggering. He ran back and positioned his shoulder underneath the man who had fallen to lend support and the three stumbled out to the ambulance.

Paramedics were everywhere now. They grabbed the middleman as his head fell back in apparent unconsciousness. His helmet came off with a jerk. Jesus, it was Vince. Beside him, Bud removed his helmet and gasped for air. Tears filled his eyes and he trembled.

"Oh my God. Oh my God," he choked, falling to his knees and starting to cry. "Are they okay? Oh my God."

Adam gasped for air as well, struggling to catch his breath. He knelt beside Bud. "Take it easy, man."

Bud was sobbing now. "I never...I couldn't...Oh my God."

"Calm down, Bud." His own heart raced. The air in his lungs pinched. Other firemen gathered around the ambulances now, concern for their brothers etched on their faces. "Snap out of it, Bud. No one has time to take care of you, too."

The words were better than a slap across the face. Bud's head jerked up, he nodded and ran his grimy coat sleeve across his face. He laid his hand on Adam's shoulder and together, they struggled to normalize their breathing. The fire was manageable now and starting to fizzle, but firemen continued to douse the side apartment wall with water. It looked like an oversized dollhouse with a panel missing.

He saw into the exposed rooms of each apartment on the first, second and third floors. The force of the water from the fire hoses blasted pictures off their nails and toppled furniture. Most of the contents of every room were thrust against the back wall.

Bud regained his composure, nodded, and they stood. "I owe you man." He wrapped his arm around Adam's shoulder. Through the heavy fire-resistant coat, he could feel Bud still trembling.

"I couldn't have gotten them both away. I don't know what we would've done. Thanks."

Cozza appeared in front of them. "You all right?" Bud wiped the last of his tears away and muttered yes. He focused on Adam. "I hear you played hero tonight."

"Not at all, chief. I was scared to death. Are they going to be okay?"

"Thanks to you, I hope so. It appears Vince was overcome by smoke but not burned. The paramedics are taking him to the hospital as a precaution, but they expect he'll recover quickly." He rubbed the stubble on his chin. "No word on Chester. He's already on the way to the hospital.

"We should notify Vince's sister. Otherwise, she'll hear it from one of the other departments. We'll be here for at least another two hours cleaning up. Any chance you can go get her? She's probably at the radio station already."

Adam raised his eyebrows in surprise. "Why me?"

"We take care of our own, son. You're the only one I can spare."

His heart surged. He was no longer the outsider. He'd earned a place in this fire family. He was one of the boys now, someone who unselfishly looked out for his brother firefighter. His blood rushed through him followed by a surge of anger. Who the hell was setting these fires? How dare they jeopardize these men? His brothers.

The chief snapped him back to the present. "Will you go to the radio station?"

A new urgency encompassed him. Valerie. He needed to go to Valerie. He nodded and the chief signaled for a Benton Falls policeman to escort him back to the station to retrieve his SUV. Once inside his own car he programmed the navigation system to guide him to the radio station.

He called Rick Martellan to make sure he was monitoring the early morning events, then he called Gina. She answered on the first ring, saying she'd been awake for hours and had sensed something was wrong. His voice cracked as he relived his anxiety at seeing the firemen drag a body wrapped in a fire coat from the flames, and his fear about rushing toward the burning building with only the thought that he had to help.

"Adam, that was crazy. You could've been hurt."

He clenched his teeth. His mouth was as dry as Styrofoam. If he said anything more, he might actually surrender to the panic that had crept into his mind while he'd spoke.

"Where are you headed now? I'll meet you."

"I'm on my way to WARJ to notify Valerie Daniels and transport her to the hospital. The chief asked me to do it," he said quickly to justify his actions. Gina wasn't a Valerie Daniels fan and she'd worried aloud that Adam was too much of one. She'd told him multiple times that Valerie was a woman who would use whatever means necessary to move ahead. Adam ignored it all, including the fact that the lower part of his body seemed highly interested in the woman whenever she crossed his mind.

"Call me when you're done. I want to see you after you drop her off."

"Ten-four."

A security guard opened the radio station door when he rang the bell. It wasn't quite eight o'clock and regular office staff hadn't reported to work yet. He showed his fire inspector's badge and asked the guard to notify Valerie. Valerie's smile faded when she saw him standing in the lobby.

"What are you doing here? I'm working." She crinkled her nose. "You reek of smoke."

"What did the guard tell you?"

"Just that someone with a badge was out here. And by the way I've got some questions about that badge. I—"

He interrupted her. "We had a fire this morning."

"We?" She propped her hands on her hips. "Since when are you part..." The look on his face must have stopped her from finishing the sentence.

"Your brother was hurt. I came to take you to the hospital."

The color drained from Valerie's face. "Vince? What happened? Is he okay?"

"Gather your things and we'll talk in the car."

She wanted an answer now. "Is he okay?"

"They believe he'll be fine. Just too much smoke is all."

Tears rimmed her eyes. "I'm-I'm sorry. Give me a minute." She disappeared through the door and returned in minutes with her purse and a hooded sweatshirt. She brushed past Adam toward the front doors. "Let's go."

Valerie walked to the passenger door and waited for him to unlock his vehicle. Her eyebrows rose when he opened the door and allowed her to slip inside and get situated. It must have been a while since she'd witnessed chivalry. The radio came on when he started the engine. It was tuned to WARJ. "I thought you only liked country music."

Adam smiled at the windshield, ignoring the flip in his chest. "Only after the morning show."

"Can you tell me what happened?" He started by saying the fire bell scared the hell out of him, which made her smile, before giving her the sketchy details on the fire and its victims.

"How bad was Chester?"

"Pretty bad."

"Where was this fire? What was the address?"

"I don't remember the number. It was a Rippey Street building."

They arrived at the emergency room entrance and Valerie jumped out of the SUV and rushed into the hospital. She hadn't even said thank you.

He drove to his hotel, desperate for a shower and sleep. But sleep didn't come easily. The image of Bud and Vince dragging Chester from the bright orange flames stayed in the forefront of his brain. There was something wrong in the picture his mind recalled, but he couldn't pinpoint it. His own impulse to immediately help surprised him. He was apprehensive running toward them. Downright scared, to be truthful. But he didn't think once about not helping.

What angered him was the mounting evidence that some-body on the inside was setting the fires. One of the brothers was deliberately endangering a family member. Bud had really panicked. Was there more to it than seeing a fellow firefighter go down?

On the spreadsheet he'd created, the big picture looked bad

for C.J. Kwin and Vince Daniels. A plot of all the recent fire locations placed them within a mile of where each man lived. If they
were looking for someone on the inside, those two were always at
the fires, sometimes the first to arrive even if they were off duty.
Good firemen or eager to watch their handiwork? Or ensuring
that key evidence was doused? But Vince was on duty with him
tonight when the blaze broke out. How would he have managed
that?

Rick Martellan ran background checks on both men, but the
profile on Kwin was incomplete. Rick was still in the process of
verifying the dates and employment references on his
application.

The check on Daniels offered Adam a small insight into
Vince's and Valerie's childhood. They'd both worked hard to get
where they were today. Both had earned scholarships and
worked part-time jobs to pay their way through college. Vince
signed an apartment lease when he was seventeen, and he and
Valerie struggled to pay the rent each month. A credit history
check showed late payments in their past but each had excellent
credit ratings now.

They chose jobs that kept them close to each other and
appeared to lead sensible lives. Vince seemed to have found his
niche in the fire department. Valerie was a more intriguing
puzzle. There were reference checks on her from prospective
employers in two other cities but, based on what Vince said, she
wouldn't move too far from him.

She didn't seem to know the words "thank you." An ice
queen, maybe. Still, there was something he liked about her.

8

Valerie's heart catapulted to her throat, choking her worse than when someone snuck up behind her and screamed "boo." She shot straight out of her chair and held her hand to her mouth to stifle a gasp.

Seven typed addresses stared at her from her computer screen, numbered with dates and times beside each. The last entry was fourteen twenty-eight Rippey Street, the address of yesterday's fire.

Chester would be hospitalized for several weeks. The intense heat and smoke he'd inhaled had damaged his esophagus and larynx. He couldn't speak, but he wrote on a notepad that his radio malfunctioned and he'd stupidly lifted his mask to yell to one of the men just as the explosion occurred. Vince had swallowed an enormous amount of smoke and would recover but had spent the night in the hospital as a precaution. While gathered around his bed, the men had recounted in detail how Adam raced to help Vince and Chester. She'd stood beside her brother's bedside clinging to his hand, listening to the specifics.

They'd rehashed the Rippey Street fire and, at one point, compared it to the Crandon Circle fire. The address typed in capital letters above the Rippey Street entry was a Crandon Circle address. She uncovered the first two notes she'd printed more than a week ago and propped them next to the monitor. Each was typed in capital letters and used the same font. This newest e-mail, like the others, would not let her send a reply.

Earlier in the week, she'd asked the station tech team if it was possible for a hacker to block reply mails. They said it was. She printed the list of addresses and carried all three notes to her supervisor.

"Hey, boss. How about authorizing a little overtime for me today?" She showed him her notes and explained that she wanted to file a public records request and review the Benton Falls fire logs. If the addresses listed on the newest note matched the recent fire addresses, she could be on to a big story. He agreed.

Valerie arrived at the fire station shortly after lunch. Jimmy and C.J. greeted her and asked about Vince. "He expected to be released today. He's going to call me. Is the chief in? I'm here in an official capacity. I'd like to check the fire logs for a possible story I'm working on."

Jimmy escorted her to the office. "Hey, Adam. Think you can help Valerie?"

Her heart stopped. Adam sat at the chief's desk and when he looked up and grinned, her stomach did a somersault.

"Ya'll need to be more specific." His Southern drawl was so damn sexy. "What kind of help does the little lady need?"

She straightened her spine and glared at him. Jimmy chuckled and said over his shoulder, "He'll help you, Valerie. If you need anything from us, just yell."

She stood in the doorway staring at him. He'd saved Vince and Chester. He'd rushed to her rescue in the parking lot and at her home. Was Adam Mitchell some kind of superman? But what kind of a hero had no public record to prove he existed? Not even a social media presence.

His eyes roamed over her slowly, down her torso to her feet and back up, as if he were a tailor sizing her for a new outfit. She held her breath under his perusal. He made no move to stand or speak. He simply leaned back in the chair with his hands folded on his stomach and returned her stare.

"I suppose I should thank you for what you did yesterday."

There was that damn grin again. "Go ahead."

She drew in a sharp breath and raised her chin. "I'm here in an official capacity for WARJ news. I'd like to see the logs for the fire calls for the last three months."

"Why?"

"I don't have to tell you."

"You do if you want to see the files."

She knew the open records law. "They are a matter of public record."

"Right now they are part of an arson investigation. That means I decide whether or not you see them."

"Arson? Are you sure?" She walked into the office and stood on the opposite side of the desk. She had copies of Favfan's e-mails in a manila folder that she laid on the desk underneath her purse. "What do you know?"

Adam chuckled, stood, and walked to the filing cabinet behind her. "I know better than to answer your questions. Why are you interested?"

She turned and leaned against the desk. Adam's back was to her and she admired his broad shoulders. He wore a white shirt neatly tucked into black suit pants with gray stripes as thin as a thread. The pants must have been tapered because they fit him snugly. What would it feel like to have those shoulders beneath her fingertips? He probably had plenty of women dreaming of doing that. She'd bet he was a pushover when it came to women.

"I'm interested because this is my brother's passion, and I

want to learn more. You understand passion, don't you?" Adam
didn't respond. She took a deep breath, lowered her voice, and
dropped her gaze. "I could be interested in a lot of things around
here."

"I'll be sure and let Bud know." His back remained to her
while he searched the files.

She was undeterred. "Bud wasn't who I had in mind."

Adam turned, cocked his head, and regarded Valerie. She had
one hand on the desk and was leaning back on that arm, trying to
strike a provocative pose. She watched him with half-closed eyes.
He slid the file drawer shut.

"I thought country wasn't your thing, Ms. Daniels."

She smiled and fluttered her eyelashes, except it looked more
like she had dirt under a contact lens. "I never really meant that."

He resisted laughing out loud. "Really?" He took three steps
toward her, into her space, moving as close as he could without
making physical contact. His heart beat faster than normal and
the scent of her perfume teased him. He towered over her, and
she had to look up to give him that come-hither look. He'd bet it
took all of her reserve not to flinch.

"Ever had a cowboy?" Her face was flawless, the skin on her
throat as smooth as glass. Damn tempting.

She swallowed hard enough for him to see and whispered.
"Not yet."

He kept his eyes locked on hers as he lowered his mouth closer
and closer. Their lips almost touched.

She detected a hint of musky cologne on his body and
peppermint on his breath. She closed her eyes in expectation of

his kiss. Butterflies danced the two-step in her stomach. When he spoke, she felt puffs of warm air from his mouth on her lips. Desire pulsed through her body.

"Know something about cowboys, Ms. Daniels?" He was so close. "We know bull when we hear it."

With that, he backed away, leaving her with her head tilted up and her lips puckered. Adam returned to the desk chair and sat.

She spun around ready to lash out at him but he held up his hand to interrupt her tirade. "Don't play games with me, Ms. Daniels. You play with fire, and you'll get burned. Even in a fire house." He riveted his eyes to her face.

She seethed, partly because she'd wanted him to kiss her and he'd embarrassed her by not. She'd just made a fool of herself. Why couldn't she think clearly around this man? He was right. She had been toying with him. Perhaps it would be better just to tell him why she was there. She took a deep breath and looked around for a chair. There was one in the corner.

She eyed Adam. "I'm sorry. I was, ah, I'm sorry. Could we start again? Please? Mind if I sit?"

He maintained his cool reserve, never looking up from a report in his hands. "Suit yourself."

She dragged the brown metal folding chair up to the desk and sat across from him. She waited patiently for him to look at her, then she reached for the folder, opened it, and removed the three printed notes. "I received these e-mails. They reference unspecified fires that I can't identify. This e-mail is a list of locations that I'd like to check against the addresses of the suspicious fires."

Suddenly, she had Adam's full attention. She shrugged. "I'm not exactly sure what I'm looking for."

He reached for the notes. "When did you get these?" He looked at her with one eyebrow arched. "And who is Favfan?"

"I don't know. I tried to reply to the messages but I couldn't. Every time, it comes back with an error message."

"Why do you think someone would send these to you?"

"I don't know. Until this morning, I didn't even make a connection. I thought it was just some prankster or something."

"What happened this morning?"

"This note with the list of dates and addresses was in my inbox. Yesterday at the hospital Jimmy and Bud rehashed the Rippey Street fire and then mentioned Crandon Circle and it all came together. Are these the dates and addresses of the fires you're investigating?"

Adam compared it to the master list at his elbow. He nodded as his eyes moved back and forth between the pages. From what she could see reading upside down, they appeared to match. "Are they all arsons?"

"Right now they're all suspicious. I can tell you that at least two were deliberately set. We don't have confirmation yet, but it appears yesterday's fire also was intentional."

He set the pages aside. "What I want to know is what you have to gain by all this." His question stunned her and she glared at him.

"What do you mean?"

"What does 'do your homework' mean?"

Her voice raised an octave. "I don't know. What are you implying?"

"These notes are almost a confession. They say the fires were set. What do you gain by knowing that? An exclusive story?" The insult was a low blow.

"How dare you. My brother was hurt fighting one of these fires."

His finger tapped the printouts. "Your brother was also a first responder for every one of these fires. Do you think that is more than just a coincidence?"

She jumped to her feet. "Who do you think you are making accusations like that? Who are you anyway? I ran your name, Adam Mitchell. No such person exists. For all I know, you're Favfan. Who are you and what are you doing here?"

Adam stood as well and closed the office door. Then he turned and approached her slowly.

"You think I'm not real? I'll be glad to show you how real I am." His words should have frightened her, but that deep voice summoned those butterflies for another dance. His eyes turned almost smoky. "What do you say, Ms. Daniels? Minutes ago you wanted to play this game for your own benefit." He narrowed his eyes. "Let's play it on my terms now. I think you would thoroughly enjoy finding out just how real I am."

Valerie backed up two steps but the chair blocked any further retreat. Adam was in her space again, towering over her again. They breathed hard, their chests rising and falling in unison, each focused on the other's mouth. If he kissed her right now, she'd faint. She raised her hands to his chest to block him, discovering rock solid pecs beneath his shirt. Oh God. He felt as good as he looked.

"Who are you, Adam Mitchell?" she whispered, wanting to know so much more than that. "Who are you really?"

A knock on the door caused them both to jump apart when Jimmy walked in. "You two fighting in here? Sounds like yelling from outside."

She laid her hand against her chest to cover her pounding heart then started digging in her purse to retrieve her ringing cell phone.

Adam cleared his throat. "Just some First Amendment issues. Seems the press thinks it has the right to know everything." Jesus, he could barely speak. He'd been ready to drag her into his arms and devour her, beginning at her dark red mouth that dared him. It had started with her defiant stance in the doorway, daring him then, too. And that little show she performed, leaning back on the desk and tempting him. She hadn't been serious, but she'd looked damn sexy with her eyes partly closed and her perky breasts pressing against her shirt. His legs had propelled him toward her against his will. More like the lower half of his body had led the way.

When had she taken control of that? Usually he was the one setting the pace, tempting the prey and then taking his good old time capturing it. Valerie wasn't falling all over him like most women. Was that what made her so damn appealing? Because sure as hell, this woman was sneaking beneath his skin.

Jimmy laughed and glanced at Valerie, but she was absorbed by the phone call. She sank onto the folding chair and the color drained from her face. "What? Oh my God, when?" Tears welled in her eyes and began a slow crawl down her cheeks. She shook her head to whatever the caller was saying. "No, no. I'm coming right now. I'll meet you there."

Jimmy frowned and waited for her to end the call. "Is everything all right, Val? Is it Vince?"

She rose slowly, shaking her head, and spoke barely above a whisper. "A friend of mine died last night. Please excuse me."

Her hands trembled when she reached for her car keys and purse. She didn't appear to hear when they expressed their condolences.

"We better check with the hospital," Adam said after she was gone. "If Vince is being released today, she's in no condition to pick him up."

9

In Valerie's confused state, she'd left her manila folder on the desk. Adam and Rick Martellan had no qualms about scrutinizing the notes and trying to e-mail Favfan. They received an error message each time. The sender obviously knew how to hack programs.

There was little Adam's agency technicians could discern from only the paper copies. They traced the root of the e-mail address, only to discover it was somehow diverted and re-routed. He doubted Valerie would surrender her desk computer to a crime lab tech to investigate further. The arsonist seemed to be inserting Valerie into the action. Why? Was it to promote her career and if so, did that point a finger directly at her brother?

He was a first responder at every fire, including the one in which he and Chester were injured. If it was Vince, he certainly wouldn't deliberately incur an injury, and Adam doubted he would allow a fellow fireman to suffer an injury, especially Chester. Vince worshipped Chester.

The other consideration was that these notes inserted Valerie into a perilous position, possibly dangerous. That made him uneasy. Rick wasn't as convinced. He suggested that Vince and

Chester sustaining injuries could have been a miscalculation or a plan that went awry, He speculated a connection between Valerie and Favfan.

Was the arsonist's plan to endear himself to Valerie by giving her an exclusive scoop on a sensational news story? If that was the case, what kind of man had she attracted? Certainly a dangerous one.

Was it Richard, the parking lot molester, trying to pay her back for her rejection? He'd made a veiled threat that night, but the suspicious fires began prior to his attack. He may like to strong-arm women, but Adam didn't think Richard had the balls for arson. Nevertheless, Favfan seemed to have Valerie in his crosshairs.

If only he could simply sit down and discuss these various theories with her. But for some reason, nothing seemed simple where she was concerned. Certainly not the emotions she stirred in him. He liked her ambition and her intelligence. Listening to her on the radio each morning, it was obvious she was smarter, better educated than her colleagues. She had a quick mind and a quirky sense of humor. Gina had made him appreciate a woman who took pride in her appearance. Any time he'd seen Valerie, she'd been professionally dressed, her makeup done and her nails polished. He could only imagine what those dark red nails would feel like running the length of his back. Too bad he'd never find out, especially if her involvement in these arsons was not as innocent as he wanted to believe.

Later that day, he tossed around their suppositions with Gina. He cautiously told her about Valerie's admission that she'd tried to trace his identity. That was potentially a problem, and it concerned him. Gina hit the roof.

"That bitch. Who does she think she is?"

"She's a news reporter trying to flush out what her sixth sense is telling her. She's no different than a cop playing a hunch. She hasn't done anything that you wouldn't do if you had an odd feeling about someone."

Gina wasn't happy. "Well, she's not a cop. And why are you defending her? Remember, you're on a case, Adam. Getting involved with her could cost you your job. Please don't tell me you are attracted to her."

"I'm not attracted to her." He recalled that moment in the chief's office when he came so close to kissing her and she, with her eyes closed and her face upturned, seemed ready. A flush of heat spread through him. He hadn't told Gina that part of their encounter. What might have happened if Jimmy hadn't knocked on the door?

It looked like it was going to be a slow Friday night at that corral. He gave Gina a peck on the cheek and headed to his hotel suite for some much needed down time.

"I'll wait for you tonight after we close," Gina cooed in case anyone was paying attention to them. They doubted it. There were fewer than ten people in the bar tonight. But to be safe, Adam ran his hand down Gina's back and over her ass and nuzzled her ear. To the casual observer it was the promise of things to come. He strolled through the hotel lobby contemplating a cold beer when he heard raucous laughter coming from the lounge. How could this out-of-the-way spot be jumping tonight when Shots in the Dark was dead? The commotion drew him to the entrance.

Sue and Valerie were sprawled over four seats at the bar, rip-roaring drunk. Their voices were loud and they wobbled in their chairs, grabbing each other for balance. Wads of tissue sat in tiny mounds around them along with several empty glasses.

Adam walked in and signaled the bartender. Since he was

staying here and stopped often on the way to his room, the staff knew him.

He nodded toward the women. "What's up with them?"

"From what I can make out, someone is dead. They've been bawling all night. I shut them off about an hour ago, but I think they drank somewhere else first. I already took their car keys off the bar and neither one of them noticed. I'm about ready to call a cab, but I'm not sure either of them can recite their address."

Adam smiled. "Thanks but I'll handle it. I know them." A look of relief crossed the bartender's face and he handed over two key fobs. He strolled to the women and touched the brim of his hat. "Ladies. What are you doing here?"

Sue shrieked, attracting everyone's attention. "She's dead." She started blubbering and reached wildly for Adam, practically falling off the barstool.

He looked at Valerie and grinned at the sight. Her mascara was smeared beneath her eyes, like a cute little raccoon. She sat with her shoulders slumped and a vacant look on her face as if she recognized him but couldn't place him. He turned his attention back to Sue, who tugged on his arm.

He steadied her on the bar stool. "Where's Dolan tonight?" But Sue didn't answer. She folded her arms on the bar, dropped her head onto them and moaned like a wounded animal. "It's our fault."

He dialed Dolan. "What's up, man?"

He didn't waste time with the amenities. "You better come to the Benton Falls Hotel bar now. Sue and Valerie are here and they are wasted. You have to take them out of here."

"I've been trying to find her all night. I'll be right there." While they waited for Dolan, he tried to calm the women. Sue was inconsolable. When she wasn't crying she was demanding that the bartender serve her another drink. He filled a rock glass with ice, added water and a lemon twist and placed it in front of her. She didn't know the difference. Valerie remained in a drunken stupor.

"How much have you had to drink tonight, ladies?"

Sue pounded her glass on the bar. "Not enough."

Dolan's arrival caused Sue to wail and throw herself into his arms, almost knocking him over. He signaled to Adam.

"You handle Valerie, and I'll take Sue home. Thanks, man."

"Wait a minute. Stop. I'm not going to take care of her. Why can't you take them both home with you?"

Dolan struggled to hold Sue up, grab her purse, take her keys from Adam, and maintain his own balance. "Help me out here, buddy. I'll call you tomorrow." With that, he stumbled with Sue out of the bar.

Now what? She stared without seeing him. "What do you say I call a cab for you, Ms. Daniels?"

She blinked once, twice, her lids dropping and raising slowly over those dark brown eyes. She offered him a lopsided smile. "Hey, Tex."

He snaked his arm around her waist, registering somewhere in his brain how tiny she was, and helped her off the stool. But Valerie had no legs to support herself so he wrapped both arms around her and felt a rush of excitement having her so close. She laid her full weight against his chest, threw her arms around his neck, and giggled.

Removing her purse from the back of the chair, he opened it to deposit her cell phone and car keys inside and draped it over his shoulder. Valerie threw her head back and laughed loudly. "Really, Tex. If you nee money I loan you some. You don aft to steal purse." She clung to his shoulders with both hands and squinted, as if that might clear her vision.

"Thank you, Ms. Daniels. That's generous of you." Her head bobbed in agreement. He advanced them toward the door, well aware that the other patrons in the bar watched their progress.

Once in the lobby, he maneuvered Valerie toward an overstuffed sofa near the hotel entrance.

"You sit here, and I'll call for a cab."

Suddenly, she clutched at his shirt and croaked, "I gonna be sick." She bent over and threw up on the lobby floor, then started to cry.

He acknowledged the horrified look on the desk clerk's face. "I apologize for that. Charge the clean up to my room." He leaned Valerie against his side, splayed his hand across her hip to keep her close, and whisked her down the hall. She didn't give a warning the second time and puked on her shirt and jeans before bending over into a waste can just outside the suite. When he thought it was safe, he nudged her inside.

Over the course of various assignments, he'd spent weeks in fleabag motels and in deluxe accommodations, and these rooms were right up there with the best of them. Straight inside the door was a living area with two plump chairs and a sofa grouped in front of an entertainment center on the back wall. To the left of the front door was a fully equipped efficiency kitchen. A small dining table for four and matching hutch served as a dining area off the kitchen and opened onto one of two private patios.

He'd spent several nights sipping his favorite port outside on the patio and relaxing to the sounds of a small waterfall in the center of the common area. The living room opened out to the second patio and served as the divider between the living space and two large bedrooms that shared a master bath. There were two spacious clothes closets, a full china cupboard and other accessories to make someone staying long-term feel right at home. He stumbled along with Valerie to the bathroom, where she bent over the commode and was sick again. Her nose was running, she was crying and slobbering.

"He, hel, help me. I can't stop throwin' up." She fell to her knees and clung to the sides of the toilet bowl.

Adam brushed the hair back from her sweaty forehead. She

was in for a long, miserable night. "Nothing we can do until you get it all out, honey. Hang onto this porcelain throne for a couple minutes, can you?"

He strode to the living room and deposited Valerie's bag on the sofa. He took off his hat, removed his boots and socks, and his shirt. Barefoot, in just a T-shirt and blue jeans, he returned to the bathroom.

Valerie was in the position he'd left her, coughing and gagging. The odor of vomit permeated the room. He flushed the toilet and squatted behind her, positioning her between his legs. Gently, he leaned her back against his chest.

"You stink, darlin'. Let's get you out of these."

She wore a short sleeve shirt with a contrasting cotton sweater. Adam eased one arm and then the other through the sleeves of the sweater as if he were undressing a toddler. Her head wobbled from side to side as he lifted her shirt off. He tossed the garments into the bathtub.

He paused, seeing faint marks from the bite on her neck. It had healed nicely but remembering the source of the scar made his temper flare. Had the hang-up calls stopped?

"Wha you doin?" she mumbled.

"This hotel has a fantastic laundry service. They work wonders with puke. Let's give them the jeans, too." She didn't appear to comprehend his words. Removing the jeans would be harder, but they were pretty rank. Reaching around her from behind, he unsnapped the snap and rolled down the zipper. They fit her nicely, clinging to her thighs and her tight butt. "Valerie, can you help me take off your pants?"

"Are we makin' luv?" She was bleary eyed but smiling. The sight made him laugh. "No honey, I like my women to remember when I make love to them. C'mon, help me here. Lean back." He leaned her against the wall and removed her blue high heels. Then he tugged and wrenched on the denim. Valerie screwed up her face. "Donne you wan a make luv to me? I'm not attractive you?"

Adam slid his hands beneath her bottom to lift it and eyed the smooth skin of her breasts while he yanked at the jeans. Her belly button was pierced with a gold jewel that had three vertically hanging small diamonds. She wore a lavender lace bra and matching lace bikini panties.

She was a tiny thing and he'd guess a regular exerciser. Her arms were toned and her belly flat. He liked the feel of her skin, soft as puppy fur, and felt a surge of longing course through him as the jeans came off. Even reeking of alcohol and puke, she was beautiful. Her bewilderment made him smile.

"Actually, you have no idea how attractive you are right now, sweetheart. But I don't think you're in the right mood."

A wave of nausea wracked her body again and he quickly bent her over the toilet. But she no longer had anything to bring up. Now she sobbed.

She cried uncontrollably, mumbling about Sue and her dead friend and her own lonely life. Adam sat on the floor, leaned against the bathroom wall and positioned her between his legs and onto his chest. He wrapped his arms around her.

"Take deep breaths," he whispered. "Relax." He caressed her face and her back and swept the sweat-soaked hair off her forehead while she sobbed and her stomach involuntarily heaved.

"Deep breaths, honey. You have to calm your stomach muscles. Shh, try to relax."

He woke and blinked against the blinding fluorescent bathroom light. He checked his watch. Three-thirty in the morning and he was pinned against the wall on the cold tile floor with Valerie sprawled across his stomach. She snored and drooled on his T-shirt.

He shifted slowly, every inch of him stiff. He raised his legs and straightened his back to stretch those muscles. She didn't stir. Dead to the world. He slid himself out from the wall and hung onto her when he stood. Bending over, he lifted and carried her into the spare bedroom. As gently as he could, he laid her on the bed and drew a comforter over her.

She'd be miserable when she woke up and likely have no idea where she slept. He switched on the bathroom light and left the door partially open so that if she awakened she'd be able to see her surroundings. He went to the living room, stretched out on the couch, and fell back to sleep.

It was after eight when Adam woke again. He walked barefoot into the kitchen to set the coffee pot to brew, then peeked in at Valerie. She slept soundly. He tiptoed into his bedroom, removed a dress shirt from the closet and draped it at the bottom of her bed. She'd need something to wear when she woke up. Walking out onto the patio so he didn't disturb her, he dialed room service to order breakfast. While he waited for the double order of eggs, bacon, toast, and fresh fruit, he called Gina. Valerie and Gina were the same size, a detail he'd noticed when he removed Valerie's jeans. Recalling that moment sent a pleasant wave of heat through his body, and he shifted in his chair. "Hey, partner. How was your night?"

"You sound chipper," Gina said. "My night was lonely. I didn't get to see my fiancé, and my partner stood me up. I thought you were coming over last night. Did you end up cheating on me?"

Gina could usually sense when he spent the night with a woman. Only her radar was a little off this time. "Well, I ended up running a goodwill mission, and I need a little favor in that regard."

"I don't understand."

"Will you bring over a pair of blue jeans and some kind of sweater or sweatshirt?" Silence emanated from the other end of the line for fifteen seconds before Gina spoke slowly. "Um, I don't think they will fit you, my friend. Care to tell me what's going on?"

Sheesh. He was as nervous as a school kid caught cheating on a test. The minute he told Gina that Valerie Daniels was asleep in her underwear in the other room, she would go ballistic. She did.

"I knew that woman was going to be a problem. Did you sleep with her? Please tell me you aren't that stupid."

"I didn't sleep with her. She threw up all over herself. I missed the laundry pick-up this morning. She'll need some clothes. Just come over. I ordered breakfast for both of us. You can lecture me in person over breakfast. And bring one of your migraine pills. She's going to have a whopper of a headache."

Hearing a noise, he went to check on Valerie. He knocked softly on the bathroom door and she raised her eyes to look at him through the mirror. She stood at the sink trembling, inhaling deeply. Her makeup was smeared and she held her hands to her head, jamming her index fingers into her temples. The circles beneath her eyes looked darker. Earlier he'd put a glass of water and one aspirin on the sink vanity for her.

He walked up behind her and reached for the glass. "You should go back to sleep. Take one small sip. Let's see if it stays down." The glass shook as she took it, cupped it in both hands, and sipped. She stared at him in the mirror, her eyes searching his face.

No sign of a reaction "I think your stomach has stabilized. Take this with another small sip of water." He handed her the pill, and she obeyed.

"Gina is on her way over. If this stays down, she has a headache pill that should help you."

Valerie shivered, and he wrapped his arm around her shoulders and walked her back to the bedroom. He tugged the blankets back and watched her crawl into bed and curl into a fetal position, never taking her eyes off him as he covered her. "I'll be in to check on you in a little bit."

Gina arrived with clothes, drugs, and an attitude. She said out loud everything that had gone through his mind for the last few hours. What was he thinking? Did he realize he was risking his undercover status as well as his career? Who was Valerie Daniels to him really? Was he attracted to her? What really happened last night? What had he wanted to happen? That last question took him by surprise because it made his heart leap. Last night, as he held Valerie in his arms, he'd asked himself what he wanted for his life. He'd kissed the top of her head, run his fingertips over her sleeping face, and thought about what it would be like to share his life with a woman like her, passionate about everything she tackled. He'd wanted to hold her forever.

He poured Gina a cup of coffee and asked her to wait on the patio. With the migraine pill in hand, he gently shook Valerie awake. When she opened her eyes he smiled at her.

"Take this, Valerie. You'll feel much better when you wake up."

"What is it?" she whispered. "Why should I?"

Adam brushed the hair off her forehead. "It will ease your headache. Take it because you trust me to take care of you." He leaned over, supported her beneath her shoulders, and helped her sit up. She kept wary eyes on him but dutifully swallowed the pill he offered. Then she lay back down and closed her eyes. Adam rejoined Gina on the patio.

"Is she okay?"

"I think she'll be better when she wakes up. Thanks for the meds." He sat at the table, lifted the metal lids from the serving bowls on the room service food cart and began preparing a plate, hoping to delay a confrontation. It didn't work.

"First the parking lot incident, Adam, which I realize was a coincidence and a good thing you were there. Then you risk your life to save her brother. Now you're playing nursemaid, letting everyone see you bring her to your room.

"You're on an undercover assignment, remember? Who appointed you her personal protector? And what if she is connected in some way to the arsons? What if this is all a ploy to deceive you?"

"I hardly think a tragic accident and a drinking binge are part of some master plan on Valerie Daniels' part to divert my investigation." He handed her a full plate.

"Valerie Daniels was a total stranger to you just a few weeks ago. Now she's asleep in your bed. You don't find that strange?"

"She's not in my bed. She's in the other bedroom."

"What really happened last night? Are you telling me the truth?" He dished up a second plate of scrambled eggs, bacon, and fresh fruit and settled it in front of him. He held his fork poised over the dish and regarded his partner, appreciating her loyalty and her protective concern

"I've never lied to you and I won't start now. I did not sleep with her last night. Not unless you consider sleeping on the bathroom floor with a drunken, drooling woman a sexual encounter. It's not my idea of a good time. My back is still stiff even though I stood under the hot shower for a long time. I told you everything that happened. It was the simple truth." He dug his fork into the eggs. Gina tasted a bite of bacon, chewed, and swallowed. Then she used the crisp bacon strip as a pointer. "But?"

"But what?"

"But she's different than any other woman you've known."

How could she be so damn perceptive? "She is."

"And after last night, you feel sorry for her."

"I do." He bit into a piece of toast, hoping the interrogation was over. It wasn't.

"And if she has nothing to do with the arson notes then she could be in danger. And that concerns you."

"It does."

"And that combination makes her vulnerable, which is your weakness, my friend. Somewhere, in your head or your heart or your pants, I'm not sure where, you're attracted to her. That's a problem, Adam."

She was right on all counts. All three of those places she named were attracted to Valerie. "I might be."

Gina threw up her arms and leaned back in her chair. "Dammit."

"Relax, partner. Maybe it's more fascination but whatever, it won't go anywhere. I'll be careful. You and I both know there's no time for a relationship when we're undercover. Your fiancé hates your current assignment. I'm not about to be derailed by Valerie Daniels, even if I do find her fascinating. The feeling isn't mutual, believe me. She has no interest in me so you don't have to worry. Besides, I have you to keep me on the straight and narrow. It's under control."

Gina leaned forward shaking her head slowly and raised her fork. She obviously didn't believe that any more than he did.

10

Valerie lay still in the bed and looked slowly around the unfamiliar room. Where was she? Every muscle in her body screamed when she sat up, as if she'd been beaten to a pulp. She ran her fingers through her hair. Thankfully, her head didn't hurt. Her mouth was dry and her breath sour. Where were her clothes?

The digital clock's orange numbers on the nightstand glowed one-thirty three. Was that morning or afternoon? She eased her legs over the side of the bed, using the furniture to steady herself, and stood. Was she ill? She was so weak. The partially opened door across the room offered a glimpse of a white pedestal bathroom sink. Taking tentative steps, she reached the door but decided against switching on the bathroom light.

The toiletry case on the back of the commode emblazoned with the words "For our guests" puzzled her but she gladly used the toothbrush and toothpaste to scrub her teeth twice. Then she turned on the faucet and stepped into the shower.

The pulsating hot water invigorated her and she stood like that for a long time, letting the heat and steam soothe her swollen eyelids and relax her muscles as it cascaded down her neck, her breasts, and her legs, before washing her hair and scrubbing her face and body with the sample bottles of shampoo and body wash. When she reached for a white bath towel, she felt decidedly better. She towel-dried her hair and used a black comb from the toiletry bag to comb her hair straight back. It parted naturally in the center with a few wet wisps falling over her forehead. Once dry, she wrapped herself in the towel, returned to the bed and scanned the room. Where were her clothes?

She didn't recognize the shirt at the bottom of the bed, but she slipped into it, finding no other alternative in sight. It hung below her knees. Definitely a man's shirt. But whose? She rolled the French cuffs three times to reveal her hands. Her stomach growled, but her throat felt raw. She opened the bedroom door and peered out. Where the hell was she?

A quick scan of the room showed it was neat and clean but not homey. There was nothing personal in the room. Okay, she was in a hotel. That was obvious. But where? How had she arrived here? Voices drifted in from outside and she walked barefoot toward them.

Gina and Adam were comparing multiple pages spread on the table in front of them. When Adam noticed her standing inside the opened sliding glass door, he stood and came toward her smiling, his hand outstretched.

"Hi. How are you feeling?"

Gina stood as well and moved behind him.

"This, this isn't what it looks like." She clutched the shirt collar closed at her throat.

Gina glowered at her. "It looks like you're wearing my boyfriend's shirt and coming out of his bedroom."

Adam's jaw dropped and he raised an eyebrow at her.

"Lucky for you I trust Adam implicitly. He told me all about last night. I'm sorry about your friend."

Well, that stirred one memory: the accident. Valerie dropped her gaze and mumbled thank you.

"How are you feeling?" Adam asked again.

"I'm not sure. How did I get here?"

"You were in need of assistance." That sounded so formal.

"And I called you?" Why hadn't she called her brother? Why ask a strange man for help?

Gina had gathered all the files and folders from the table and stuffed them in a briefcase. She picked up her purse and came up behind Adam. "Yes. In his spare time, Adam likes to play Sir Galahad. Don't feel too special though. He takes in stray puppies, too."

Adam snapped at the comment. "Gina. That's uncalled for."

Gina's gaze shifted from Adam to her. "I'm sorry. That was a mean thing to say. I'm glad he was able to help you." She wrapped her arm around Adam's waist. "I have to go to the bar. I'll see you in a little while, won't I?" She emphasized each word in the last sentence, making her point to both of them.

"You will. I'll come over soon." He leaned toward her and she kissed him on the cheek. As she brushed past her she said, "I hope you feel better."

Neither of them said anything until the door closed. He held out his hand to her. "Come out and sit in the sun. You'll feel better. I'll pour you some coffee. Do you feel like you could eat something?"

She slid her hand into his big, warm hand and stepped through the door. It seemed as if he transmitted strength through his fingers. He escorted her to the table and retrieved the portable hotel phone. "I like a greasy burger and fries after a drinking binge. That appeal to you or do you want something lighter? Breakfast maybe?"

She slipped into a chair at the glass-topped patio table with her back to the sun. "Maybe just some toast and coffee, please. I'm not sure I can handle even that."

The mere subject of food threatened to make her retch again. Adam disappeared inside while he ordered room service. He returned with a glass of ice water and set it in front of her. "Water should be your friend today."

She offered a soft "thank you."

"It'll be about fifteen minutes." He sat in the chair across from her. "Are you okay?"

What had she done last night? Had she embarrassed herself? Worse. Did she throw herself at him? Nausea threatened. "I have no recollection of last night. How did I get here?"

Adam recounted finding her and Sue in the bar and calling Dolan to take Sue home.

"And I came here? To your room with you?"

He smiled. "Yes ma'am, you did." She clutched the collar of his shirt closer to her throat. "Did we, um, did I sleep with you?"

The seconds ticked by in slow motion in direct opposition to her racing heart. Her body began to overheat. He didn't smile. He didn't nod. He didn't react at all. Just two words: "You did."

It was devilish but he couldn't resist. She looked like she might throw herself into the waterfall if she thought they'd slept together. Her breath caught in her throat and her jaw dropped. She covered her face with her hands and muttered, "Oh dear Lord." Did she find the idea so repulsive?

"Relax, Valerie. You slept with me on the bathroom floor because you couldn't stop throwing up and I wasn't about to leave you alone in there." He winked at the look of relief on her face. "Unfortunately, we were not intimate."

She released the air locked in her lungs with an audible sigh. Teasing her was too much fun. "But it wasn't because you didn't throw yourself at me. It's because I'm faithful to Gina."

She ran a nervous hand through her wet hair. With her face scrubbed clean, she looked even younger and very sexy. Her eyes were big, her lashes long, and her cheeks rosy from blushing. He liked it. He liked a lot about this woman.

"Was I obnoxious to you last night? Did I say things I should be embarrassed about?"

He laughed at her concern. "Relax, sweetheart. You were drunk and what you don't remember I'll never reveal. You needed someone to take care of you and I ended up being that someone." He shrugged. "That's all it was. Not a big deal."

For the first time, she smiled at him. "Yeah but it seems that lately, you end up taking care of me all the time. Me and my brother. That wasn't something you signed on for, I'm sure. And I've never even said a decent thank you. Not really. I've always treated you terribly."

He couldn't suppress a grin. "So say thank you and get it over with."

A knock on the hotel door interrupted their conversation. He went inside and returned with a full breakfast tray, which he placed in front of her. "You said only toast, but I know you must be hungry so eat whatever you want."

The aroma of the eggs, toast, bacon, hash browns, and coffee wafted up and teased Valerie's senses. She was ravenous. She dug into the food with a gusto that made Adam laugh. He watched her eat with a smile on his face and declined her offer to share something from her plate or from the coffee carafe. She cleaned the plate and poured a second cup.

"Where are my clothes?"

"You threw up on them." Oh God. She'd embarrassed herself after all. She covered her face with her hands and muttered another prayer.

"I sent them to the hotel laundry, but they won't be back until tomorrow. I think you look mighty fine in my shirt, but Gina brought you some clean clothes if you want to change into them. She's your size. I think they're in the living room. But don't change on my account."

He flashed that killer grin again. As she stood, her knees went weak and she wondered if it was Adam's smile or the events of the previous night. He'd jumped up ready to catch her if she lost her balance. If she did, she'd fall right into those strong arms.

She raised her hand to reassure him she had her footing, even though she walked tentatively into the suite in search of the clothes. Minutes later, she returned, still barefoot, wearing Gina's jeans rolled up into wide cuffs and a white cotton button-down shirt.

She resumed her seat across from Adam. They sat in silence, enjoying the warmth of the sun, until he finally spoke. "The newspaper has an account of your friend's accident. How long have you known her?"

She studied the blue sky while she calculated the years. Sue had introduced them and they became friends fast. Their birthdays were two days apart and they shared a lot of the same characteristics, she said.

Adam made her laugh when he started counting on his fingers. "Stubborn, bullheaded, pushy..."

She contradicted him. "More like vivacious, fun-loving, witty." She related the memory of the first time the trio went bar hopping together and one story led to another. They'd been a terror and he laughed at her accounts. She laughed, choked up, had a brief breakdown, reaching for tissues Adam somehow produced without her noticing, and felt decidedly better after two hours of rambling. He'd listened to every word.

"Thank you for allowing me to cry on your shoulder."

He pointed at her. "Don't forget throw up in my bathroom."

Damn, he made her smile. She agreed. "Thank you for everything you've done for both of us."

Adam simply smiled and waved away her words and her heart skipped.

He walked her to her car and she drove home. Drained emotionally and physically, she ate a piece of toast for dinner and went to bed at seven o'clock. She drifted to sleep recalling Adam's words, "Unfortunately, we were not intimate." Maybe someday.

11

C.J. Kwin was a tall, lanky man with thinning hair and a know-it-all attitude. No matter what book you read, what movie you saw, or what song played on the radio as you drove to work, Kwin knew one that was written better, ended better or contained stronger lyrics.

Kwin always had to be right, even when he was wrong. It frustrated Adam simply making small talk with the man. He logged an overnight shift with Kwin, Jimmy, and Dave and the hours spent with Kwin were maddening.

The shift kicked off with a rocky start. Adam arrived at the firehouse shortly after five. The men changed shifts at six o'clock each night but regularly arrived early so that Jimmy, Kwin, Dave, Bud, and Vince were all on station when he walked in.

He'd just passed through the open bay doors with his backpack when he heard a screech from the rear of the garage. Suddenly Bud charged him sputtering something about Valerie and threw a weak punch. Adam deftly ducked it but the commotion caught everyone's attention, and they gathered around to see what Bud was so worked up about.

Tears wet his eyes as Bud yelled. "I trusted you. I thought you were one of us."

Adam raised his hands defensively. "Bud, take it easy. What's this about?"

"Yo-you sp-spent the night with Valerie." His emotions had the best of him. "We respect her around here. She's like a goddess. But you-you treat her like trash. And your girlfriend is just blocks away." He waved his hands wildly and spit flew from his lips when he spoke. "Does she know? Huh? How'd you like me to tell her?"

Adam was taken aback by his words. He doubted Valerie would confide in Bud about anything, let alone the night she'd spent sleeping it off in his hotel suite. He measured his words as if he spoke to a frantic five-year-old threatened by a nightmare.

"What are you talking about?"

"Yeah, Bud," Vince piped in. "What are you talking about?" Bud pointed an accusatory finger toward Adam. "She spent the night in his hotel room. Ask him." Then he boldly stepped toward Adam and spit. Most of the spittle fell down the front of his shirt.

He wasn't easily riled and most times, as an easy-going Southern boy, it took a lot for him to lose his temper. But being spit at coupled with hearing Valerie maligned just about pushed him over the edge. He clenched his fists and consciously inhaled two slow, deep breaths. Bud flailed his arms in an attempt to take another swipe at him but Dave and Jimmy intervened and shoved Bud away from the fray. Through clenched teeth, Adam snarled, "Keep him away from me." He moved past the men into the chief's office.

Seconds later, the door closed and he turned to find Vince standing there, his bottom lip tucked between his teeth. He'd seen Valerie do that when she was nervous. "My sister is a big girl. What she does is her own business. But, is that true?"

Adam met Vince's riveting gaze eye-to-eye. "You should ask your sister. It's not my habit to discuss my personal life and I'm not saying anything about Valerie."

But Vince continued to stare at him. "Bud's right, Adam. There's a code among fire brothers."

Did he dare say he knew it, appreciated it and, what's more, respected Vince for standing up to him in defense of his sister's honor. These Daniels kids were made of strong stock.

"Have a talk with your sister, Vince. If she wants you to know, she'll tell you."

Vince scowled. "Fair enough."

The subject didn't come up the rest of the night. Dave was quiet most of the shift. Jimmy whispered that he was recently divorced and still coming to terms with it. Like Adam, Jimmy was a country fan and the two of them talked about current radio hits, favorite singers, and bull riding. Neither one of them had ever ridden one but both imagined it. Jimmy shared that he played the guitar and thought he was good enough to become a singer.

The men sat around the kitchen table playing gin rummy. "What made you become a fireman?"

"It's in the blood," Jimmy said, throwing down a third winning hand. "My dad and his brother were firefighters and my granddad. Ever since I can remember it's what I wanted to do." Adam asked Dave.

"Me, too. I used to chase the fire trucks on my bicycle. My mother would have fits. But it was all I thought about doing with my life."

He'd initiated a similar conversation with Chester, Vince, and Bud when he signed on with their night shift. Almost to a man, it was a career that each lived and breathed. Except for Kwin. He released a nervous laugh. "I was out of work. I answered an ad. They offered training and a stipend. I didn't have any other offers."

Jimmy leaned over and playfully punched Kwin in the shoulder. "But he's got the bug now, don't ya C.J.?"

Kwin grinned and nodded. It didn't strike Adam as very sincere.

As usual, Valerie was running late. Vince sat at the bar in Shots in the Dark drinking a beer and watching Gina work. She was an attractive woman and had an easy way with the customers. He noticed that she garnered more tips than the other bartender.

She'd flashed a warm smile when he sat down and placed a fresh draft in front of him. "My treat," she'd said with a wink. Then she'd turned her attention to another customer. If his sister spent the night with her boyfriend, Gina must not know it. She was being too friendly.

That was one of the reasons he suggested meeting Valerie here. He wanted to see both women's reactions before he asked Valerie what was going on.

She rushed in and planted a kiss on his cheek. She apologized for being late and climbed onto the stool next to him. "I'll just have a diet whatever," she told the male bartender. She breathlessly told her brother it had started to rain and she'd run from her car. "How was your day?"

"Okay until the end of shift."

"What happened at the end of the shift?"

Vince turned in the chair to face her. "Bud accused Adam of sleeping with you. I know it's none of my business Sis, but is that true?"

Valerie's eyebrows shot to her hairline. "No, it's not true." The "no" came out in a long high-pitched squeal.

He detected something off in her voice. "Why would he say something like that?"

"He's crazy, that's why. You know he obsesses about me."

"Did you spend the night in Adam's hotel room?"

Valerie stopped halfway through a swallow of soda and studied her brother. His forehead wrinkled with concern. She'd never lied to him when he asked a direct question like this. She had no reason to lie now. "Yes, I did. Unfortunately I don't remember any of it. I was falling down drunk."

Gina came to them, eyed Valerie's choice of refreshments and propped her hands on her hips. "Soda?"

Valerie returned the smile. "I know it's not what a bartender wants to hear, but I may never drink again. Did Adam find your clothes? I left them at the registration desk under his name."

Gina nodded.

"Thank you again for everything you did."

"Don't mention it. Once I thought about the whole situation, I'm glad Adam was there for you. Sorry for what I said when I wasn't thinking." She left to wait on another couple.

She turned back to her brother. "She's tough, but I like her. I guess she has to be in this business. Adam and Gina helped me through a difficult night after my friend died. All I remember is Sue and I drinking in a couple different spots before ending up in the hotel bar. I'm not even sure how I drove there but my car was in the parking lot. I barely remember seeing Adam in the bar, let alone going to his room.

"I woke up the next afternoon in the second bedroom in Adam's suite. I wasn't even in his bedroom, Vince. Gina loaned me some clothes because I threw up all over mine. Doesn't that sound attractive?"

"Why didn't you call me?" His tone had changed to brotherly concern.

"I was too blotto. From what Adam told me, I could barely talk or walk. All I did was throw up. He said he planned to summon a cab but he was afraid I'd never make it home. I guess I was pretty much a blubbering idiot. I'm embarrassed when I think about it. If I never see him again I'll be happy.

"And anyway, when was the last time I had a casual fling like that? That's not my style and you should know he's not my type. I hate cowboys. Let's order, I'm starved. And I want to tell you about some weird e-mails I've received."

Which reminded her, she should return to the fire station for those and find out if Adam was able to trace them to the sender.

"Either one of you know much about computers?" Adam asked when the card game ended and they were collecting the match sticks. "I think I have a virus on mine and I can't figure out how to clean it off."

Dave muttered a few curse words about the Internet and e-mails and walked outside to smoke a cigarette. "That's how he found out his wife was having an affair. She left an e-mail from her lover open on the computer screen. It had a time and meeting place and Dave found them together. He went home and smashed the computer."

Adam raised his eyebrows. "Wow, that's rough."

That might eliminate Dave as a Favfan suspect if he didn't have a computer to send notes to Valerie.

Kwin added his two cents. "Poor schmuck. Serves him right for trusting a woman in the first place. We should all have a program to detect deceit. Something that gives off an alarm when a cheating woman signs on." Adam and Jimmy stared at him. Apparently, he was oblivious to the looks on their faces.

"I hate them all. Sashaying around, flaunting their stuff. No matter what they say they always lie. You can't trust none of them. I think they exist solely to destroy our lives."

Jimmy stayed silent. Something tweaked Adam's curiosity. "That's a little harsh, don't you think?"

"No, I don't think so at all. You're pretty trusting of your woman and she's flirting with men every night, dressing the way she does. Unless you're in that bar all the time, you have no idea what goes on. Do you really think she always tells you the truth?" Kwin's nostrils flared, like a bull ready to attack.

Adam shrugged. "I don't think Gina lies to me because I don't lie to her. Trust is a fundamental element in any relationship."

Kwin rolled his eyes. "If you believe that you're not as smart as I thought you were."

Jimmy finally found his voice "Don't you trust your wife?"

Kwin threw his head back and laughed. "She got knocked up to force me to marry her. How can you trust someone like that? She'd do me a favor if she got the hell out of my life. The only people I trust are the men in this fire station who wear blue uniforms like me."

He focused on Adam. "Only men know about loyalty and trust. If you don't believe me, ask Dave." With that, he threw a balled up napkin on the table, rose and walked to the sofa. He grabbed the remote and switched on the television. Jimmy tossed the napkin in the trash and looked to Adam.

"I'm pretty good with computers. I took a couple of courses and I mess around with different programs and stuff. What kind of virus do you think you have?"

"I don't know. It seems to block responses I try to make to certain e-mails."

Jimmy looked surprised and said he'd never heard of that. Kwin yelled to Adam from the couch, "Maybe you should be checking her e-mails."

Jimmy shook his head at the comment. "Let me do some research and see if I can find anything like that."

"Appreciate it."

12

Adam arrived at the daytime fire on the squad truck but instead of suiting up, he studied the crowd, wondering if the arsonist stood now among the spectators admiring his work. The middle-of-the day blaze was reported anonymously as an explosion. The timing—daylight—was unusual but maybe, as he grew bolder, he wanted an audience. Was he bold enough to stay and watch?

Adam observed the teens with the dog huddled together. The girl was cute, with a pink headband in her shoulder-length black hair and a pink shirt with a white shirt over top of it in the layered look the kids wore. She had a fresh-looking red scratch on her cheek, scratches on her arms, and her clothes were dirty.

The boy next to her bore similar dirt marks down the front of his clothes. Fresh scratches decorated his forearms. Neither one of them looked like the kind of kid who wore dirty clothes.

Starting a slow advance toward them, he called the police dispatcher to inquire about the caller reporting the blaze. The caller only gave his first name, Jason, and a dog had been yipping in the background. The kids noticed him approaching and sepa-rated, each walking a different direction. The girl was the closest and he whistled to catch her attention, simultaneously flashing his badge. The boy stopped and watched, concern etched on his face.

"How ya doin?" he asked the girl. "Can I chat with ya'll for a minute?" He let his Southern drawl come through as he gently grasped her elbow.

"Come on over here next to your friend, honey." The boy wasn't about to abandon her. Adam placed his hand behind her shoulders and guided her back toward him. The kid jammed his fists into his jeans and kicked an imaginary pebble with his shoe as they neared. She clutched her dog so tightly, it yelped.

"I'm Fire Inspector Adam Mitchell. Are you Jason?" He showed his credentials to the boy and registered the surprised look on his face.

Kids. He loved them. He smiled and tried to appear less official, despite his three-piece suit. "Relax. You aren't in any kind of trouble. Thanks for calling in the alarm. How'd ya'll happen to discover the fire?"

Jason straightened his shoulders. "I was, ah, I was just walking by."

"Were the two of you here together?"

In unison, they immediately denied being together. The girl nervously surveyed the people eavesdropping and squeezed the dog tighter, eliciting a second yelp.

"No. No. She wasn't with me. I was alone."

He smiled at Jason and gently touched the girl's hand. "You're pinching your pup. What's your name, honey?"

"Tracey."

"Whaddaya say you and me and Jason take a little walk, over here where we can speak privately." He gently nudged Tracey to separate her from the group and Jason followed. When they were out of earshot from everyone, he turned his back to the onlookers.

"As I said, neither one of you is in trouble. I'm just glad that neither of you was hurt. Let me guess. Not allowed to see each other, and doing everything you can to be together, right?"

Tracey's mouth dropped open and Jason took a step backward. "I find myself facing a similar situation in my life right now. I seem to be attracted to someone I shouldn't be and can't stop thinking about her. It's problematical. I'm not here to add more complications to your life."

Their wide-eyed reactions told him he'd hit the bull's eye. "How about we make a deal? You tell me truthfully what you saw and heard today, everything you know, and it stays between us. No one needs to know you were here together. It's pretty important that I learn as much as I can about this fire." Turning to Tracey he added, "Your name will stay in my notebook and only Jason's name will appear on any official report since he was the one who called in the fire. Does that work?"

Adam watched Tracey's forehead visibly relax and Jason expel the breath he'd held. The kids used the next thirty minutes to tell him about their past rendezvous at the vacant house, where they sat on the porch to be together. Both were adamant they'd heard a ringing bell that sounded like a school bell between classes, or like an old fashioned wind-up alarm clock, shortly before the explosion. It scared the hell out of them and they'd jumped from the steps, landing face down on the pavement as the house exploded.

The only thing they could recall out of the ordinary was the day they saw a blue car in the driveway.

Adam looked up from his notebook. "What blue car? When?"

"Right when we arrived. I don't think it was anything," Jason said, "just a car turning around in the driveway."

Tracey disagreed. "It was parked in the driveway and just backing out. I kept worrying that the car would come back and we'd be caught."

"Did you see a driver?" The kids said no. "Can you describe the car for me?"

Jason said that, based on its sound, the car was a standard shift and that the last two numbers on the license plate were six nine. "How do you remember that?"

Jason blushed. "I remember thinking how cool it would be to have only sixty-nine on your license plate."

Adam threw back his head and laughed. Oh, to be eighteen years old again. He gave them each a business card, shook their hands and wished them luck. He winked at Tracey. "Mum's the word."

Like the other fires, the house was saturated with a combustible liquid. The kids had told Adam they'd noticed a pungent smell when they were sitting on the porch but they thought it was the garbage dumpster behind the house next door. If they hadn't heard the ringing sound and jumped to safety, Rick Martellan confirmed both kids would have been killed by the explosion.

He was intrigued by the alarm clock theory. Since the place of origin for ignition would be the clock, that would burn as the hottest spot of the fire. No remnants of a clock or starter device would remain.

"Theoretically, he could give himself a twelve-hour head start, designating an explosion time long after he was gone, thereby establishing an alibi when the blaze was discovered. Like setting it up and then going to work at the fire station, ready and waiting."

Adam eyed the spreadsheet in front of him with the fires plotted and the names of the men who had reported for duty. He highlighted two recurring names: C.J. Kwin and Vince Daniels. "How the hell am I going to establish where these men were twelve hours before they reported to work?"

"Do we have enough to put a tail on those two?"

"No, it's all circumstantial. And weak at that. Let's look for that car the kids saw. We have a partial license plate." He awakened the chief's computer and keyed in the search words, recalling that each fireman had to list the make, color, and license number of the vehicle he parked in the city lot while on duty.

Dave Oswalk and Vince Daniels both drove blue cars but neither listed the digits six or nine as part of their license number. Adam flashed back to Chez Cher's parking lot the night he'd encountered Valerie fighting off Richard Fredtoni against her car. He hadn't taken note of her license plate as she sped from the parking lot but he remembered the vehicle. Valerie drove a blue Pontiac.

13

V alerie stared at the list of new messages in her inbox. She had another message from Favfan. Her heart raced. She held the computer's cursor on the message line but couldn't bring herself to highlight and open it. She read a few other fan e-mails, but her eyes bounced to Favfan's each time she returned to the inbox. She finally clicked the left mouse button with a faltering finger and watched the note expand onto her computer screen.

THIS IS YOUR CHANCE. BREAK THE STORY.

BE CAREFUL WHO YOU TALK TO

Favfan was a madman, whoever he was. Her conversation with her brother three nights earlier convinced her that something was seriously wrong and someone wanted her to know it. Vince was surprised that she'd received the messages, mad that she hadn't told him about them from the very first, and insistent that she tell him and Adam if she received another message. He placed more faith in Adam than she did. Vince thought that

Adam seemed more focused on the arsons than whether the department complied with the state fire regulations.

"Isn't that unusual?" Her reporter's radar was whirling.

Vince shrugged. "I'm new so I don't know what is involved with annual inspections. We need help with these fires, Sis, and he's experienced with incendiary cases. Bud told me the chief grilled him about his background that first day. The way I see it, maybe it's just good timing."

"I don't believe in coincidence. I don't think he's simply a fire inspector. What if he's Favfan?"

Vince laughed so hard his eyes watered. "For once, do what I ask you to do and promise me if you find another note or anything else even remotely related to these fires, you'll tell me or Adam." She'd promised.

As soon as she finished her first news broadcast, she went to her cubbyhole-turned-office and closed the door. Taking a deep breath, she reached for the phone and dialed the Benton Falls fire department. She knew another vacant building had mysteriously exploded and, thankfully, no one was hurt fighting the blaze. Like the others, the structure had been consumed in flames by the time firemen arrived. The building was a total loss.

It sounded like chaos in the background when C.J. Kwin answered the phone. Valerie heard a truck backing in and, assuming Vince had his hands full, she surprised herself by asking if Inspector Mitchell was available. Her heart fluttered while she waited on hold.

"Mitchell," Adam's deep voice oozed through the phone, sending a wave of heat through her like hot chocolate at a Friday night football game.

"Hi, it's Valerie. I promised my brother I'd tell him or you if I received another weird e-mail. I know he's probably busy since there was another fire so I asked for you. Was this one another arson?" The words tumbled from her lips. On the other end of the line, Adam chuckled.

"I'm fine, Ms. Daniels. Thanks for asking. How're y'all?"

She smiled at his indirect reprimand. "I'm sorry. I didn't mean to sound rude."

Adam remained silent on the other end of the phone. "Um, I found another e-mail today."

"What's it say?"

She'd written the thirteen-word message on day twenty-one of the desk calendar. It was the longest message yet and an unlucky length. A shiver ran down her spine as she read it out loud.

"What story are you going to break?"

"I'm not breaking any story. At least not yet. I'm not sure I know the story."

"Do you have it on your screen now?"

"No, but I can call it up." She swung her chair around to face her computer and honed in with the cursor on the message. Two clicks and the bright green note briefly blinded her. Adam asked her to forward it, but when she touched the forward button the recurring error message popped up. "Can you print it and fax me a copy?"

"I think I have the fax number for the station in my files. What do you think it means?"

He didn't respond and she cleared her throat. She was more nervous talking to him than when she'd interviewed with the station owner for this job. "May I have the copies of the other e-mails back?"

"Didn't you save the originals?"

"Oh, yeah, I guess I did. I'll print new copies. Sorry."

"I don't suppose you'd let me and a technician take a look at your computer, would you?"

"What kind of technician?"

"A computer technician, honey." The endearment was meant as sarcasm but her heart skipped. "A computer technician from where?"

"From my office, of course." His words were laced with sweetness and she made hers sound equally as rich.

"What office is that exactly? The state fire inspector's office?"

"Where else?"

She hoped he was sitting at the chief's desk squirming in his chair. She'd searched the entire state's website and couldn't find an Inspector Mitchell in any department. The website broke the state down by regions and then into smaller districts and then listed every conceivable contact. She was no dummy. The sooner he learned that, the better.

"You tell me what other office it might be. I'm familiar with the state's website and I can seem to find what district you're assigned to. I'm curious about your credentials. And where did you say you were from originally?"

Adam snickered. "I don't recall saying."

"Well, this is as good a time as any to answer those questions, don't you think?"

"You didn't answer mine. Will you let me take a look at your desk computer?"

He was trying to change the subject. "No."

"I could get a subpoena and compel you to turn over the computer, you know."

The hairs on the back of her neck bristled and she instantly changed her tone. Damn him. "Do what you have to do, sir. I tried to be a good citizen and report the latest communication regarding a series of suspicious fires in your city. Next time you might just hear it on the news."

She slammed the phone down in its cradle. Adam Mitchell infuriated her. Just when she was beginning to think he might be a decent person, he had to flex his muscles and outrank her. She printed two copies of the newest message and called up the others to print new copies. The fax machine was in the copy room with the printer so she took the page of the most recent e-mail, scribbled 'Mitchell???' across the top, wrote the initials "G.C." on the bottom and faxed it to the fire station.

She'd have to remember to tell her brother that Adam Mitchell had redeemed himself as a jerk.

Her conversation with Adam annoyed her the rest of the day. Everywhere she looked for the facts, she encountered a roadblock. Why had he shown up on the scene the same time Favfan dropped into her mailbox? They had to be connected. With renewed determination to track his credentials, she carried a glass of wine and her laptop to the couch that evening. She balanced the computer on her knees. When her screen opened automatically to her personal e-mail inbox, she practically choked on her drink.

Three new e-mails stared at her. The first one was from Favfan, and the subject line read: "I'll see you."

Her heart ricocheted in her chest. How had he discovered her private e-mail address? Should she open the message? She reached for her wine glass with an unsteady hand, all the while keeping her eyes on the computer screen as if the note might disappear if she looked away. It didn't. She'd left her cell phone on the kitchen table. Should she call Vince? Or Adam? The first thing either of them would ask is what the note said. Her breath came in spurts, as if she'd just completed a five-mile run. She closed her eyes, mentally trying to calm herself. *Relax. You're safe in your own home. It is just an e-mail message.*

From some lunatic. She opened her eyes and focused again on the computer screen. Her hand trembled as she moved to the center of the keyboard and tapped it. The message bloomed before her with one word typed in capital letters on the screen: "SOON."

Jesus. She ejected from her seat, barely snagging the laptop before it hit the floor. She was sick to her stomach as she rushed to the kitchen, her hand outstretched in the direction of the phone.

Vince was on speed dial at number one. She hit the digit and paced the kitchen, waiting for the connection. When Vince's recorded message came on, she snapped the phone shut, annoyed with her brother for not answering. She tapped the contact list button and stared at the listing for Adam. Should she call him? After their conversation this afternoon, he'd probably want to confiscate her work computer and her personal laptop. She couldn't have that. From the kitchen she eyed the laptop on the coffee table. "I'll see you soon," the message said. Favfan must plan to reach out to her.

Okay. She was on alert now. She'd wait for him to contact her and set a trap for him. She wouldn't meet any strangers without Vince and the other firemen knowing where and when it would happen. She could help set up a sting operation like she'd seen in so many movies.

And she'd have the exclusive story of the arsonist's arrest when it went down. This was a much better plan than calling Adam and having him step in and take over. She knew enough to be careful now.

She returned to the living room and repositioned the computer on her lap. She'd forward the e-mail to her work computer, print it and file it with Favfan's other e-mails. And tomorrow, she'd tell Vince about it when they spoke, keeping her promise to him. Valerie moved the cursor to the forward button and pressed. An error message appeared on the screen, restricting her from sending it anywhere. Just like at the radio station. Well, no matter. She could send it to her printer upstairs and take it into work. She read the other two new e-mails in the inbox and was ready to sign out to surf the state website again when her eyes locked on her index of messages and she gasped. Favfan's message was gone.

Vince Daniels arrived twenty minutes earlier than usual for his shift the next day. He went straight to the chief's office where Adam sat at the desk. Vince knocked on the open door and, when Adam waved him in, he closed the door behind him. "I owe you an apology."

He strode to the desk with his hand outstretched. Adam rose and shook hands with him.

"Ah, thanks but it's not necessary."

"Yes, it is. I jumped to the wrong conclusion without reason. I should thank you for saving my sister's drunken ass. In fact, I am thanking you."

Adam smiled. He liked this kid. There was something almost innocent about him. He saw it in Valerie, too, but she worked hard to conceal it. "You're welcome."

Vince shoved his hands in his pants pockets. "Can I talk to you about her?"

Adam's heart skipped. He'd love to talk about Valerie. There was so much he wanted to know about her. Maybe when this investigation was over, he'd contact her. Maybe try to start fresh. Their relationship, whatever it was, was as choppy as Lake Erie. "What about her?"

He motioned for Vince to sit and watched him drag the same folding chair that Valerie had used to the front of the desk. "I'm worried about these e-mails she's receiving. I know you're looking at all of the fires. I'm not certain that's part of your routine inspection, but I don't care. I think they were deliberately set."

"What makes you think that?" Was he talking to the arsonist right now? His gut told him no.

"The way they burn, so fast and hot, we don't have a chance. We responded to that last fire in minutes and it was already beyond saving. You don't have to be an arson specialist to know there was more than one hot spot at those fires."

He pointed his forefinger at Adam. "Based on the fire patterns, I'd say the arsonist used some kind of accelerant to saturate all those places. As a fireman, that worries me. The fact that someone is e-mailing my sister about those fires scares the hell out of me."

Adam leaned back in his chair with his hands in front of his mouth. His fingertips touched, forming a small pyramid, like the church and steeple game he'd played as a kid.

Vince continued. "Valerie doubts you're an actual fire inspector. In fact, she told me you hinted that I might be a suspect for the fires. I—"

He interrupted. "Does that concern you?"

"No, sir." Vince looked him in the eye as he said it, clear and strong. No revealing body language here. He wasn't nervous, he was confident. "I'm very aware that these fires began when the newbies came on board and it looks bad for me. But you don't need to waste your time looking at me. I'm not your firebug, Adam. I'll tell you anything you ask if it helps you find the bastard. I'll climb in your back pocket so you know where I am and what I'm doing every minute of the day. What worries me is the thought that this sicko who is sending Valerie e-mails is connected to the arsons. Hell, he may be the arsonist."

He rose to pace the small office. "I'm not concerned about me. I'm concerned about Valerie being dragged into this. Especially now that she received a note at her home."

Adam's jaw dropped and he sat forward. "When?"

"You didn't know? She didn't contact you? She opened her laptop last night and there was a note that said 'I'll see you soon.' I told her to call you. I guess she didn't."

Adam shook his head and sifted through the pages inside a thick manila folder. He showed Vince the newly faxed page from Valerie.

"I thought this was the most recent note she received." Vince read it with his mouth pinched tight. Then he grinned and pointed to the last name with the series of question marks beside it. "My sister is a trip sometimes." He spotted the initials at the bottom of the page. "G.C.?"

Adam chuckled. "Good citizen."

Vince let out a small laugh. "Well, at least she called you about that one. I made her promise to tell one of us."

Adam raised one eyebrow. "Next time make her promise not to slam the phone down in my ear." He laughed again and, after a second or two, Vince did too.

"Sorry. You gotta love her though. When she hooks on to something, she's passionate about it."

Adam's heart flipped. He'd love to be the object of some of that passion, in the right context. He cleared his throat and willed the lower part of his body to retreat. "Could you two have an enemy trying to score two strikes with one swipe?"

Vince couldn't think of anyone.

"How will your sister handle all this? Will a big story make her career?"

Vince narrowed his eyes and glared at him. "My sister is a responsible news person. She won't hurt other people, especially me, just to move ahead. If I can help you in any way, I will. In return, if you discover she's in harm's way, please tell me. Don't let anyone hurt her."

Adam nodded slowly. "I don't want to see her get hurt either." He really didn't.

14

———

V alerie parked in her garage after returning from a lively dinner with Sue that did not include alcohol. She double checked the dashboard clock against her watch and groaned, seeing it was almost midnight. Two alarms might guarantee she woke up on time in only a few hours.

She walked through the door between the garage and the kitchen and stopped at her kitchen counter, dumping her sweater and purse on top of it. A noise behind her startled her and she spun around. A fist smashed into her face.

"Did you have fun with your cowboy?"

Slowly, the room came into focus through blurred vision. A weight pressed into her face, challenging her breathing. She inhaled through her mouth, blinked twice, and shook her head. That hurt.

She scanned the room. Everything was sideways and her right arm was twisted uncomfortably beneath her. She lay on the kitchen floor. Judging by the cool breeze on her feet, the inside door was ajar and the garage door open. She lifted her head to look and saw darkness outside. The movement made her dizzy and she rested her head on the floor. The breaths through her mouth came fast and panic washed over her in tiny beads of sweat along her back. Her purse, with its contents spilling out, had fallen by the refrigerator. Her neck muscles protested when she lifted her head again and peered toward her feet. Blood covered her legs and her slacks and panties were knotted around one ankle. She blinked away the dizziness and nausea rising in her throat and lowered her chin. Her ripped shirt and bra failed to cover her bloody breasts.

Slowly, bits and pieces of a nightmare flashed before her eyes like a horrifying peep show. A struggle. A scream. Richard. Another punch. Rape.

She squeezed her eyes shut but tears still escaped, running down the side of her face and into her hair. It was so hard to breathe. She touched her hand to her mouth and brought it back bloodied. Dear God.

Her cell phone lay on the floor near the strap of her purse, awakened and shining a bright light like a beacon. She raised herself up on her right elbow and waited for the room to stop revolving. Pressing her arm into the floor, she inched forward. The lower part of her body towed behind her like stone. Jesus. She'd left a trail of blood on the hardwood floor, like a snail's path leaving marks in the sand.

She dragged herself another inch, and then one more. With her right arm outstretched, her fingertips barely touched the phone. Why couldn't she breathe? Every muscle in her body strained to reach the lifeline. Working her forefinger and middle finger, she edged the phone closer until she snagged it. One of her fingers must have hit the contact icon because when she looked at the display screen, Adam's name was highlighted.

She started to sob and tapped the phone number. Please God, let him be there.

Cursing the ringing phone, Adam yanked his head from under the pillow. Whoever was calling at one-thirty in the morning had better have a good reason.

He eyed the cell's caller ID. V Daniels. Which one? "This better be good," he snapped.

All he heard was heavy breathing, almost like an obscene phone call. But not quite. He sat up. Now, he heard crying. "Valerie?"

"Please help me."

He pressed the phone tighter to his ear, already out of bed and reaching for his jeans. He could barely hear her. "He raped me."

"Where are you?" He shoved bare feet into his boots.

"My place." More croak than spoken words.

"Is he still there?"

"I don't think so."

"I'll be right there."

He snatched his sweatshirt, grabbed his credentials and his keys and ran out the door. Was Vince on duty tonight? He couldn't recall who was scheduled. He floored the gas pedal and prayed for a police cruiser to spot him speeding through the city and follow him to Valerie's condo. There wasn't a damn cop in sight.

He drove eighty miles an hour and squealed the tires when he rolled to an abrupt stop in her driveway. The garage door and inside door stood open. With the headlights shining into the condo he saw Valerie lying on the floor, curled in a ball on her side with her back to the door.

He bolted through the garage and into the kitchen. He knelt behind her but didn't touch her. "Valerie, did you call the police?"

She was sobbing with her face on the floor. He barely

detected a negative nod. "I'm going to call the police, honey. You're going to be fine. I'm here now."

Son of a bitch. He gave the dispatcher Valerie's address and reported the rape. Then he dialed Gina. She'd worked as a crisis counselor specializing in rape victims before joining the agency. In the many hours they'd spent together on assignments, she'd often discussed various cases and the things that were most important in those first few critical moments.

A lump formed in his throat as he stood over Valerie. She was covered in bites and blood. One leg was tied with her pants to the kitchen chair leg. She must have been kicking at the bastard. He ran to the living room and yanked an afghan from the back of the sofa. Carrying it into the kitchen, he carefully knelt beside Valerie, remembering Gina's word's that the first touch for a rape victim was the worst.

He whispered. "Valerie, I'm going to cover you with this blanket. The police are on their way."

He eased the afghan over her and lightly touched her arm. Valerie screamed and swung at him.

"It's okay, it's okay, darlin'. It's me. It's okay. Honey, I'm going to untie your foot."

He crawled toward her feet and grabbed the chair, leaning it backward until the chair leg released from the knot of material. But he left the pants wrapped around her ankle. The police would need to see that. Sirens sounded in the distance.

Valerie had stopped crying but her breathing was ragged. He gently touched her shoulder and leaned toward her. "Valerie, let me..." his words caught in his throat. Her nose spread wide across her face, which was smeared with blood. One eye was swollen shut.

He closed his eyes and swallowed hard. She was covered in bite marks. Richard's trademark. He'd kill the bastard. Red flashing lights filled the room and a siren switched off. Adam went to the door to meet the police and paramedics. Directly behind them he saw Gina park across the street. She came running up the driveway and through the garage, ran past Adam and right to Valerie. She may not have liked Valerie but she believed that no woman deserved to be raped. She'd make sure compassion was first on everyone's agenda.

Adam began telling one of the police officers what little he knew. The second officer snapped pictures as the paramedics gently rolled Valerie onto her back. Gina was on the floor on her knees clutching Valerie's hand and whispering non-stop. Valerie's eyes were open wide but she appeared to be in shock.

The paramedics strapped her to a stretcher and prepared to take her to the hospital. She gripped Gina's hand so hard, Gina's knuckles were white. His partner didn't seem to notice.

Adam approached them and whispered to Gina, "I need Richard's last name."

"Who?"

"The bastard I'm sure did this. The parking lot biter. I want his full name."

Gina was annoyed. "Do you need it now? What are you going to do?"

He ran his hand though his hair. "I'm going to give it to the police for their report. And then I'm going to the firehouse and take Vince's shift so he can go to the hospital."

Still clinging to Valerie, Gina leaned over and whispered, then leveled her ear close to her mouth. The paramedics had packed Valerie's nose and padded a gash on her lower lip. Gina whispered a second question, moved her ear over Valerie's mouth and then stood.

"Fredtoni," she said. "Richard Fredtoni. I'm going to the hospital with her."

He used his key to open the side door to the fire station, hoping the men remembered to turn off the public doorbell. He climbed the stairs as quietly as he could. The sleeping men all snored from their beds. Adam shook Vince awake, holding his finger to his lips in the universal sign for quiet. He motioned for Vince to follow him into the living area.

"What's the matter?" Vince stood in his underwear, his hair tousled like a child's. Adam ran his hand through his own hair.

"I'll cover for you," he whispered. "You need to get to the hospital. Valerie's been hurt."

Vince rubbed his forehead. "Was she in an accident? What happened?"

Adam hated being the one to inform relatives when something bad happened to their loved ones. He laid his hand on Vince's shoulder. "This isn't the time for questions, Vince. You should go to the hospital. Valerie was raped."

15

When the men woke in the morning, Adam said simply that Valerie had been in an accident and he'd covered for Vince.

The chief called Jimmy and authorized his overtime so that Adam could leave. He drove to his hotel, showered and changed his clothes. Then he called the Benton Falls police and asked if they had filed charges against Richard Fredtoni.

The detective said Fredtoni was in custody and they planned to hold him for twenty-four hours, until his scheduled court appearance the next morning.

"He's mad as hell that we picked him up," the detective said. "He claims to have an alibi for the entire night. We're holding him on Ms. Daniels' positive ID."

"Glad to hear it. I'll see you tomorrow." He headed for the hospital. He hadn't slept at all last night, in part because of those damn uncomfortable bunks and because he'd wanted to be with Valerie, holding her and reassuring her everything would be okay. Seeing her helpless on the floor, sobbing, had made him want to cry, too. How could anyone hurt her like that? He sure as hell wasn't going to let anything else happen, if it was at all in his power. He called Gina while en route. She'd spent the night with Valerie, staying by her side for the rape examination and the police interview.

Valerie's memory wasn't clear on every aspect of the attack, but Gina said that the portions she did remember sounded horrific. Valerie had waged one hell of a fight. Bruises covered her body and two ribs were cracked. The police pressed her to make a second positive identification of her assailant and she did without hesitation. She was certain it was Richard Fredtoni.

"I think it's to Valerie's advantage that she's worked with these men and covered this department. I'm not sure they'd hold him otherwise," Gina said. "Two patrolman who were here on another call poked their heads in to check on her and the nurse told me she received inquiring phone calls from other police departments. Everyone is concerned about her, almost as if they're taking it personally."

"That's good. I am, too. I'm on my way over."

Vince and Gina flanked Valerie's hospital bed when Adam arrived carrying a bouquet of pink roses and baby's breath tied with a bow of wide, white ribbon. A plastic surgeon had already operated and Valerie's nose was packed and bandaged. Her left eye was black and swollen shut. Her bottom lip was twice its size, more black than purple underneath two butterfly stitches. Tears filled her eyes when Adam entered the room. She bowed her head and droplets rolled down her cheeks. Adam cleared his throat and looked at Vince.

"That's the usual reaction from women when I show up with flowers. Must be my charisma."

Vince laughed nervously, cleared his own throat and looked at his sister. She swiped the tears from her face with the back of her hand but they wouldn't stop falling. Finally, she raised water-filled eyes to Adam and said softly, "I don't even know what to say to you."

His heart stopped beating for a full three seconds. Had they been alone, he would have embraced her and never let go. He mustered up a wide smile, laid the flowers on the tray table and perched on the bottom of the bed.

"How about 'Hi, Tex'?"

Valerie offered a quivering smile as more tears cascaded down her cheeks and whispered, "Hi, Tex." Gina squeezed Valerie's hand as she addressed Adam.

"Valerie can leave the hospital tomorrow. We were just discussing where she should go. She doesn't want to go back to her place yet."

He turned to Vince. As if reading his mind, Vince said, "I told her to stay with me but she doesn't want to do that. She's not ready to be alone and you know I'll be gone twenty-four straight. Plus, I have my paramedic classes."

He returned his gaze to Valerie. "What about staying with Sue?"

"I'd feel like a fifth wheel there. Dolan spends the night there pretty regularly. I don't want to impose."

He considered suggesting Gina's place, but staying with her would jeopardize their case against the Sanchillios and be too risky for Gina and her fiancé. They called each other several times a day.

He knew the answer, even before the words rolled from his lips. From somewhere deep inside the thought started small and exploded, scary and exciting simultaneously.

He fixed his gaze on Gina's face. "I have a second bedroom. I'd be there at night. I could probably manage to work from there the first few days as well. 'Til you're back on your feet. You're welcome to stay with me."

No one said a word.

"Also, you'd have a whole hotel staff at your fingertips if I had to leave." He had no intentions of leaving her alone there.

Gina turned to Valerie and winked, breaking the uncomfortable silence that stifled the room. "It's not like you haven't slept in that bedroom before. That might be a good idea, if you're comfortable with it. It eliminates concern that Richard might resurface plus Adam is a pretty good caretaker."

Valerie appeared stunned. "Gina! You're suggesting that I stay with your boyfriend. What will people think?" With her nose packed each word came out clipped off at the end.

Gina narrowed her eyes, studying Adam, but he kept his face expressionless. He wanted this ball in her court.

"The only people we need to be concerned about are in this room. I don't give a damn what anyone else thinks. If you'd be comfortable staying with Adam temporarily, I don't have a problem with it. I'd be able to check on you every day and that will make counseling easier."

She refocused on Adam and he recognized the questioning look in her eyes. But she was playing out this hand he'd dealt. "Valerie and I are going to some sessions together until she feels comfortable enough to go on her own."

"That's good." Gina had impressed upon him that a rape victim usually needed professional help to move forward. He knew she'd experience guilt, anger, fear—a myriad of emotions before she recovered from this. Damn that spineless prick. For Richard's sake, he'd better stay in jail.

Valerie turned to her brother, not needing to pose her question. Vince shrugged. "I'm okay with it if you are, Sis. I'm sure you'll be safe. I like the idea actually. I won't be as worried about you. And I can spend my days off with you so Adam can work at the station. I think it's a good plan."

Tear-filled eyes leveled on him. "It would only be for a little while. Are you sure?"

"Of course I'm sure. It will give me a chance to change your mind about cowboys."

Valerie's head snapped up. A look of fear crossed her face.

She turned to Gina. "Cowboy," she repeated in a shaky voice. "Before he hit me, Richard said—no, he asked me if I had fun with my cowboy."

He clenched his teeth. "Did you tell the police that?"

Valerie shook her head. "I didn't remember it until just now." Her eyes filled with tears again. "I'm sorry. You don't need dragged in to my problems."

A muscle tightened his jaw. Seething was an understatement for what he felt. Fredtoni might be Valerie's problem but Adam had just become Richard Fredtoni's worst nightmare.

"My offer stands, more now than ever." He tried to control the growl it sounded like. "It was obviously a reference to me. That makes your problem my problem. You need a place to stay where you will feel safe. I have a spare room. And I won't let anything happen to you. No one is going to hurt you again."

He locked into her gaze, willing her to feel warmth, comfort and safety. Silently, pleading with her to let him be the one to care for her.

Her response was whispered. "Thank you, Adam. I can't think of any place I'd feel safer."

They agreed that Gina and Adam would pick up Valerie the next day when she was discharged. Vince was scheduled for duty. Gina planned to go to Valerie's condo with Vince to pack Valerie's clothes and other essentials before he reported to the fire station. She and Vince also wanted to clean the place. Gina and Adam left Vince sitting at his sister's bedside.

Gina waited until they were in the elevator. "We need to talk about this. Are you coming to the bar?"

"You bet. I could use one or ten beers."

At Shots in the Dark, Gina ordered sandwiches brought to her office and a beer for Adam. They sat opposite each other at the small round conference table eating their burgers and fries. Adam drained his mug of beer in two gulps and Gina ordered a second. Neither spoke until their plates were emptied. Adam had half a mug of beer left and Gina sent for a third. She placed it on the table in front of him.

"What do you make of Richard's comment?"

"Besides being pissed off? I'm just as puzzled as you. It's obviously a reference to the night Valerie sobered up in my hotel suite. How the hell does he know that, especially if he hasn't been around? He could be stalking her. I still haven't figured out how Bud knew. Is there a connection between them? A note writer and a firebug?"

He shook his head. "I don't have any answers. And quite frankly, I'm too tired to think it through right now." He needed sleep and a clearer head.

"What about Valerie? That came out of the blue, offering up your suite. Did you think that through?"

His heart jolted. "I threw you a fast ball, I know. Good catch. I might not have thought it all out but it will only be for a couple of days, Gina. A week at most. Where else would she go? She looked so helpless in that hospital bed. And I think she's in danger."

"It was a magnanimous offer, Adam, and on some level, I don't disagree with it. I think you made it for reasons you don't even comprehend yet. I was wrong about her. I spent some very intimate time with her and I've gotten to know her. She's smart and strong and I like her. But you need to remember why you're here. And you need to keep in mind that her brother looks suspicious in all this, and that she is suspicious of you."

He drained his glass. "I don't think her brother is involved with the arsons." He related his office conversation with Vince and his offer to let Adam know every move he made. "He's a good kid. He's going to make a hell of a fireman. And he's devoted to his sister. I like him."

"And Valerie?"

There was that sensation again in his chest. He grinned. "You're right, as usual. I like her, too. I like her spunk. I like her backbone. I like her mind. Under different circumstances, I'd chase her. But you don't have to worry. She'll have enough on her plate recovering from this trauma. From what you've always said, she won't be looking at men for a while. And, if you want to know the truth, when she is ready to start looking, I wouldn't mind if it was me she saw.

"But that will never happen. We're like fire and water if we say more than ten words to each other."

He leaned back in his chair and stretched his long legs forward to release the tension in his spine. "This temporary living arrangement could be a good opportunity to get closer to Vince and pick his brain about C.J. Kwin. Kwin is still a question mark for us. Those two started on the same day and were roommates at the fire academy.

"Kwin's an odd duck. His background information doesn't check out completely. But it's obvious Kwin feels some sort of kinship toward Vince. Jimmy told me that Kwin struggled through some of his classes and Vince tutored him through. Maybe he thinks he owes Vince. If he's our firebug, he could think that one way to pay Vince back is to help Valerie climb the career ladder."

Seeing the look on Gina's face, he shrugged. "It's a stretch, I know. But at this point, I'm not ruling out anything."

"But Adam, don't forget that while you're cementing a relationship with Vince, you'll also be forging a bond with his sister. She's in a vulnerable place right now. You have to tread lightly."

"Gina, if there is one thing that registered from all the horror stories you told me, it's that a rape victim needs time to heal and more time for a relationship. I'm offering her friendship right now, nothing more. I told you already, we don't get along." His eyes slowly closed.

"I heard what you said. But fire and water make a sizzling hot combination, you know."

16

Adam wore his three-piece suit to court the next morning and stood in the back to make sure Richard Fredtoni saw him. Fredtoni appeared before the judge with a high-dollar attorney and pleaded not guilty. His attorney argued a convincing case and the judge agreed to release Fredtoni if he posted fifty-thousand dollars cash bond.

Adam lingered in the hall while Fredtoni wrote a check for the bond amount, then followed the pair out of the building. He kept a short distance between himself and the men, walking slowly behind them through the parking lot. By the way Fredtoni kept looking over his shoulder, he was making the bastard nervous. Good. Squirm you piece of nothing.

The attorney urged Fredtoni to keep moving toward the car. As they drove past him, Adam tipped his hat. Nothing more than Southern hospitality. Fredtoni made an obscene gesture.

Gina had Valerie dressed and ready to be discharged when Adam arrived at the hospital. Seeing her, he grinned. She looked almost fragile, sitting in a wheelchair with his bouquet of roses in her lap. She returned a quivering smile of her own. A hospital aide stood ready to wheel her to the front door as hospital policy dictated. Gina planned to drive Valerie to the hotel and spend most of the day with her to dispel any awkwardness Valerie might feel. When Adam finished his day and returned to the suite, they'd order dinner.

On Gina's suggestion, Adam had purchased containers of fresh fruit, iced tea and soft drinks, and snack items to stock his kitchenette. Two of Valerie's suitcases waited in the spare bedroom.

"She's going to be tired and probably feel a little uncomfortable so once we get to the hotel, try to disappear without being too obvious," Gina had ordered. "The weather should be nice enough for us to spend most of the day on your back patio. That will feel less like a hotel, I think."

Adam agreed. Despite a path that wound through the common area, the patios were fairly secluded. Valerie's nose was still packed and bandaged although he thought the swelling had started to subside already. But on the private patio, she wouldn't have to worry about her appearance, and Gina said the waterfall might be soothing.

Feeling somewhat out of is element, Adam let Gina run the show. She was like a schoolteacher taking her kids on a field trip. She eased Valerie into her temporary living quarters with chatter about fashions, interior decorating and other insignificant topics. They hung her clothes in the closet and filled the bureau drawers. They puttered in the kitchen cutting up fruit, mixing lemonade and, later, dishing up pizza. Vince called twice from the fire station to check on his sister. At about eight o'clock, with Valerie looking like she was running out of steam, Gina said she had to work at the bar.

"Gina are you sure you're okay with this arrangement?" Valerie asked one more time.

Gina squeezed her shoulder. "Absolutely. Call if you need me."

He walked Gina to the door. "Give her a pain pill and let her sleep. She needs it."

"I do, too. If I'm awake, I'll call you later."

With Valerie watching from her seat on the patio, Gina kissed Adam on the cheek and left.

He returned to the patio barefoot with his hands in his jeans pockets. "Can I get you something?"

"I'd love to stand in a nice, hot shower for a while."

"Help yourself. But leave the door open just in case you need help."

Valerie looked uncertain. She cast her eyes downward and fidgeted with her fingers. He sensed her embarrassment.

"Sweetheart," he said as gently as he could, "there isn't much left of you I haven't seen, so there is no need to be embarrassed. I respect your need for privacy but you've had surgery and been pumped full of pain medicine and in a hot bathroom you could become dizzy and pass out. I'd feel better if you left the door open. I promise not to peek."

She nodded ever so slightly. She clamped her lips between her teeth and her eyes rimmed with tears as she gingerly stood and walked toward the bathroom. For a while, he leaned against the wall outside the opened door with his eyes closed, his hands balled into fists in his pockets, listening to sobs that all but tore out of his heart. He wanted to tell her so many things, to reassure her somehow that everything would be okay. Without any idea how to do that, he left her alone.

It was her first chance to have a really good cry. The gut-wrenching, heart-breaking, pain-relieving kind of cry best done in a steamy bathroom under a pulsating spray of hot water. Valerie leaned her head against the side of the fiberglass shower stall and sobbed and cursed and sobbed longer. Why had this happened to her? Why should this happen to anyone? The platitude about taking lemons and making lemonade raced through her head, followed by the recollection of the sharp knife she'd used a short while ago while she and Gina chopped up fruit in the kitchen. The dagger seemed much more appealing.

She inhaled deeply, deliberately, allowing the hot steam to fill her lungs and, when she exhaled, taking all the ugly with it. Once again, her will to fight took root in the pit of her soul. She would overcome this. A piece of slime like Richard Fredtoni would not ruin her life. She could move forward. Certainly, she was strong enough.

The tears stopped. With a new resolve to face this crisis head-on just as she and Vince had attacked every life obstacle, she reached for her lilac body wash and scrubbed her skin until it glowed. She wasn't dirty and used. She was fresh and new. She emerged from the steamy bathroom with her hair wrapped in a towel and wearing her oversized cotton robe. Only her red eyes hinted of her therapeutic breakdown and she doubted Adam would notice.

"I'm beat." She offered him a tremulous smile. "I'm going to bed."

Hours after he'd fallen asleep, he sensed more than saw that someone was in the room. He was in bed, lying on his side with his back to the door, but he heard labored breathing behind him. He rolled over to find Valerie standing beside his bed silhouetted by the bathroom light behind her. She wore a black and gold football sleep jersey. Her arms were folded as if she were shivering and trying to warm herself. Even in shadow, he could see her trembling. He sat up, letting the sheet fall to his waist.

"What's the matter?"

Her voice was unsteady. "I-I can't sleep."

"Do you want a pain pill?"

Despite the shadows, he saw her shake her head. Heard her catch and hold her breath before she said, "I can't close my eyes without seeing him."

"What should I do? Do you want the light on? Do you want to talk?" He was desperate to help but how?

"I-I'm sorry. I, please, I don't want to be alone."

She reached for a pillow from the head of the bed and placed it in the middle. She dragged the blankets back and crawled underneath them. "Y-you said I could trust you. St-stay on your side. Please."

She stretched out on her back and heaved the covers up to her chin, shaking so violently, the entire bed vibrated.

He sat for a minute watching her. He'd never fall asleep with the bed shaking this way. He finally flung his own blankets back and threw his legs over the side of the bed. He stood, ignoring the fact that he was naked, walked to a chair in front of the window, and reached for his jeans. In the silence, the sound of his zipper and his jeans snapping shut seemed magnified. Returning to the bed, he ran his fingers through his hair, eyeing Valerie uncertainly as she stared at him wide-eyed. He straightened the blankets, drawing them high to cover his pillow. Then he reached for the makeshift blockade that she'd placed as a barrier between them and tossed it toward the headboard. Crawling on top of the bedcovers, he edged toward her.

She watched his every move. Slowly, he stretched out beside her shaking body. He gently placed his right arm across her stomach and drew her closer to him.

"Go to sleep," he whispered, laying his head next to hers on the pillow. "You're safe."

Valerie's trembling ceased.

17

Adam slowly roused from sleep aware of two things. He wasn't alone in bed and his bedmate was crying. He lay still collecting his thoughts. Valerie. She was against his back, crying. Her anguish was muffled.

The clock was on her nightstand and he couldn't see what time it was. But tiny beams of daylight usually filtered through the window curtain in the morning and he saw only darkness in that direction. It must still be the middle of the night. He rolled over and waited for his eyes to adjust to the shadows cast by the light escaping from the partially open bathroom door. When he propped his head on his hand, Valerie stiffened and stifled her sobs. Her back was to him, her face buried in her pillow.

He tapped her shoulder and whispered, "Hey. Anything I can help with?"

Her response was muffled. "Un un."

"Are you in pain?" It looked like she shook her head no, but he wasn't certain. Her distress ripped at his heart. "You know, it's been a long time since I've had a woman in bed with me who cried. This isn't at all good for my ego."

That resulted in a muffled laugh before she withdrew from the pillow and turned onto her back, rolling into him. She repositioned her head to face him and he casually laid his arm across her waist.

"Nice to know you're so concerned about me. Thanks, Tex," she whispered. She sniffled and averted his gaze.

"Well, at least I got you to stop crying. Do you want to talk?"

"Not really."

"Ahh. Feeling sorry for yourself?"

Her head jerked toward him and she caught her breath. Finally, she whispered, "Pretty much."

"Is that helping?" Tears clung to her eyelashes, dancing in the dim light, and one escaped down her cheek toward her ear.

"Not really."

"What would help?" His thumb moved idly at her side, willing her to relax. She remained silent for a long time, staring at the ceiling before she whispered, "I'd like to undo it all."

"Well, I can't do that. What else would help?"

She faced him, showing the slightest smile. "Can you kill Richard?"

He chuckled and her smile grew wider.

"Probably. But not without serious consequences that I'm not willing to face, even for you." He reached up and gently released a strand of hair caught to the adhesive bandage at her hairline. "What else?"

"Can you make it go away?" He inhaled deeply. How he wished he had that power.

"If I could, I would darlin'. What I can do is tell you that you are a strong woman and you will get through this. But not by crawling into a hole and feeling sorry for yourself. That ain't gonna cut it."

She snapped, regaining some of her fight. "What do you know? You've never been a rape victim."

He gazed into her eyes and nodded. "That's true. I can't really know what you're feeling. But I do know that rape is about power, not sex."

He'd heard Gina say that at least a hundred times. "If you lie here crying and feeling sorry for yourself you continue to let Richard have power over you. And you continue to be his victim."

She listened silently. "That's not a word that suits you, sweetheart. And I don't think that's what you want. But if it is, just roll back over and boo-hoo some more. I'll go back to sleep."

Her jaw clenched. A good sign.

"You getting mad at me yet?" he whispered.

"I'm getting close."

"Good. I was beginning to think I had a stranger in my bed, not the stubborn, bullheaded Valerie Daniels that I know." She smiled.

"There's a song that tells you to shake it off, be strong and stand." He softly sang the chorus.

Valerie giggled "It sounds like one of those sappy country tunes."

"It's country wisdom, honey." She returned her focus to the ceiling and when she spoke, her voice quivered.

"I thought I steeled myself against it. I told myself I could overcome this. But lying here in the dark, all alone, it looks like a mountain."

Another tear escaped to roll into her hair. He tightened the arm across her waist. "You're not alone, sweetheart. It's like learning to ride a horse. You're bound to take a couple spills. But the people who care about you will be right there to help you back up into that saddle when you fall off."

He watched her, trying to read her face in the partial light. Did she know he was one of those people? She'd turned to him in one of the darkest moments of her life. Did she want him to be someone who cared about her?

Teary-eyed, she whispered, "I don't know how to ride, Tex." His heart was pounding. She looked beautiful in the semi-darkness, even with stitches and bruises. He wanted to wrap himself around her and protect her from everything that was bad. A slow smile crossed his face.

"Maybe you need a cowboy to teach you." They stared at each other in the darkness, their noses almost touching, their mouths close. He wanted to kiss her. What was she thinking?

Finally, she grinned. "Maybe." His heart leapt.

"I'm just scared, is all. Thanks for talking me down from the ledge. I'll be okay."

"I never doubted it." He laid his head on the pillow beside hers. "Get some sleep. You'll feel better tomorrow." A few moments passed in silence.

"Adam? Can I ask you something?"

"Sure."

"Could you really kill a man?"

Should he answer honestly? "Yes, if I had to. You could, too."

Her head moved on the pillow. "I don't think I could, not really. Are you special forces or something?"

"Something like that. It's late. Can we just go to sleep?" She readjusted her position, moving closer to him and laying her hand over his at her waist. The silence didn't last long.

"Tex, are you asleep?"

"Yes."

"How come a woman you took to bed was crying? Was it too awful for her?" She laughed, lightening his heart.

He cleared his throat. "I'll have you know they were pure, ecstatic tears of joy. She was overwhelmed. Are you ready to go back to sleep now?"

"Yeah," she murmured. "Thank you."

He coaxed her closer. After a few minutes he whispered, "I'll work on that Richard request for you." He closed his eyes to her soft giggle.

∼

He woke the next morning to find Valerie curled against his back in the spoon position but with layers of blankets separating them from the waist down. He lay very still, listening to her labored breaths. The packing in her nose kept her from breathing normally. She felt warm against his bare back.

He thought about how his heart drummed hours earlier when he held her close, close enough to kiss her had the circumstances been different. A wave of emotion had washed over him unlike anything he'd felt before. With Valerie in his arms he became strong and weak at the same time.

He quietly slipped from the bed and went to the kitchen to brew coffee, puzzled by his musings. This wasn't the first time he'd awakened with a woman beside him. Usually they were both naked together under the covers, which made it different. Valerie had simply been a sleeping partner and yet, waking up beside her excited him beyond the physical erection.

Filling the coffee carafe with cold water, he conceded it felt comfortable. It felt right. He poured the water into the coffeemaker, probably just like hundreds of men did every morning for their...*whoa, fella, hold your horses.* This was bad timing at its utmost, for both of them.

He quietly opened the hotel door and retrieved the daily newspaper from the floor. With a steaming mug of black coffee in his hand, he walked barefoot to the patio. He settled into a chair with the sun at his back and stretched his legs to the next chair. Valerie found him engrossed in the sports pages when she came out barefoot a half-hour later and sat opposite him. He offered her a bright smile.

"Mornin' darlin'. I waited for you to order breakfast. What would you like?"

"Maybe just some cereal and coffee. But you have to let me pay for it. You can't keep buying my meals." She still sounded like she was speaking through a muzzle. He waved his hand in the air as if shooing a fly.

"It goes to the room. I'll settle up the personal charges when I check out."

"No. That's not fair."

He grinned. "You must be feeling better. You're bossy again." The comment made her smile.

"All right. If you insist, I'll give you a copy of the final bill and you can reimburse me then, okay? That's the easiest way." She nodded her head in agreement.

He punched the number for room service and waited for the connection to go through. "Are you feeling better this morning?"

She nodded. "Thank you. I apologize. I'm not usually a cry baby."

He winked at her and smiled. "No problem, ma'am. Cowboys are good listeners. What's on your agenda today?"

"First, I'm going to remove this packing from my nose. The doctor said I could. My face will feel a hundred times lighter once I do.

"I should check in with work and review my e-mails and upcoming program schedules. I'm not ready to go back to the radio station yet but I can accomplish a lot from here. Maybe line up some interviews for future shows or find some interesting items that the morning show jocks can discuss.

"I'm supposed to contact the detective handling my case. He said I might need to go to the police station and provide additional information, although I don't know what else I could tell them." She wrung her hands in her lap. "I hope I don't have to."

"If they insist on interviewing you again, I'll go with you."

Valerie looked surprised. "Really?" He nodded.

She studied Adam as he returned his attention to the newspaper. What was happening here? They were sitting at a table, waiting for breakfast like, like...she took a deep breath through her mouth and continued her conversation.

"Vince clocks out at six tonight. Is it okay with you if he comes here? I'm not comfortable going out looking like this." She gestured toward her face.

"Absolutely. Feel free to have anyone here any time. Breakfast will be about twenty minutes. How about a cup of coffee?"

"I'll get it." She rose and reached for his mug. Returning from the kitchenette with two fresh cups, she set one in front of him and nodded when he thanked her. As she sat down again she asked, "May I ask a favor?"

He waited for more. "I don't want Sue to know what happened. I don't want anyone to know, actually. I'm asking you not to tell anyone, especially Dolan. Please."

His eyebrows shot upward. "I'm not in the habit of discussing other people's business, honey. You needn't be concerned."

That was a weight off her mind. She murmured thanks as Adam's cell phone rang, negating any further discussion of the matter. She could tell by his responses that it was Gina. Adam offered a cheerful hello then kept his eyes on her face as he responded to Gina's questions.

"Yes, she is...about ten minutes ago...she seems okay...not yet, probably in about fifteen minutes." Then his voice faltered. "Ah, she had a little trouble sleeping...no she didn't want a pain pill...eventually...no, she's fine...she's sitting right here, why don't you talk to her yourself and take me out of the middle? No, I'm going to work from here today."

Valerie's stomach somersaulted.

"Okay, see you shortly." He ended the call and rose to answer the room service knock. When they sat with their plates in front of them she asked, "Gina wanted to know how I slept last night?"

"Un huh." Suddenly, his eggs were the most interesting entrée he'd ever seen. She cleared her throat. "You didn't tell her where I slept."

"She didn't ask where you slept. She asked how." They ate in silence for several minutes.

"You don't have to babysit me, you know. I'll be fine if you report to the fire station."

He looked up for the first time and smiled. "I know." But he stayed.

That evening, he and Gina by silent agreement left for a while to give the twins time to themselves. He returned to the hotel shortly after nine o'clock and found Vince and Valerie on the couch watching an old movie. It was apparent that Valerie was tired. Her eyelids drooped and the smile she greeted him with was weak. She'd removed the packing from her nose but her face remained bruised and puffy. Nevertheless, Adam told her she looked good.

Vince called it a night at ten o'clock, when Adam realized he hadn't wanted to leave his sister alone. He thanked Adam once again for offering her safe haven. Adam waved it off as nothing. After he closed the hotel door and bolted it, he turned to see Valerie standing in front of the sofa.

"The day has been exhausting. I hope you don't think it's rude of me to go to bed."

"Not at all. Goodnight." He grabbed a beer from the fridge and settled on the couch with the remote to search for a sporting event. He woke up at the end of the eleven o'clock news, turned off the TV and tiptoed to the bathroom and then into the bedroom.

Valerie lay curled around a pillow on the near side of the bed with her back to the door. The covers rimmed her ear. He slipped off his shirt, removed his belt, and quietly walked to his side of the bed. She was awake and wide-eyed, staring at him like a frightened child. Without a word, he turned off the light, crawled on top of the blankets and stretched out beside her.

"I'm sorry," she whispered, "I tried. But I—I ..."

"Don't worry about it." He rolled closer, removed the pillow and wrapped his arms around her. "Get some sleep."

Valerie was awake and up before Adam the next morning, reversing the events of the day before. She had coffee ready and the newspaper spread on the patio table when he came out of the bedroom.

"About time you woke up," she teased, immediately brightening his day. "Breakfast should be here in five minutes. The coffee is hot in the kitchen."

He smiled, poured a cup and sat opposite her.

"I hope to go back to work tomorrow if my face doesn't look too bad. Gina says the sooner I resume my normal routine, the better. It's easier said than done, though." She fidgeted with her thumbs when she talked about returning to work, obviously nervous about it. She kept talking.

"Gina said she'd come over this morning. There is a group that meets at the hospital she wants me to join. I'm not sure I'm ready for that, but I'll try it."

He sipped his coffee, remaining quiet. It was as if she were giving herself a pep talk, trying to convince herself it was a good idea. "I just hate to go somewhere looking like this." Her hand fanned her face.

Did she need his reassurance? He smiled. "I think the bruising has already faded. It might be a nice touch to put a stars and stripes Band-aid across your nose. Or maybe little horses. Try going country."

That worked. She snickered and the fidgeting stopped. "Vince switched shifts with Jimmy because Jimmy has a wedding to attend this Saturday. So he's off today and is coming over tonight again. I hope you don't mind. You seem to have lost your privacy."

"Not a problem. I'll go spend time with Gina again tonight when your brother is here. If business is slow, maybe she can leave the bar for a while."

She eyed him, took a deep breath and a hard swallow. "I can't help myself. I have to ask this. Are you two really a couple?"

That sent a zing to his stomach. "A couple of what?"

"You know, a romantic couple. Two people in love."

He raised his eyebrows but didn't respond. He'd already figured out Valerie carried a conversation just fine all on her own.

"I've never known a woman to offer up her man to someone like this." She spread her hands palms up to indicate herself. "And I've never seen you two kiss on the lips. She always kisses you on the cheek."

He loved how observant she was. "I'll be sure and kiss her romantically next time we're all together." He rose when room service knocked. "For your sake, of course."

Gina rang in on Adam's cell while he and Valerie ate breakfast to announce her arrival. Valerie thought he sounded disappointed. Or was she the one disappointed that their cozy breakfast had been interrupted? He showered and announced he was reporting to the fire station. But before leaving, he embraced Gina and kissed her hard on the mouth. So hard, Valerie felt the jolt. Or was that something else she experienced? She looked away when Gina leaned into his kiss, wrapping her arms around his neck. She was sorry she'd said anything.

It was close to midnight when he crept back into the hotel suite. She'd been dozing on the couch under a blanket with the television on. She sat up the minute the door opened.

He leaned against the door with his hands behind his back.

"I'm sorry, I didn't mean to wake you." His baritone voice was more gruff than usual.

She'd removed the remaining bandages from her face and applied makeup to cover the remnants of the bruises as a test run for the next day when she returned to work. She'd been pleased with the results. And if she were being totally honest, she hoped he thought she looked pretty.

"It's fine. I wasn't asleep." She eyed him curiously. Had he just crawled out of Gina's bed? He looked a little disoriented. Was he drunk? He strode to the dining room table, took off his hat and sat on a chair to remove his boots. "You should be in bed."

She watched him. His hands appeared red and she saw scratches on his knuckles. "What happened to your hands?"

He viewed the top of his left hand as if seeing it for the first time. "I had some car trouble. I guess I got scratched up."

"Did you see Gina tonight?"

Adam took a deep breath and rested one arm on the table. He pointed with his forefinger in her direction. "This is why I'm not married. I don't need an inquisition when I come home at night. I'm going to bed. Are you coming?"

He stood and walked, a little unsteadily she thought, toward the bedroom. She gathered up the blanket and followed behind him. He brushed his teeth as she crawled into her side of the bed and waited for him to come out. He was dressed like the other nights, bare-chested and in his jeans. He lay on his back on top of the covers. Valerie sat up and spread out the blanket she carried from the living room, covering him from his feet to his chest. He was already asleep.

Three hours later, the alarm on her side of the bed went off. She quickly reached out and thought she'd silenced it fast enough so as not to disturb him. So it surprised her when she closed the door of the spare bedroom to dress and heard water running in the adjoining bathroom. She peeked around the door and saw Adam at the sink in jeans and a sweatshirt.

"What are you doing up?" she whispered.

"I'll drive you to the radio station. I can come back and go back to sleep."

He didn't have to do that but she was grateful. She'd fretted about making the trip in the dark by herself. They rode to the radio station in silence with country music playing softly on the radio.

"Someone will pick you up at one o'clock," Adam said when he drove up to the employee entrance. She nodded and walked into the station. Her co-workers welcomed her back and eased the awkwardness of her cover story of being mugged with off-color jokes. Being the brunt of their comedy was good therapy. She fell back into the groove immediately and began assembling briefs for her first news broadcast, surprised and pleased that several of the dispatchers welcomed her back.

One news item in particular caught her attention. Benton Falls police discovered an assault victim lying face down in a pool of blood in an alley shortly after midnight. He was in critical condition in the hospital with a concussion, broken bones, and multiple bruises. He hadn't recognized his assailant. Police identified him as Richard Fredtoni.

She switched on her cell phone after the morning show ended. There was a message from a Benton Falls detective saying that the hearing scheduled for her case was postponed indefinitely because of the attack on Richard. The detective asked Valerie to call him and when she did, he asked if she knew about the assault.

"I found out about it this morning when I made my police rounds."

"Was that the first you heard of it?"

She paused before answering. "Yes, of course, why do you ask?"

The detective said that Richard was incoherent in the hospital emergency room but that he kept repeating her name. "Mind if I ask where you were last night?"

The question surprised her. "I was with my brother and a friend for a portion of the evening. And then," she paused, evaluating her response, "I stayed with my friend for the rest of the night."

"Mind if I ask your friend's name?"

"Is that really necessary?"

"Yes ma'am, it is. I'm sorry."

She took a fortifying breath. "I was with Fire Inspector Adam Mitchell at his hotel suite."

"All night?"

She swallowed the lump in her throat. "Yes, sir. All night."

"Was Inspector Mitchell at the hotel the entire evening with you and your brother?"

Like a child, she closed her eyes and crossed the fingers on her left hand. "Yes, yes he was." She didn't doubt Vince would support her story. The detective thanked her for the information and said he would let her know when the court rescheduled her case.

At the end of her day, it surprised her to find Adam waiting in his SUV on the circle. She'd expected Gina or maybe her brother to pick her up.

"Hey, sweetheart. On the air it sounded like it went well. How was it being back?" He shifted into gear and eased away from the curb.

"It went pretty smoothly, I think. Did you listen to the show?" He nodded.

"Did you hear the report about Richard Fredtoni? He's in the hospital."

He nodded again.

"The police called me this morning to ask where I was last night. And you."

For the first time, he looked at her. Then he returned his eyes to the road.

"What did you tell them?"

"That you were with my brother and me for part of the night and that I was with you for the rest of the night. All night."

Adam smiled. "Good answer."

18

Two more abandoned buildings were set on fire in Benton Falls, but one of the houses provided shelter for a homeless man who died in the blaze. The arsonist had elevated himself to murder.

The minute Valerie learned of the death she wrote a report stringing the suspicious fires together by date and reporting that fire investigators were in the city working to solve the arsons. WARJ had broken the story and her boss was ecstatic. And hungry for more.

He suggested that she interview the fire chief and press him to find out if there was a suspect. If not, why? Valerie could hardly contain her excitement. She called the fire station and set up an interview with Chief Cozza for after lunch. Fortunately, she'd driven herself to work today. Adam had seemed hesitant to let her go alone, but she'd insisted.

By next week, she'd be making the trip herself anyway. She'd spent the last seven nights in Adam's hotel suite. Vince spent the evenings with her when he wasn't on duty or at class. When her brother couldn't be there, Adam and sometimes Gina kept her occupied. Valerie planned to return to her condo that Friday.

She continued to share Adam's bed when they called it a night, using the blankets as a divider between them. He never said anything about her sleeping in the extra bedroom and she didn't want to relocate. She was certain Gina didn't know about their sleeping arrangement.

It wasn't as if they were sleeping together, she rationalized. They simply slept side by side. As they had agreed, Vince told his colleagues only that Valerie was mugged. He said the refurbishment of her condo was scheduled before the assault, and that she was staying with a friend until it was complete. No one knew where she was outside of work except the four of them.

When she arrived for her appointment with the chief, Vince greeted her with a kiss on the cheek.

"Valerie, you look great," Chief Cozza said, coming out from behind his desk. He gave her a quick hug around the shoulders. She returned his greeting with a warm smile and turned to Adam, who stood in the corner leaning against a four-drawer file cabinet with one arm on top of it. He nodded. "Ms. Daniels."

She mimicked the nod. "Inspector." She had a list of points she wanted to cover in the interview, but Cozza pre-empted her questions by saying there wasn't much information he could provide because the fires were part of an ongoing investigation. Still, he said, he wanted to help.

Adam watched her remove a small reporter's notebook and a compact tape recorder from her purse. She was poised and professional and it was apparent she'd done her homework. He smiled with pride.

During her stay with him, he'd seen Valerie in several different modes—playful, serious, vulnerable, determined. Now, he watched the professional reporter emerge. He hated to admit it, but he liked all that he saw. He was going to miss having her around his hotel suite. He wasn't sure how to handle that. Or if he should do anything about the feelings he couldn't deny. He enjoyed spending time with her and wanted to do it more.

Valerie questioned the chief about the timing of the fires in relation to the new hires, surprising them by including her brother in the list of names to be scrutinized. She asked about the background checks for all the men in the department and handed the chief an official request for copies of their personnel files. She also wanted to know the times of each fire and requested a breakdown of the costs for each blaze. In all, she interviewed the chief for nearly an hour.

Cozza did well, giving her a little new information so that she was satisfied but not enough to compromise the investigation. The two of them hadn't anticipated the records requests, but that was easily satisfied. The chief agreed to fax copies of what she wanted by noon the next day. Finally, Valerie turned to him.

"Inspector, may I ask you a few questions?" Her tape recorder pointed at him.

"I have no comment."

Resigned, she turned back to the chief. "I expected as much. Thanks for your cooperation, chief. I appreciate it."

His pulse fluttered. He'd have to tease her about that remark tonight in bed.

Valerie returned to the radio station to file a report that would begin broadcasting on the five o'clock news. She'd learned that the same accelerant was used in all the fires, indicating the same person or persons were likely responsible. She also was able to narrow the window of time in which all the fires ignited to a three-hour time frame. WARJ was out ahead of all the other newscasts on this one. Her boss e-mailed to the higher ups suggesting a merit award for her good work. She was thrilled. It would be her first.

Before she signed off from her computer, she quickly checked her other e-mail messages. Favfan was waiting again.

KEEP ASKING QUESTIONS. YOU SHOULD FIND OUT WHO IT IS

The news report wasn't on the air yet. The only people who knew she did a follow-up interview were at the radio station or the fire station. Impulsively she spun around in her chair and scrutinized her surroundings, as if Favfan were standing behind her. Then automatically, she reached for the phone to call Adam.

"Fire district four two. Eagle."

"Hi, Bud, it's Valerie Daniels."

Bud caught his breath. "Hey, Val, sorry I missed you this afternoon. We were out on a fuel spill."

"I missed you, too." That ought to set his head spinning. "I need to talk to Inspector Mitchell, please. It's urgent."

Music filled her ear while she waited on hold. "Mitchell."

"It's Valerie. I just found another Favfan e-mail and it's pretty creepy. It sounds as if he knows I did the interview today."

"How so?" Was he pleased to hear her voice? He was all business so she couldn't tell. She read the message to him.

"Who knew you were coming to the firehouse?"

Her boss, who only made the decision that morning, and likely his executive assistant. Valerie hadn't mentioned it in the control booth during the morning broadcast and she doubted anyone else at the radio station knew. That left only the men at the fire station who saw her there.

"You're right. It sounds like he knows you were here. Just for the heck of it, give me your boss' full name and his assistant's name. If you know their addresses, that will help."

"What are you going to do with the information?" The reporter in her wanted to know.

"I'll give it to Inspector Martellan to run a check. We checked the backgrounds of all the men here at the station but no one who works with you. It's just routine. I'll feel better knowing their specifics. At this point, I don't want to overlook anything. Are you able to find their addresses?"

"Yes. We have a master employee list."

"Any chance you know their birthdates? It would make it quicker for Inspector Martellan to search."

"I'll have to look that up and call you back, but I can find that information."

"Good. Call me back when you have it. And print a copy of that e-mail for me, please. Bring it home with you tonight."

Bring it *home*. A small thrill ran through her.

Adam returned his attention to the spreadsheet in front of him: Eleven suspicious fires that didn't include the car fire on Adam's first day at the fire station. Rick Martellan thought that was a legitimate coincidence.

All the arsons appeared to be set using an accelerant.

One death. They'd identified the vagrant they now knew had died penniless and without family or friends.

One blue car seen by the teenagers and two firefighters with blue vehicles. Vince Daniels and Dave Oswalk. But no match to the partial license numbers. Three months' worth of schedules that placed two firefighters first on the scene at each suspicious fire, even when not on duty. Daniels and Kwin.

And five e-mails to Valerie Daniels, all appearing in her mailbox within twelve hours or less of a fire or, in today's case, within two hours of her visit to the firehouse. Was that because she was related to Vince or because she was a news reporter? Or was there another explanation?

That was an unknown that made him uncomfortable. He drew an arrow from the e-mails column to the margin and penned in Richard Fredtoni's and Bud's name with question marks beside each. Both of them knew that Valerie spent the night at his hotel suite when she drank too much.

That was a puzzle. He wrote his thoughts beside their names. "How did they know?"

Stepping back and looking at the spreadsheet, Vince Daniels' name was highlighted in every column. Still, his gut instinct told him Vince wasn't involved. He walked to the door of the office and called Vince to come in.

"What's up?" Vince asked as he closed the door behind him. Adam turned the master spreadsheet around so that Vince could read it standing on the opposite side of the desk. The bright yellow Daniels highlights popped off the page. Vince glanced at it then leaned over and used his finger to read each line slowly.

"Inspector, I swear. I had nothing to do with starting these fires. This looks bad but I swear to God…"

His words trailed off and he looked at Adam with the same wide-eyed stare that Valerie often displayed. Adam studied his body language and reactions.

"I believe you, Vince. But someone sure wants it to look like you or Valerie, or maybe both of you, are connected to them. Valerie just called me. When she returned to the radio station after her interview this afternoon, an e-mail from Favfan was waiting for her. He knew she was here."

Vince's jaw dropped.

"Someone is plugged into this place or watching her or both. Valerie moves back to her condo this weekend. I don't like the timing but I don't want to stop her. She's done well with her recovery."

Vince nodded in agreement.

He ran his hand through his hair. "Vince, will you do some investigating for me? Valerie and I are like water and oil when we start talking about these arsons." His words made him smile. "Nah, it's more like cat and mouse, both trying to catch the other.

Neither of us wants to give up any information, although I think finding that e-mail when she returned to the office today scared her. But she won't let me see that she's scared. She'll let her guard down with you.

"Can you pin her down and ask her some questions about rejected guests who wanted to appear on the show or maybe an advertiser she has difficulties with. I'm looking for anything that could be problematic and might offer a clue as to who has her in their crosshairs."

Vince listened intently, appearing to run through his own list of suspects.

"It could be some whacky secretary who doesn't like the spotlight that shines on Valerie or, I don't know, the way she dresses." Adam rubbed the back of his neck, acknowledging the tension when he thought about Valerie in danger.

"If I try to ask any of these questions, she'll get defensive. But she'll tell you. Maybe you can help jog her memory." Vince bobbed his head.

"Ask about her co-workers. Is she having any issues with them, maybe about time on the air? I thought I heard that the one jock on the show was somewhat jealous of her rising to the top so quickly. She has quite a following. She told me she received more than a hundred cards and e-mails when listeners learned she was mugged."

He shrugged, hating this feeling. "I'm at a loss. I don't know who to look at or what to look for. But I do know that someone is going out of his way to connect Valerie to these arsons, and I don't like it. You have to pick her brain, Vince, for anything and everything. We're out of places to look."

Vince nodded again and shrugged. "I don't know of anyone off hand but I'll talk to her. I'm coming over tonight. Are you planning to be there? We could both sit her down. You might think of questions that I won't. If you two start to square off, I can referee."

Adam laughed. He already was regretting the coming weekend and Valerie's departure from his hotel suite. Any chance to spend more time with her appealed to him.

"All right, I'll stick around. How about if we all have dinner in the hotel restaurant tonight? We can call it a going-away dinner. My treat."

Vince smiled. "That's a good idea. You don't have to buy though. I can't possibly repay you for everything you've done for my sister but I can start by picking up the tab tonight. I'll call Val and set it up. I'll meet you two there."

Vince touched the spreadsheet again with his index finger, his eyes narrowing as he reviewed it. "You said anything and everything, right Adam?"

He nodded.

"Bud has had car trouble twice since I've worked here. Both times, the loaner he drove was blue. He commented about it matching his uniform. And Kwin's wife has a blue car. I don't know what make it is. But he complains whenever he has to drive it that she trashes it."

"Good. That's good. I'll check into that."

"See you tonight."

19

The dinner designed to pick her brain was unsuccessful, mainly because seconds after he joined Vince and Valerie at the table, Dolan and Sue walked in and Valerie insisted they dine together.

Now, he watched Valerie deposit her suitcases beside the hotel door. It was time for her to go home. He sat on the couch with the TV remote in his hand searching for a ballgame. Valerie plopped into the chair opposite him.

"Vince is meeting me in a half hour at my place. I have a rough cost estimate of what my share of the hotel bill should be. I'm keeping it to compare to the bill you promised to split with me."

He kept his eyes fixed on the TV set.

"That was the deal, remember?"

"Yes ma'am." He couldn't look at her. She was regaining her independence while he was losing his heart. She took a deep breath.

"I hate to say this, Tex, but I'm going to miss you." She held up her hand. "Not that I've been converted to a country fan, mind you. But I just might be an Adam Mitchell fan. I could have never gotten through all this without you and Gina. What can I do to thank you beyond paying my share of the hotel bill?"

He eyed her for the first time. "Go out with me next Saturday night."

He wasn't sure where it came from or why he said it. He'd been thinking about how much he didn't want her to leave, how much he wanted to be a part of her life. More than that, he wanted her to be a part of his life. Once she walked out of this hotel suite, there'd be no reason to talk to her every night. For sure there'd be no one to curl up with in bed. How was he going to sleep without her?

Still, the invitation surprised him as much as it did her. After all, this was an undercover assignment and a personal relationship, especially with someone who might be involved, violated every ethics code imaginable. It was grounds for dismissal.

Not to mention he was supposedly involved with Gina. Valerie's moral standards didn't include extramarital anything.

Valerie stuttered. "Adam, what are you asking? I—I can't. Gina. I...you don't mean that."

But he did mean it. Despite all the alarms sounding in his head, he was serious. He couldn't let her walk out of his life. He snapped off the television and leaned back on the sofa.

"Go out with me." His tone was deliberate. "I'll square it with Gina. Give me a chance to show you a real country good time. We didn't really have time for that this past week. We'll have no expectations beyond two friends having fun together. I think we can at least call each other friend. It will be our freedom celebration. You said you want to thank me. That's what I want as thanks. Go out with me. It's not like it's a date."

Valerie's heart hammered in her chest. It was a ridiculous request.

It was a bad idea. It was an exciting offer. She shook her head. "It's not a good idea, Adam. I can't."

"You don't want to?"

"I didn't say that." Damn, she answered too quickly. He had her rattled. "It's just that you are involved with Gina. And I've become friends with her. It would be wrong."

"Aren't you my friend too?"

If he only knew. "Yes, yes you are a one-of-a-kind friend."

"Well, friends go out together. I promise Gina will be okay with it. I'll tell her right up front that I'm taking you out and where we'll go. I won't be cheating on her, and neither will you. If you want, you can call and talk to her yourself."

She threw up her hands. "How can she be okay with it, Adam? I haven't understood how she is okay with my staying here with you for over a week, let alone going out with you on a Saturday night. What woman would be okay with that? And she doesn't even know we slept in the same bed. Your entire relationship doesn't make sense to me. For that matter, our relationship doesn't make sense. What are we? Friends? Adversaries? Bedmates?"

"If you insist on a label, leave it at friends. Friends have fun together. Yeah, you've been here over a week but it hasn't been much fun. I want us to enjoy a night out together. Let me worry about Gina. You owe me."

"That's not fair. Ask me to repay you some other way."

"No. That's what I want. Go out with me."

Butterflies did a line dance in her stomach. Even as she shook her head no she knew that she'd go. She wanted to. And after all, he said it wouldn't be a date.

"You swear to me you'll clear it with Gina?"

He nodded. She agreed.

~

She didn't hear from him for the rest of the week except for the brief phone message he left on her machine on Thursday. "Don't forget. Eight o'clock Saturday. Wear jeans." Now she stood in front of the full-length mirror in her bedroom straightening her denim jacket and smoothing the front of her jeans. She chose a long-sleeved light blue sweater with tiny crocheted rosebuds scattered across the front to wear beneath the jacket. Dark brown peep pumps showed her toes, which were polished dark red to match her nails. It was as country as she could manage.

All week she admonished herself for agreeing to go out with Adam tonight. She'd even dialed his cell phone around noon, ready to cancel the date. But she hung up before the connection went through. If she were truthful, she wanted to see him tonight, even knowing it was wrong. This week without him had seemed empty. So many things had happened at work that she wanted to share, none of them related to Favfan. Just everyday incidents that she thought would interest or amuse him.

She spoke to Gina every day, but Gina never said anything about tonight and Valerie was too much of a coward to bring up the subject. Every day she'd checked her cell phone the minute she signed off the air, hoping he'd called. She'd replayed his brief Thursday message four times over.

Now, as eight o'clock approached, she convinced herself these were feelings she should quash as soon as possible. They were more than feelings that friends shared. It was wrong to feel anything for Adam beyond gratitude for his help.

She paced the living room floor rehearsing what she intended to say when he arrived. Nevertheless, her heart jumped to her throat when he knocked at three minutes to eight. She took a deep breath, smiled, and opened the door.

Adam looked her over from head to toe and smiled. "You look nice, darlin'. Not quite country enough, though."

She straightened her shoulders. "Adam, we should rethink this evening. It's not a good idea."

He was undaunted. "Instead of the sweater do you have a shirt you could wear? Maybe something with a collar that buttons down the front?"

She was taken aback. "Did you hear what I just said?"

"Yes, ma'am. This evening is not open for debate. Gina knows I'm here. She knows our plans. Do you have a different shirt?"

"I beg your pardon. Never has a man picked me up for a date and asked me to change my clothes first. What's wrong with this sweater?"

He held up one finger. "Technically, sweetheart, it's not a date, remember?" He grinned. "It's a nice sweater, but I know you can't wait to wear this." He reached behind him.

His grin was like a Cheshire cat's when he removed a red paisley bandanna from his pants pocket, folded it into a triangle, then folded it a second and third time. He walked to her and tied the cloth around her neck, his eyebrows coming together as he fussed with the knot.

"Go look. It doesn't work with the sweater."

She was ready to argue but instead, she dutifully walked into her bedroom and stood in front of the full-length mirror. He was right. The neckerchief, expertly tied in a square knot and flared at both ends, looked awful with the sweater. If he wanted her to wear it, she had to change.

She jerked off the blue jeans jacket as she headed to her closet and yanked the sweater over her head, tossing it on the bed. She chose a long-sleeved white cotton shirt with red pinstripes and shrugged into it. She swapped out the brown pumps for red. She saw her reflection in the mirror and shook her head at the cowboy scarf around her neck. Of all things to give her.

But she couldn't help smiling. She tucked her shirt into her jeans, slipped back into the jacket and returned to the living room tugging on the shirtsleeves to extend them full length.

Adam sat on the sofa but jumped to his feet when she re-entered the room.

"Will this do, sir?" She held her chin in the air. He walked to her grinning and adjusted the bandanna. His knuckles brushed against her chin and her skin burned where he touched. She gazed into his eyes and hoped he couldn't see her heart beating wildly in her chest. With him so close, his cologne tempting her and his eyes locked on hers, her breath quickened.

He ran his gaze down her body to her feet and then back to her face. "Damn." He shook his head slowly, grinning even wider, "I should've thought about boots for you."

Her eyebrows shot up and Adam burst into laughter, raising his hands defensively. "I'm kidding, sweetheart. I like the shoes. They're hot. You look great. Please relax. I want us to have a good time tonight."

He took her arm to move her toward the door, but she didn't budge. She focused on his face, her own as set as a statue's. "That's the problem, Adam. I can't relax. This doesn't feel right."

He cupped her chin and gazed into her eyes, then slowly ran his thumb along her jaw line to her bottom lip, spreading heat to her heart and soul. He caressed her mouth gently, keeping his eyes locked to hers.

"It does feel right, darlin'," he whispered. "That's the problem."

She was paralyzed in his hands, as vulnerable as a baby bird. She stared at him and whispered, "It's not a good idea."

He ran his hand down to the small of her back and nudged her to move. "C'mon. You've always trusted me. Let's go."

She studied him as he climbed into the driver's seat. His black jeans were skin tight and he filled them nicely. He wore a long-sleeved gold and silver striped black shirt with white pearl buttons. Gold piping extended across the front and back yokes and small gold embroidered galloping horses decorated each shoulder. The shirt also had two front pockets with pearl buttons on the flaps.

On any other man it might have appeared feminine but the shirt fit him snugly and emphasized his broad shoulders and chest. He'd tucked the shirt into his jeans with a wide black leather belt that appeared braided. A similar braided band encircled his black hat. Heat crept up her cheeks and below her waist as she admired him. He carried off the cowboy look rather well.

"How was your week?" he asked after he backed out of the driveway.

She smiled, recalling all the incidents she'd wanted to share with him. "It was mostly uneventful. I fell back into my routine right away. Wake up in the middle of the night, go to work, do more work from home and go to bed when most folks are just thinking about what they want to do with their evening. It's not much of a life. But it's what I need to do for now to have the career I want."

She told him about the caller who believed in aliens and the Cub Scout troop that toured the station, leaving behind chocolate finger smudges on her boss's computer screen. No anonymous e-mails and only one insult from a caller who referred to her as an amateur. Adam turned toward her.

"You're not an amateur, sweetheart. I admired the way you handled yourself when you interviewed the chief that day. You were extremely professional. When you're famous, I'll be proud to say I know you."

Her eyebrows shot up. "Wow, Tex. I'm flattered. Thank you."

"How did it feel being back in your condo? Were you comfortable sleeping there?"

"I was a little nervous the first night. I almost called you."

He glanced at her quickly, then refocused on the road. "You could have."

She smiled and continued. "Did you know that Vince installed a security system and outside motion detector lights? And you saw the new deadbolt. That makes me feel better. I was fine by the second night. It's my home. I can't be afraid to stay there.

"One of my counseling sessions focused on returning home. In my case, returning to the scene of the crime, if you will. I wasn't going to let it beat me. Gina was spot on with every emotion I experienced. She's an incredible woman."

She paused, waiting for him to comment. When he simply shook his head, she continued, "Gina checked on me every day and Vince called me at least ten times."

"I thought about checking on you, but Gina always told me she spoke to you. She said you were all right. You've done really well, sweetheart. I'm proud of you."

He wasn't like anyone she'd ever met. After thinking about him all week, wondering, her question exploded from her lips before she could stop it. "You're not the average fire inspector here for a routine annual inspection, are you?" It looked like his hands tightened on the steering wheel, but she couldn't be sure.

"Why do you ask that?"

"I've seen you take a gun from your glove box and move across the lawn like a cop. I've listened to you talk and watched you work. I can't find your name anywhere on the state website. And that first night in the restaurant parking lot, you said you were 'sort of the police.' Call it a gut instinct or just pieces to a puzzle that don't fit. We've slept together and now we're out together, just the two of us, so I think I deserve an answer. You're either not what or not who you say you are. I'm curious to know which. We'll get to the why."

Adam threw his head back and laughed. "I like that I'm a puzzle to you sweetheart. It means you've been thinking about me."

"No, I haven't." She'd said it much too quickly, like a five-year-old denying a guilty deed. She prayed that in the dim light, he couldn't see her blushing. Now he had her flustered.

"Ah, too bad because I've been thinking a lot about you." Her head jerked in his direction.

"You're not supposed to be wearing your reporter's hat tonight. If you must know, I'm here for a state inspection but my timing coincides with events that need investigated. I already told the chief, it doesn't hurt to have another set of eyes looking at these arsons. That's all I'm doing."

"Are those the eyes of a fire inspector or the eyes of a police investigator?" He looked again from the road to her and then back to the road.

"Are you a reporter or an investigative reporter?"

"There's no difference. A good reporter is an investigative reporter."

"Exactly." He turned up the radio. "Do you ever listen to country music? They are the best short storytellers in the world."

"Are you going to answer my question?"

"This is my girl Reba. You'd like her if you listened to her songs."

He'd effectively closed the subject so she temporarily gave up. They rode on the turnpike heading out of the state. "Where are we going?"

"To a fun little honky tonk bar just over the state line. I think you'll like it. It's a lot of dancing and a lot of fun."

"Well hell, I'm only going to embarrass both of us. I don't know how to do any country dances."

He smiled. "Don't worry, sweetheart. I'm an excellent teacher. By the end of the night you'll be a pro."

The club parking lot was packed. A bright red neon sign spelled out Dancin' Cowboys in rolling letters. People were pouring into the place, all wearing western hats and boots. Adam offered his hand as she climbed out of his SUV. She thought he was simply helping her out but he kept hold of it, locking his fingers with hers.

"Are you going to know a lot of people here?"

He hit the electric lock and the horn sounded twice. With Valerie's hand in his, he started toward the door. "I doubt I'll know anybody here. We should both be rather anonymous so you don't have to worry about being seen with me, if that is your concern. It shouldn't be though. I told you Gina knows I'm bringing you here. Let's relax and have some fun."

He paid the cover charge and then weeded through the crowd, still clutching Valerie's hand. At the far end of the room he found a tall, round bar table with two high bar chairs. She stepped onto the first chair rung to climb onto the seat. Adam stood beside her.

They were positioned directly in front of a huge dance floor half the size of the room and roped off like a corral. The dance floor was packed with an equal number of men and women clapping their hands and stepping in unison in a line dance. In the opposite corner was a mechanical bull surrounded by a circle of inflatable mats to catch the riders who were flung off. It seemed everyone went soaring within seconds of mounting the thing.

Adam yelled over the music. "Do you want a beer?"

She leaned close to his ear. "I don't think so. Maybe later. Since the night I over indulged, I haven't had a drink."

He smiled. "Don't worry. I won't let you drink too much. I'll buy you a soft drink for now. Diet or regular?"

She asked for diet and he maneuvered his way to the bar. She surveyed the room. Several groups of women stood together and openly assessed the men around them. Men in twos and threes likewise checked out the female prospects. There seemed to be just as many couples. A cluster of men congregated around the bar, trying to appear cool. Adam stood out among them as just a touch taller and just a bit more handsome.

She watched a young blond off to the side give him the once over and then step toward him. She sidled in beside Adam and flashed an inviting smile.

Adam tipped his hat and returned his attention to the bartender. The blond lightly touched his arm and leaned in to speak to him. When he smiled and responded, a surge of jealousy roared through her. How dare that bimbo? The woman was intruding on their evening.

Date or no date, Adam was here with her. Should she go to the bar and stake her claim? A warning voice sounded in her head. How could she be jealous when Adam belonged to Gina? She had no more claim on him then the blond trying to pick him up. What was she thinking? Worse, what the hell was she feeling?

Adam paid for their drinks, tipped his hat to the woman and displayed a wide smile as he approached her.

"Thank you. Who was your friend?"

He grinned. "Just some young thing hoping to get lucky. I have to fight them off regularly, you know. I hope I didn't break her heart when I told her I was already spoken for. I tried to be gentle."

"I was beginning to think I'd have to rescue you, for Gina's sake, of course. After all, you belong to her and she is my friend."

The color of his eyes deepened to a dark purple as he stared at her, running his eyes over her mouth and then locking his gaze with hers. Something akin to an electric shock shot through her, sending heat waves down to her toes. She cleared her throat and averted his stare.

He took a deep draw from a longneck bottle of beer and leaned toward her, nudging her shoulder and nodding toward the dance floor.

"You ready to try this?"

"It looks complicated."

"It's easy. I bet you're a natural." He grasped her hand and gently eased her from the stool.

"This is the two-step. Two quick steps and two slow steps. I'll lead you."

Adam placed his right hand on her waist and held her right hand in his left. His fingers were strong on her back and in seconds, she felt them prodding her to turn and move.

"It's six steps and then it repeats. Don't lift your feet too high and don't look down. Stay close and look at me. Let me see those big brown eyes. Relax and follow me."

They went around the floor twice and by the second spin, she had the pattern down. She flashed a victorious smile at Adam and he winked, smiling as well.

He was a big man but extremely light on his feet. The song ended and the first chords of "Boot Scootin' Boogie" filled the room. Adam positioned her in one of several lines that were forming. "Just follow me. It's not hard."

Everyone started to move in unison and he yelled directions to her, telling her when to kick, when to slide and when to clap. At first, she was awkwardly out of step and bumped into the dancer beside her but it was all repetition, if only she could remember the order of the steps. When the lines turned and she was behind him, a woman to her right picked up the cadence and announced the steps for her to follow. She mouthed "thank you," and the woman grinned and nodded.

Halfway through the tune she knew the dance. She caught Adam's eye and laughed. The music ended and he applauded her. "Nicely done. Nobody would know you're a greenhorn."

She winked. "Thanks, Tex. I surprised myself but this is fun."

The next dance was a promenade and Adam moved her to his right side and locked his arm around her waist. As he had done previously, he recited the steps and guided her into the moves with the hand at her waist. She made a few missteps, stomped on his toes twice causing both of them to laugh, but made the rounds of the floor with ease. At the end of the song she looked at him out of breath with beads of sweat dotting her upper lip.

"Want a break?"

"I want a beer!" She threw her head back and laughed. When was the last time she'd actually had fun like this? She couldn't recall. He deposited her at their table and returned with two bottles of beer and a basket of popcorn.

"I hope you like nachos. I ordered a plate for us. We'll order something else to eat later." She nodded enthusiastically and sipped her beer.

The first chords of a Trace Adkins ballad filled the room. Adam snagged her hand. "I know you know how to slow dance. C'mon."

He led her onto the dance floor and embraced her, placing her right hand over his heart and covering it with his left hand. The spot on her waist where his hand lay burned hot, with fingers that spread like fire through her body. *Oh my God, I'm falling in love with this man.*

She looked into his eyes and he slowly raised her right hand, placed a kiss in her palm and then returned it to his chest, all the while peering deep into her soul. Beneath her hand, his heart thudded and his embrace was so close, the tops of their thighs touched.

She and Sue often joked that a woman could tell a lot about a man by the way he slow danced. Adam was by far the best slow dancer she'd ever taken the floor with. The heat between them was so intense, she feared she might melt in his arms. The man exuded sex appeal and confidence. They remained locked in each other's arms for two more slow dances. When the final ballad ended, he kept her hand and led them back to their table where an oval serving plate of covered nachos waited. She hungrily grabbed a cheese smothered chip.

She needed to bring herself back to reality. "What exactly did you tell Gina we were doing tonight?" She watched for his reaction.

"I told her I was bringing you here. I said we'd probably close the place and have breakfast somewhere. And then I would take you home and see her at her place after."

"What did she say?" Their relationship confused her. She couldn't imagine being so willing to share Adam if he were her man.

"She said this was a fun place to take you. She told me to tell you to have a good time."

Gina's words picked a hell of a time to echo in his head. "She thinks she's going out with Adam Mitchell, a fire inspector. Not who you really are, Adam Michaels. How far do you want to take this relationship based on deceit? I understand that she's important to you and now that I know her like I do, I think she's perfect for you. But this isn't the time. You can't assume your true identity until we catch the arsonist."

"I can't lose her either," he'd countered.

"If there is truly something there, it'll wait. It'll be there when you can go to her and be you. Every woman wants a man who is honest with her. Adam Mitchell isn't honest."

Everything she'd said was true. Becoming involved with Valerie right now was just plain dumb. But he was well on his way anyway. He'd never experienced such a powerful need to be with a woman. And it wasn't at all physical, although the thought of making love to her someday actually made him giddy. Christ. He'd lost all control of his heart already.

Valerie waved a chip in front of his face. "Earth to Adam. Did you hear what I just said? How can a woman be fine with her boyfriend taking out another woman? I don't understand—"

"Let's not talk about me and Gina, okay? There are things I'd like to share with you but I can't. Please drop it."

The look on her face said her mind was spinning. Fortunately, a man decked out in black from hat to boots dropped a flyer advertising a midnight bonfire on the table. He pointed to it. "You game?"

She read it and nodded. "Sure. But are we done dancing?" The beginning chords of a slow song filled the club.

"Do you want to be done?"

She glanced toward the couples moving slowly, wrapped tightly in each other's arms. He held his breath, hoping she'd surrender to the notion that tonight, it was only about the two of them. She shook her head and he led her to the dance floor, taking her in his arms, excited for the chance to hold her close again. He breathed in her perfume, a soft scent like spring rain. They danced the slow set and then kicked up their heels to a dozen more honkytonk tunes.

"I hate to admit it, Tex, but this is one of the best nights I've ever had."

He prayed there'd be more. It was shortly before midnight. He grabbed the bonfire flyer and suggested they leave to find it.

"You don't know where it is?"

"Nope. But there is a map and directions on the back of the page. Let's see how good we are as a pair of navigators." It wasn't the only thing he wanted to pair up with her on. They held hands walking to his vehicle. Before turning the key in the ignition, he sat for a moment with both hands on the wheel staring out the windshield, wondering if he dared take this further. His heart wanted him to.

"What's the matter?"

His voice cracked when he asked, "Do you trust me?"

Her eyebrows knitted. "Do I...yes. Why?"

He reached behind Valerie's head with his right arm and drew her toward him. At the same time he leaned toward her, his eyes locked with hers.

∽

The move startled her and her heart skipped as his mouth came closer and closer. She closed her eyes in anticipation.

He was tentative at first, as if unsure how she'd react. But she wanted this kiss. Had wondered about his kisses almost from the first time she'd seen his mouth. Would it be soft between that mustache and goatee? Would he be assertive? Did he like to use his tongue?

She leaned into him and his kiss intensified. Boldly, she moved her tongue against his lips in response to this long-awaited moment. He responded with his tongue and a small moan escaped her. The moment was pure bliss.

He drew back and stared into her eyes before leaning in and kissing her mouth one more time. Then he slowly and deliberately kissed his way along her jaw line to her right ear where he whispered, "I've missed you in bed, sweetheart. I don't like being there without you in my arms."

She turned her face and their foreheads touched. They leaned against each other like that in silence until Adam inhaled, cleared his throat and returned to a sitting position in the driver's seat. He dropped his hands onto the steering wheel like it was a safety zone.

Watching him, she gulped. The kiss ignited a spark inside her chest and belly that she had imagined never feeling again. There was no fear, no threat. No traumatic recalls. Only warmth and love and craving for this man. Her heart beat to its own country rhythm while her thoughts stampeded out of control.

What were they doing? Why had he kissed her? Would he kiss her again? Did she want him to?

"Now what do we do?"

Adam clung to the steering wheel. "We find the bonfire. You have the map. Which way do I turn?"

The trip was an easy one, thank goodness, because his mind centered on one thing. Valerie. Inside of ten minutes, they could see the glow of a bonfire on a farm in the middle of a huge plowed field.

The number of cars driving onto the grass in an orderly fashion and creating makeshift parking rows surprised her. He explained that country folks knew how to gather. Her laugh seeped under his skin.

He held her hand, loving the feel of it in his, and they walked through the field toward the flames. The air temperature warmed with each step. Bales of hay were stacked in groups a safe distance from the fire and formed a circle around it. This was a guaranteed good time.

The fire roared and crackled as bright as high noon on a summer day. He pointed to a bale of hay and Valerie sat on it.

"Coffee or hot chocolate?"

"Hot chocolate, please." Couples sat everywhere, most of them cuddling on the hay bales and whispering. Lucky dogs. A handful of folks were tuning guitars.

"You're about to experience an authentic country moment, sweetheart. I hope you aren't disappointed." He handed her a steaming mug, moved behind her to straddle the hay bale and sat.

"Yum, what's in this?"

"A little butterscotch schnapps. I hoped you'd like it." He shifted his body forward, pressing his legs against hers. She immediately tensed, straightening her spine and catching a mouthful of air.

He leaned in to whisper, "I would never hurt you, sweetheart."

"I know that. I'm sorry. It's just that...he—he came from behind and you...I...."

"I know."

She twisted to see him better. "Do you know it all?"

He did but he didn't want to embarrass her. "I know most of it."

She caught a ragged breath. "Does it make you look at me any differently? I mean, if you were a man just finding out about what happened to me. Would it matter?"

Her question saddened him. How could he reassure her she was a beautiful woman, not damaged goods? "I am a man, sweetheart. And I see what any man will see who looks at you."

"What's that?"

She needed to hear that she wasn't somehow tainted by the acts of a monster. He studied her face while he slowly extended his right hand, palm up, and motioned for her to take it.

Tentatively she slid her small hand into his huge one and he squeezed it reassuringly. "You are an incredibly beautiful woman, Valerie Daniels. Any man who has the privilege of spending time with you is lucky. It won't matter what happened in the past.

"As for this old country boy, you've taken me on a wild rodeo ride, one that surprised me. And now, you hold the reins to my heart."

Liquid eyes stared at him. "I wish that were true. Tonight has been like Cinderella living her fairy tale. But I'm afraid tomorrow, when the fire has gone out, reality will slap us like a cold rag in the face. I'm not going to like myself much."

"I asked if you trusted me and you said yes. Please trust me now and let me worry about tomorrow. Besides, this fire isn't going out."

"I meant—"

He interrupted her. "Shh. It's just us now. I want you to hear this."

The guitar players were synched and the first chords of a country ballad filled the air. Within minutes, most of the spectators were humming and singing. She kept hold of Adam's hand and relaxed against him. They were a perfect fit. He gently wrapped his arms around her and began humming the song in her ear, rocking slowly. She stared into the fluorescent orange flames, mesmerized by the warmth from the fire and his embrace.

She'd feared she'd never want another man to touch her again. But she didn't want this one to let her go.

"This is magical. Can we stay here forever?"

"No." His voice was low and deep next to her ear. "But we can come back."

She closed her eyes. How she wished it was so. More than an hour later, she jolted when Adam announced the time, declared that he was starving, and suggested they go for breakfast. She couldn't remember when she'd felt so content.

"I have a better idea." She brushed hay from the seat of her pants and reached for his outstretched hand. "Let's go back to my place. You didn't have a chance to see the new paint and wallpaper because you were too busy criticizing my outfit."

She giggled when his head snapped up. "I'm kidding, Tex. Not about going back to my condo. I'd like to kick off my shoes and have a little quiet time with you, unless that sounds too..." Adam waited "... too friendly. I'm not that good a cook but I can scramble eggs and Vince stocked my pantry so I probably have whatever you like in them. Eggs, toast, bacon. Does that work for you?"

His half-smile said it all.

Once settled in the vehicle, she laid her hand on his arm before he switched on the ignition. "Do you trust me?" Her voice sounded higher than normal in her ears.

His forehead wrinkled. "Do I trust you? Absolutely. Why?"

Just as he had done, she reached across the console and threaded her fingers through his hair. She drew his face toward hers, her eyes already closed and her lips begging him to respond to her daring move. He did, kissing her deeply. When she leaned away, tears rimmed her eyes.

"Adam..."

He touched her lips with his forefinger. "Shh, don't say anything, sweetheart. Words will just ruin it." He caressed her face. "You make me think things I shouldn't think."

"What kinds of things?"

He smiled, winked at her and shifted into drive.

Dare she ask? "Gina things?"

Adam straightened his spine. "No ma'am. Valerie things."

"But what about Gina?"

"We'll discuss her later."

When they arrived at the condo, Adam wandered from room to room while Valerie clanged pans in the kitchen. Vince had hired a professional decorator who transformed the condo into a new home, blending solid colors with a floral theme. The bright blue reminded him of the Louisiana sky on a clear day. The sky never looked quite the same here in the city.

The blues blended with purples on several throw pillows bunched between green floral ones scattered over her beige sofa. Soft and feminine but not girly. Faux stripes the color of a saddle lined walls of a lighter sand shade.

In the kitchen, Valerie whipped up the promised breakfast and brewed a pot of French vanilla cappuccino. While they ate, she told him about her therapy sessions and her determination to move forward.

"It's funny," she said, zooming in on an imaginary spot on the tabletop to avoid making eye contact with him, "I thought it would be hard to trust again, to feel comfortable alone with a man. But tonight," she paused, "tonight...has been...nice."

He remained silent, watching her, wondering where she was taking this.

"I wish things could be different with..." her words trailed off and she left the sentence unfinished.

"Be careful what you wish for, sweetheart. You just might get it."

She leveled her gaze on him. "Will I?"

"What did they tell you in counseling? Take it slow, right? One day at a time?"

She laughed. "I think that's the credo for Alcoholics Anonymous."

He laughed as well and shrugged his shoulders. "Well, it's something like that."

An awkward silence fell between them. He didn't like it. Valerie took a deep breath. "Adam..."

He held up his index finger. "Don't say what I'm afraid you're going to say, Valerie. Don't go there yet, sweetheart. We can't talk about what you want to talk about. Not yet. Not tonight."

"Why not? We should talk about this whole night and what happened. I need to talk about it. I want to be honest with you."

He nodded in agreement, fighting the impulse to blurt out the truth. This was a pivotal moment between them. He couldn't screw it up.

"You're right. We absolutely should talk. I want to be honest with you too. But not tonight. You said you trust me. Please, trust me a little longer."

"I'm trying to, Adam. But something happened between us tonight. You say Gina was all for us going out together but I'm sure she wouldn't be happy if she knew we'd kissed. We crossed the line and betrayed her. After all she's done for me, I don't know how to deal with that. Please talk to me."

"I'm asking you to trust me."

"And I'm telling you that's not a good enough answer. I'm on precarious ground here. I'm vulnerable and I-I have feelings for you. And you're sending me mixed signals. Don't treat me like a stupid woman. I want to discuss what happened tonight. And we should agree it can never happen again."

Well that was unacceptable. He retrieved the coffee pot, poured her a second cup, and began clearing the dishes.

"You're important to me, sweetheart. I don't like the idea of never kissing you again. The little I can tell you is that the situation with me and Gina is not what you think it is. To be quite frank, you've been right all along. I'm not who you think I am. I can't tell you more beyond that. You have to give me some time."

Her jaw dropped. What did he just say? She blinked, blinked a second time and watched him load the dishwasher, as if it was his normal task. "You can't leave it at that."

He wiped the sink, dried his hands with a paper towel, and smiled at her. "We just did, Valerie. We'll talk some other time and I'll tell you whatever you want to know. I promise. I better leave now."

She jumped from her seat as if a firecracker exploded beneath it. "Do you have to?"

The look on her face halted his walk to the door. Did he recognize desperation? Her heart raced. "Can you stay? At least for a little while longer?"

She tugged her bottom lip between her teeth and chewed. The look on his face told her he was conflicted. She was the one sending mixed signals now.

"You said you were fine staying here by yourself."

"I am. It's my home." She kept her gaze riveted on his face. "It's just that I don't want my country appreciation night to end yet."

Three steps would bring him to her but ten steps farther would take him to the door and keep them both out of trouble. Time stopped while she waited. He strode the three steps and took her into his arms.

She raised her fingers to his face, tracing his high cheekbones. Adam leaned toward her for a long deep kiss that she willingly returned.

"Sweetheart, you're intoxicating," he whispered, placing tiny kisses along her neck to her ear. He covered her mouth with another kiss that sucked the air from her lungs.

"Then don't leave me. Stay here and get drunk on me. Spend the night."

His tongue flicked her earlobe and his voice was barely audible. "I can't. I promised Gina I wouldn't take you to bed. It's too soon."

She jerked backward, stunned. What? He'd promised her that? He placed his mouth over hers, giving her a sweet kiss.

"Adam," she mumbled, her lips pressed against his, "is Gina really your girlfriend?"

"No."

For a nanosecond, the world stopped spinning. Nothing but her lips against his and the word "no" echoing through her head. "Who is she?"

His breath puffed into her mouth when he whispered, "She's my partner."

She went limp momentarily in his arms. Too much was happening too fast. She needed time to process. But right now she needed him. "Then stay with me."

"I can't. It's too soon." She straightened and took a breathless step back. Adam's eyelids hung heavy on eyes that looked at her hungrily.

Her eyes filled with tears. "No, it's not too soon. I appreciate your hesitation but there's a connection between us that I want to explore. I haven't been able to think of anything else except you. Your kiss. Your hands on me. Your mouth on me. It's not too soon if it's with you. Something sparked between us tonight and I'm not afraid. I want to try. I want to try with you."

He caught his breath, then tightened his embrace. "Jesus,

what am I doing?" He locked one hand in her hair and moved the other down her back to caress her bottom. His tongue plunged into her mouth, possessively.

Suddenly, he turned and swooped her into his arms. He carried her into the living room and eased her onto the sofa, knocking off the pillows one by one, except for the one beneath her head.

He knelt on the floor and stared at her, caressing her cheek. "I've never known a woman like you." Cupping her chin, he leaned forward and kissed her lightly, first on the forehead, then her nose and lastly, her mouth. When he made to pull away, she locked her arms around his neck and urged his mouth toward hers for a deeper kiss.

He didn't resist and instead ran his hands down her side to her hip, then upward to her breasts. Every nerve ending in her body screamed for more. They continued to kiss as he lightly caressed her breasts and stomach, and then rolled his large hand over her hip and down her thigh. Her shirt slipped from the waistband of her jeans and his warm hand caressed the skin along her side. His touch set her on fire and she moaned her approval. His tongue teased hers, rolling over her lips and her teeth, and delving into her mouth for more.

Straightening, he removed his hand from beneath her shirt and reached for the button between her breasts. With deliberate slowness, he unbuttoned her shirt, his eyes following his hand as it moved down the row, exposing the lavender demi-bra she'd worn the night she'd gotten drunk and he'd undressed her in his hotel suite. He ran his forefinger along the lacy edge.

"I remember this." His voice was hoarse. "It about drove me crazy." He cupped her left breast and kissed the cleft it created.

Her heart raced and she closed her eyes, arching her back to encourage him. She'd believed she'd never respond to a man's touch again but desire was drowning her. Her heart pumped at triple speed and she breathed in rapid spurts.

"Do you want to go upstairs?"

"We can't," he whispered. He used the tip of his tongue to trace a line down the center of her stomach, stopping at the belly diamonds. Gently, he touched the glittering stones with his forefinger. "This is so much like you. A precious jewel." His tongue teased her belly button while he deftly moved to the snap of her jeans. He tugged to release it and peeked at her with the slightest grin. "Do the panties match?"

He placed his hands on her hips and began easing off her jeans. She pressed her feet into the cushions and lifted her bottom and he quickly slid the jeans to her ankles and slid them over her feet. His grin widened at the lavender bikini panties. His hand rolled up her leg and he grasped the lacy edge of the panty between his thumb and forefinger. His touch left a trail of heat. Through half closed eyes, he shook his head and mumbled, "I've lost my mind."

He reached for her hips and eased the panties down to her ankles. One foot at a time, she freed herself from them. Her core ached for his touch. He walked his fingers upward along the inside of her thigh. She was slick with yearning.

"Sweet Jesus," he croaked before moving his mouth between her legs. Warm breath heated her on the outside while a furnace raged inside her body. The heat increased as he gently inserted his fingers inside her while using his tongue to tease her.

She groaned in ecstasy and reached to take his head in her hands. Adam's weight lay on her right leg so she raised her left, opening up for him to have her entirely. She dug her fingers into his hair when he pressed his mouth into her. Rhythmically, he moved his hand and his tongue, adding his thumb to a spot just below her nub. She arched her back and lifted her leg higher and Adam moaned.

"Give yourself to me darlin'. Let it go."

She floated on a cloud, unable to feel anything except the place between her legs and Adam's skilled tongue and fingers performing a country concert there. He probed and nibbled, then drew back to blow a tiny puff of air on her. His fingers worked their magic while he kissed the inside of her left thigh, using his tongue to draw tiny circles on the delicate skin. The fire he stoked rose to scorching. Her whole focus was between her legs. The pulsing. The licking. The sucking, all combined in a crescendo of sensations. Deftly, he urged her to full release and she arched her back and came in a machine-gun volley of spasms, gasping for air, clutching his hair and screaming his name.

Panting, struggling to catch her breath, she relaxed into the cushions. Tears rimmed her eyes when she opened them to discover Adam's face hovering above hers.

"Are you all right?"

No. She'd died and gone to heaven. She gulped and nodded slowly.

"You would've stopped me if it was too much, right?" She adored the concern on his face. She caressed his cheek.

"I'm fine on so many levels... I've never...that was...oh my God, thank you." She clasped her knees together, trying to control her quivering leg muscles, and felt heat creep into her cheeks. "I'm sorry. I'm embarrassed. That was incredible."

Adam kissed her soft and slow. "Don't be. A man likes to know he can satisfy a woman."

He took a deep breath and stood. "Get dressed. I'm going to use the bathroom, then call Gina. The three of us better talk."

Valerie's sat on the sofa, her shirt re-buttoned and her jeans in place, when he returned from the bathroom with his cell phone in hand. The wall clock showed four thirty. "You're going to call Gina now? At this hour?"

He'd already punched in the speed dial digit. He ran his hand through his hair nervously.

She listened to the one-sided conversation, trying to make sense of it. "Put the coffee on, I'm coming over. I'm bringing Valerie...No we didn't but...no, I wouldn't say that either. I can't leave her. I don't want to leave her...yes, I'm going to tell her now...I know, but I've been asking her to trust me all night. There's too much between us now." He leveled his gaze at her. "It's time for me to do a little trusting myself."

He paused while Gina spoke. "It's a risk I'm willing to take. Yeah, I know...but she'll protect us both...I'm certain of it...Okay, we'll meet you later for breakfast then and we can all discuss it." He paused again. "You're right. That's probably a good idea." He moved his mouth away from the phone.

"Gina doesn't think it's a good idea that my SUV sits in your driveway all night. Probably the whole fire department has driven past by now. She thinks we should relocate back to my hotel suite. Is that all right with you?"

His conversation didn't make any sense but she nodded. "Okay, we'll leave now. Yes, separate vehicles. Sure."

He extended the phone toward her. "She wants to speak to you." She caught her breath and eyed the outstretched phone, wary of the impending conversation.

"Hello?"

"I'm not sure what transpired between you two but are you all right?"

"Yes. I'm fine."

"Adam is going to tell you as much as he can."

"I'm pretty confused about the two of you."

"I know. I might be able to fill in some gaps. Please understand that once you know what's going on, you'll hold both our lives in your hands. But if Adam trusts you, then I guess I can, too. I'll see you later. Let me talk to Adam again."

She returned the phone to Adam, suddenly frightened by Gina's words. She'd hold their lives in her hands? What did that mean? Who were they?

She stood, waiting, expectantly.

"I understand you have a lot of questions, sweetheart, but

Gina is right. My car has already been outside much too long. Meet me at my hotel and we'll talk there."

He came to her, clutched her face in his hands and placed a light kiss on her lips. "I miss you already. I'll leave now. Gather your things and follow as soon as you're ready."

She stood paralyzed in front of the sofa. Who was he? What was he? How had she fallen so fast and so hard for this cowboy, a man she obviously didn't know?

As if in a trance, she used the bathroom, brushed her teeth and finger combed her hair. She snatched her keys and purse from the kitchen desk and locked the door behind her.

The answers to those questions waited for her at Adam's hotel suite. So did Adam.

20

There were barely any cars on the road, much like when she drove to work every day. She quickly made the drive to the hotel, although not before forming at least fifty questions in her head, starting with what Adam felt for her. A man who kissed like that, who sent her soaring to sexual plateaus, had to feel something.

Remembering his concern about the firemen seeing his SUV at her place, she drove around the building to the back entrance and parked. The area was deserted. As she stepped out of the car, Adam rounded the corner of the building.

"I was watching for you." He took her hand. "This back entrance is locked after midnight. I don't want you walking back here alone." Silently, they walked to the front entrance and into the lobby. The desk clerk looked up, smiled, and returned to whatever she was working on. Adam led her to his suite, opened the door, and allowed her to enter ahead of him. It felt like she was coming home. She turned to say that and he took her in his arms for a long, deep kiss.

In his arms, she was home. He scattered tiny kisses up her

nose to her forehead and whispered, "I wanted to do that a hundred times while you were here."

Placing a brotherly kiss on the tip of her nose, he stepped back. "I'm going to brew some coffee." He headed toward the kitchenette as he said over his shoulder, "Give me a minute, then we'll talk."

She'd learned, as a reporter, that sometimes it was better to let the story unfold at the teller's pace instead of trying to discover it with inquiries. This seemed like that kind of situation. She'd let Adam disclose his secrets in his own way.

She wrapped her arms around herself and turned in a small circle. What a wonderful night this had been. She wasn't a bit sleepy despite having been up twenty-four hours. She was half afraid if she closed her eyes, she'd awaken to discover it was all a beautiful fairy tale dream. As he opened and closed drawers in the kitchen, she wandered to his bedroom and stopped in the doorway. The bed beckoned to her. Would she finally sleep in that king-sized comfort zone with Adam beside her, this time under the blankets, skin on skin?

A small giggle escaped her throat. If that were the case, there'd be no sleeping. She remembered the feel of his hands and his mouth on her and her stomach careened as if on a roller coaster. She wanted more of him. She wanted all of him. Deciding it was better not to dwell on their sexcapade, she wandered to the small dining area. File folders and spreadsheets covered the table. A tablet with a pen resting on the top sat off to the side.

Casually, she skimmed the notes. His handwriting was neat, almost disciplined. The name Daniels jumped out at her. She stepped closer and moved the pen to one side for a better view. Then her eyes scanned the scattered pages on the tabletop, spotting a spreadsheet with yellow highlights poking out from under a stack.

She reached for the sheet and studied it. Written in Adam's

neat penmanship, it was a series of columns with dates, times and addresses. She recognized them from the list of arson fires she'd compiled. The names of the Benton Falls firemen appeared in smaller columns associated with the dates and her brother's name was highlighted in each of those columns. Small notations and arrows pointing to the sides of the page and at various columns created a spider web overtop of the information.

She followed one of the arrows and gasped as she read her name in the margin. She read it more closely. What the hell? Adam had obviously tracked all the arsons, just as she had.

He'd connected the corresponding duty roster to the fires and, apparently, based on the yellow highlights, decided Vince had something to do with them. She raised her eyes from the papers when he approached, not bothering to hide the fact that she was reading his files. He eyed the spreadsheet in her hand.

"What the hell is this?"

"Valerie—"

"What the hell do you think you're doing? Why is Vince's name highlighted on this?" She raised it in the air as if he couldn't see it in her hand. "Are you trying to connect my brother to these arsons? How dare you."

"I haven't—"

"Is that what tonight was all about? Take out the sister and see what information you can glean from her? Maybe get your jollies at the same time and have a little sex."

"I didn't—"

She tossed the spreadsheet on the table with a flick of her wrist. "You said it yourself. You're not who I think you are. Boy was that on the money. I don't know who you are. But I do know that Vince has nothing to do with these fires and I'll be damned if some good ole Texas boy is going to waltz in here and accuse him of that."

"I'm from Louisiana. Valerie, I—"

Her rampage was in full swing. "How could I be so blind?

How could I let myself...let you...oh my God. I can't believe this."

"If you'll calm down and let me speak—"

"You've been saying all night that we're going to talk. Talk about what? How you're ready to arrest my brother. Over my dead body, Tex. Vince is innocent and I intend to prove it."

She stormed past him, grabbing her purse on the way to the door. He called after her but she didn't dare turn around. She wouldn't let him see the tears rimming her eyes.

Through blurred vision, she hurried through the lobby and out the revolving door. The cool night air smacked her in the face and she shivered. She ran along the sidewalk, around the corner and to her car, oblivious to her surroundings. Only when she threw her car in reverse and looked in her rearview mirror did she see the glow of a cigarette in the car parked at the far edge of the lot. She glanced in that direction but couldn't make out a face and didn't recognize the blue car. She spotted Adam at the corner of the building just as she shifted into drive. She stomped on the gas pedal and buzzed by him.

Adam yelled but Valerie sped past him. Dammit. He spun and smashed his hand against the brick building, welcoming the jolt of pain that shot up his arm. He dropped to a squat position and caught his head in his hands. How could the best night of his life turn into the worst?

If she'd only let him explain about the analysis pages. Sure it looked bad for Vince but in his gut, he knew someone was setting him up. But Valerie thought...hell, he had no idea what she thought. Straightening to a stand, he took two steps and heard, from somewhere behind him, an engine come to life. That back lot had been virtually empty when he'd greeted Valerie just a short time ago. Turning, he blinked as a car with its high beams blinding him blasted toward him. He jumped around the corner and flattened himself against the wall. The car roared from the lot like a bat out of hell. Blinking to clear the colored dots floating in his eyes, all he could make out was the color of the car. Blue.

He stepped out and studied the spot where the car had been parked. Directly behind Valerie. With his heart pounding in his ears, he ran to his hotel suite, snatched a flashlight from his duffel bag, and grabbed the roll of paper towels from its wooden holder on the kitchen sink, sending the holder noisily to the floor. He raced back outside and rounded the building. Then he slowed, both to catch his breath and steady his impulse to rush to the site. Switching the flashlight on, he forced himself to pace slowly to the parking spot Valerie's car had occupied. Swinging the flash-light beam cautiously in small squares to create a grid, he stepped toward the rear of the lot.

In the dark, the asphalt surface reflected every oil drip and liquid spill like a pattern of abuse. As he neared the rear of the parking lot, his beam pointed out a cigarette butt. And then a second. Two more tossed slightly farther.

Could he be so lucky? Carefully, using individual paper towels to collect each butt, Adam scanned the area for anything else. A wad of gum mashed into the surface didn't look fresh. A crushed plastic water bottle appeared to have survived several days of weather but he collected it anyway. Rick Martellan could send these to the lab.

It was a fifty-fifty chance that the lab techs could collect DNA residue and an even more remote possibility they could match any sample to someone already in the system. But it was worth a try. This didn't feel like a coincidence, and he didn't believe in coincidences anyway.

One thing he was certain of. Vince didn't smoke.

21

"You look like hell." Gina brushed past him and into the suite.

She walked straight to the kitchen and poured herself a cup of coffee. Turning, she assessed him from head to toe. Black circles bordered his eyes and dark stubble shadowed his jaw. He hadn't showered or shaved.

"Did you sleep in those clothes?"

Adam refilled his own coffee cup and sipped. "I didn't sleep."

"Tell me what happened." He ran his hand through his already disheveled hair. "Do you want the good parts or the part where the shit hit the fan?"

Despite his obvious agony, Gina laughed. "Start with the good parts." He recounted the small talk he and Valerie exchanged on the drive to the honky tonk bar and the fun they had on the dance floor. He looked into his coffee cup sheepishly.

"I can't explain it, Gina. I took her into my arms for a slow dance, and I'd still be there if the music hadn't stopped. It was like you see in the movies where everybody else disappears and it was just me and her. One slow dance and I wanted her for a lifetime."

He described the bonfire and Valerie's invitation to return to her condo for breakfast. His account of the evening stopped.

"And?"

"And when I tried to go, she didn't want me to leave. And I didn't want to, not really."

"And?"

"And I held her in my arms and stayed for a while."

"You told me you didn't have sex with her."

He cleared his throat. "I didn't have intercourse with her. I didn't promise not to touch her."

"Was she okay?"

"If screaming for Jesus was any indication, she was just fine."

Gina rolled her eyes. "I meant with an act of intimacy. Never mind. Then what happened?"

"While I was putting on a pot of coffee here, she wandered into the dining room and saw the arson analysis. The minute she laid eyes on that spreadsheet, she blew up. I couldn't get a word in edgewise. She told me I'd arrest Vince over her dead body and stormed out."

"So you never told her you're undercover? You never told her we're not together? She doesn't know the truth?" She looked relieved.

He squirmed in his chair. "Ah, I may have mentioned that we're not a couple."

"May have?"

"Well, there was a point when I told her you are my partner. But there wasn't much conversation after that."

Gina filled her lungs and shook her head. The cardinal rule of the agency, of any law enforcement undercover operation, was to never ever, under any circumstance, blow the cover. He knew that's what was going through her mind.

They could fire him for this. Hell. It could get him killed. And her, too, if Valerie used the limited information she had. The question was, would she? And if so, how?

"Please call her, Adam."

"I tried her cell phone twice already. She's not picking up."

"You can't leave us both hanging out there not knowing what's going to happen."

"She may be upset with me, but I don't think she'll do anything to hurt you. Me either, quite frankly. Her whole motivation at the moment is to prove Vince is innocent. And as far as anyone else is concerned, nothing has changed."

It was Gina's turn to clear her throat. "That's not exactly true. I had a very interesting night at the bar while you were out dancing your heart away. One of the Sanchillio boys came in around nine. Usually he's a happy hour customer so I was surprised, especially after he told me I should dump you because you are cheating on me. He tells me that you are seeing that girl from the radio station."

He narrowed his eyes and stared at her through the steam curling from his coffee cup.

"He said he has a friend who has a friend who has a friend who is interested in Valerie. And he knows Valerie has spent a couple nights with you.

"I, of course, was appropriately shocked and hurt. He thinks he and I could make beautiful music together. He says I need a real man in my life and he'll treat me like a queen.

"It was all I could do to keep from gagging. Anyway, I asked why didn't this long-distance friend pursue Valerie himself as that would solve my problem, and he indicated this mystery person isn't interested in Valerie like that. Mystery man is mostly worried that she is snooping where she shouldn't be."

He straightened his back, his coffee forgotten.

"He knew I was out with Valerie last night?"

She nodded. "Who do you think Valerie told?"

"I don't know. I'd imagine she wouldn't tell anyone. Until last night, she believed you were my girlfriend and she was torn about being disloyal to you. She tried to call it off when I arrived at her place. Said going out together wasn't a good idea."

"Maybe it wasn't."

Adam raised his eyes to her. "It wasn't a good idea. It was a great idea."

~

Valerie swore and deleted the two missed calls from Adam. She wasn't ready to listen to him yet. Not until she had facts that proved Vince was innocent. She'd driven home in a rage. Betrayal was not easy to swallow. She'd tried calling Vince but the call went to voicemail. She couldn't remember if he was on duty. If so, the fire station was no place to discuss this.

Back at her condo, she didn't sleep. She paced from the kitchen to the living room, glanced at the sofa, and suppressed the butter-flies that vaulted in her stomach at the memory of what had passed between them there. Just hours ago, she'd invited Adam into her bed. Now, it seemed he was her arch enemy. None of it made sense.

She needed to talk this out. But not with Adam. The look on his face as she'd stood in his suite challenging him was a mixture of hurt, confusion, and anger. Or had she misread his features?

Was he irritated that she'd found out his true motives? What-ever his feelings, in the mood she was in right now, they'd only end up arguing and that wasn't what she wanted. An involuntary smile crossed her lips. Arguing with him was the exact opposite of what she wanted. Kiss and make up was more like it. But she had to keep her focus on Vince and the arsons. Making up, and hopefully making out, would have to wait.

There were four people involved in this mystery, herself and her brother, Adam and Gina. Right now, Gina was the unknown factor. She and Gina had spent so much time together, Valerie truly regarded her as a friend. What kind of friend, though, if she was Adam's partner? What exactly did that mean? She punched in Gina's cell number. It was pretty early to call on a Sunday, but this was important.

"Hi Gina. It's Valerie. I'd like to talk to you. Alone. Without Adam. Please."

"All right."

"No, not on the phone. Do you have time to meet me today? It's important. I think you know that."

Gina paused. Was Adam there listening? "Are you with him right now?"

"Yes. Why don't you speak to him?"

"No, please. I'd prefer to meet you."

Another pause. "Okay. It's usually slow at the bar on Sundays so I let my bartenders have the day off and I work solo. Can you meet me there and then we can move someplace more private? I'll call in one of my part-timers."

"I'll be there at noon. Just you, okay? Thanks." She checked her watch. She'd have enough time to shower and drive to the radio station to review her notes on the arson stories before their meeting.

Valerie looked around the room, somewhat surprised by the crowd, and sat in the corner of the bar. The two closest stools were empty. She smiled when Gina approached. "I didn't think it would be busy."

"Me either. Softball tournament, apparently. Sorry. My relief isn't here yet. Want something to drink?"

"Yes, please. A diet soda."

Once the tall glass sat in front of her, she asked, "Did Adam tell you about last night?"

Gina nodded. "It was all I could do to keep him away from

here. He tried calling you. He's desperate to talk to you and clear up some matters."

In fact, two more calls had come through on her cell from him. He'd sounded sweet in the first voicemail message, asking, "Please call me," and terse in the second, "We need to talk. This is important. Call me."

"I didn't take his calls. I feel a little betrayed after last night. I need some answers, and I trust you to give them to me without," she paused and studied the bubbles rising to the top of her drink, "complications."

"Well, I'm glad you trust me. But I have to warn you, the less you know, the better for everyone. Be cautious about what you ask. I can't promise full disclosure."

She left to refill a patron's glass and fill a table order. When she returned, Valerie fixed her gaze on her. "I would never do anything to put you or Adam in danger. I hope you know that."

"You're in a position to do just that, whether you know it or not. I think you'd place Vince's welfare ahead of everything else, including a future with Adam."

A future with Adam. She didn't dare dream of it now. But that was an issue that needed clarified. She glanced around and then leaned into the bar so she wouldn't be heard.

"About that. He said that you..." She rechecked her surroundings. "Things aren't what they seem with you two, are they?"

Gina smiled. "Not on any level."

She stuttered, "Then, last night, I—I, we didn't betray you?"

Gina reached across the bar and squeezed her hands. "Not at all." She walked away to take another order. Valerie relaxed her shoulders, not acknowledging until that moment the knot in her neck muscles.

Gina stood in front of her again, waiting expectantly. The seats beside Valerie were no longer empty. She lowered her voice.

"I saw the paperwork with the highlighted information on it. It's not true. How can he believe that? Why is he wasting his time looking at," she paused, then said, "looking at that name. He should be looking for the real name."

Gina glanced at Bud Eagle walking in the door. "We think someone wants it to look like that is the right name. Here comes your friend." She leveled a smile at Bud, who came up to stand behind Valerie. "Beer?" Bud nodded.

Thinking that he was meeting Valerie, the couple beside her moved over and he took the seat next to her. "Hi, Valerie."

She turned her attention to Bud and offered him a warm smile. "Hi Bud, how are you?" Bud blushed and stuttered that he was fine. "Are you glad to be back in your own place?" he asked.

The question surprised her. Bud rarely spoke to her let alone asked her personal questions. She didn't respond other than to nod her head affirmatively.

He bobbed his head like a sports doll. "It's always better to sleep in your own bed. Course I guess it depends on who you're sleeping with, not that you're sleeping with anybody." He sipped his beer.

"But if you were it might make a difference. If you know what I mean." He grinned at her until the look she riveted on him wiped the smile away.

"No, Bud. I'm not sure what you mean."

"I don't mean nothin'." He said it much too quickly for her liking. He cupped the mug of beer with both hands and stared at it as he spoke. "I just know it's always nicer when I'm with my girl at night then when I'm not. That's all I mean."

He took another sip from the frosty mug and ordered a steak and cheese sandwich with extra onions from Gina. He stood and dug into his pants pocket for some coins. "I'll play some music on the jukebox. You like country don't you?"

A chill walked up her spine. "Why do you say that, Bud?"

Either he didn't hear her or he didn't plan to answer. He stood over the jukebox reading the music selections and punching buttons.

Gina positioned a paper placemat and silverware at Bud's seat. She picked up Bud's beer mug and set it on top of the placemat. "I'm not sure I like his comments," she whispered. "Have you spoken to him recently about you know who?"

She shook her head. The question was ludicrous. She wouldn't discuss her personal life, especially anything that remotely involved Adam, with anyone, least of all Bud.

"There's so much I wanted to talk to you about. But I don't feel comfortable with him here. I have notes that show Vince couldn't be involved in the fires. I have other questions as well."

"That's what we think too." Gina winked. "Why don't you call my boyfriend?"

"I'm still too angry but, I admit, I'm confused about what exactly I'm angry over. I'm more comfortable discussing everything with you."

"He won't lie to you. You should call him."

Valerie rose just as Bud returned to his seat.

"Are you leaving? I played some music I thought you might like."

"Thanks but I have to run." She waved at Gina and left.

Valerie mulled over Gina's words while she drove home. Adam, and her feelings toward him, baffled her. Her temper flared when she thought that he suspected Vince of the arsons. Her stomach somersaulted when she reflected on the time they'd spent together, his kisses and what he'd whispered to her.

Maybe it would be better to call and suggest they meet on neutral ground for a heart-to-heart talk. The idea made her smile. Her heart was part of the problem. Vince thought the world of Adam. Was he aware of Adam's suspicions?

"The less you know, the better," Gina had said. How much did she know? She'd compiled a lot of information as she'd reported the arsons, enough to make the national news.

But what about the arsonist? He was e-mailing her, or at least he had been until the most recent fire. That was another unanswered question. Why had the e-mails stopped?

Adam couldn't possibly believe Vince was behind those. But who was? Perhaps someone who had a grudge against one of them and knew hurting one hurt them both. For a quick moment, she wondered if her mother was involved. But that would require planning and a lot of thought to carry off a scheme like this and her mother's thoughts usually focused on where she could get her next drink. It had to be someone else.

She considered Bud. He was harmless, wasn't he? What had he meant by his comments about her being a country fan? It was an obvious reference to Adam. And what of Adam? What did she know about him? He wasn't a fire inspector, he'd told her as much. Was he undercover? Her heart skipped. Would she like to be under covers with him?

"Valerie," she admonished herself out loud, "stick to the problem at hand and don't think about Adam." Ah, but that wasn't an easy task.

22

The voicemail message from the Benton Falls police detective set her free. They'd caught Richard in Ohio raping a co-worker and he was in custody without bail.

"He'll be going away for a long time," the detective's message ended.

Tears of relief rolled slowly down her cheeks. She folded her hands in front of her and balanced her forehead on them. She squeezed her eyes shut, forcing the tears out the corners. "It's over," she whispered. "Thank you, God."

Vince knocked sharply on his sister's door with a large pizza in one hand and a bottle of champagne in the other. He'd just missed grabbing the phone before it bounced into voice mail. The message she'd left was short. "Ohio police arrested Richard. It's over. Call me."

He'd sensed the urgency without returning the phone call. She'd been on the verge of breaking down as she spoke.

She opened the door with tears streaming down her face,

placed the pizza on the kitchen table then threw herself into his arms.

Vince clung to her as she sobbed into his shoulder, finally letting go of weeks of pent up fear and anger. Her entire body shuddered with her sobs, and he squeezed her tighter.

When the waterfalls subsided, she held his hands, laughing at his water-rimmed eyes. "You open the champagne. I'll find glasses and paper plates."

She laughed out loud when he popped the cork, and they smiled in unison. "I hadn't realized how long it's been since I heard you genuinely laugh, Val. It sounds good."

They were always so in tune with each other. Even those few nights at Adam's hotel suite when they'd played games and watched movies, there was a sense of dread overshadowing her demeanor. He'd sensed it.

She served up a slice of pizza for each of them while he filled their glasses. They clinked the champagne flutes and sipped before diving into dinner.

"Did you share the news with Gina? Or call Adam?"

"No, I could barely call you without breaking down." She wiped her mouth with a paper napkin. "I'll call Gina later or tomorrow after I sign off. Right now, I don't think I can discuss the subject without crumbling to pieces." Her eyes filled with tears again.

"You gonna let Adam know, too?"

She studied the lone piece of pepperoni on her plate and shrugged. "Probably."

"Probably? Don't you think he'd want to know?" She nodded but didn't offer a response. But he pressed. "I called you last night." He dished up another pizza slice for each of them. "I wanted you to come eat pasta with me and a friend, someone I want you to meet."

She canted her head. Now, he had her full attention.

"Someone special? I didn't know you were seeing anyone special."

"Maybe special, I'm not sure yet. Anyway, we went out to eat and then I went to her place for a while. It was pretty late when I came home." He cleared his throat. "I noticed you had company." He narrowed his gaze, likely wondering if she'd be truthful. With him, she always was.

"Adam was here."

"Do I want to know why he was here at two o'clock in the morning?"

She licked pizza sauce off her fingers. The events of the night set off fireworks in her belly. "We went dancing last night. And then to a bonfire. We were hungry and rather than hitting an all-night diner we came back here and I cooked breakfast. It was pretty good if I do say so myself." She chuckled, then took a deep breath.

"Vince, I had such a good time. He's so much fun to be with. I asked him to spend the night."

Her brother caught his breath. "Did he?"

"No." She bit into the pizza and chewed slowly. "He's an incredible man. And a hell of a dancer." A broad smile creased her face, upsetting him.

"And Gina Gordi's boyfriend. Have you forgotten that? The same Gina who befriended you. Or are we not addressing that particular fact?"

She stared at her brother, knowing exactly what he was thinking. It would be so easy to repeat Gina's words from a few hours before and allay her brother's concerns. He could be trusted, she knew that. But she didn't dare. *She held their lives in her hands.* The phrase scared the hell out of her

"Things aren't what they seem between him and Gina."

"Sis, every man who cheats on his girlfriend uses that line. I had a bad feeling that you were falling for him. I've never known you to get involved with a married man or a man in a committed relationship. I'm surprised at you. And frankly, a little disappointed."

She nodded, agreeing with his every word. "I know, Vince. But this is different."

His voice raised an octave. "How? Just because he says so?"

"No. I'm not sure I can explain it to you. He's not cheating on Gina. You have to trust me on this." The irony didn't escape her. She asked the same thing of her brother that Adam asked.

"Why isn't it cheating? Because he hasn't taken you to bed yet? That's a pretty slim justification."

"No, it's not that at all. Please, trust me for now and let it go."

"You should trust me enough to tell me whatever in the hell it is you aren't telling me." He practically yelled the final few words.

She bit her lip against his anger. They rarely argued. She desperately wanted to confide in him, but she couldn't. She remained silent and he spoke again, more calmly.

"Sis, you've been through a lot in the last several weeks and you're vulnerable right now. Adam stepped in like a knight in shining armor to come to your rescue. I think he is a hell of a man. I like him, I really do. I'd be happy if he was single and you hooked up with him. But he isn't single. And it was his girlfriend who stepped up right beside him to help you. Don't let your emotions confuse you and take you down a road where you can easily be hurt."

"I know, Vince, and I love you for your concern. I'm not a schoolgirl with a crush on the teacher. I've said all those same things to myself. After what happened, I never thought I'd feel anything for a man. And I was beating myself up for having those feelings for Adam because of Gina. But I found out today that there is a difference between perception and reality. I can't tell you anymore, so please don't ask."

Vince studied her, his chest rising and falling faster than normal "Does he have feelings for you?"

She felt heat creep up her cheeks and remembered his whispered words, telling her she was intoxicating. "It felt like he did when he kissed me."

He ejected part way out of his seat, slapping both palms on the tabletop. "You made out with him? Is there more I should know?"

Oh, there was so much more. The memory shot heat down her spine that pooled below her waistband. She tried to appease her brother. "Look, never mind the details about us for the moment. There is something else I want to tell you. I went to his hotel room."

She raised her hand to stop the interruption he tried to inject. "Listen to me, please. I went to Adam's hotel and was looking at several files and papers spread out on the dining room table. He was in the kitchen. I don't think I was supposed to see them but Vince, he thinks you're the arsonist. He has a spreadsheet covered with yellow highlights over your name." She waved her hands to demonstrate. "It has notes and arrows all across it. He's trying to pin the fires on you."

Vince nodded. "I know. I've seen that spreadsheet."

His words didn't register at first. "I was so mad I started screaming at...what did you say?"

"I've seen that spreadsheet. Adam showed it to me at the fire station."

Her jaw dropped and she stared at him speechless for a moment. "You saw it? Did he accuse you of setting the fires? I hope you told him where to shove it."

He laughed. "No, I didn't tell him that. I told him I'd help find the real arsonist. I don't think he really believes it's me but when everything is down on paper, it sure looks like that. Didn't he tell you about our discussion?"

"No. I, um, I didn't give him a chance. I stormed out."

He laughed again. "Boy, Sis. You must've had one hell of a night."

Valerie smiled. "I did."

Monday morning brought the usual overload of e-mails to Valerie's mailbox that included comments on national, state, and local events from the weekend. She was both relieved to find there was nothing from Favfan and concerned at the same time. She'd expected a communication about the weekend fire the station had on its log.

Adam had stopped calling and she hadn't gotten around to calling Gina to talk to her further. Calling both of them to update them about Richard's arrest was on her list of things to do as soon as she clocked out. She wanted to speak with Gina first, and perhaps ask a few more questions. A small voice in her head chastised her to apologize to Adam when she made that phone call.

She'd asked her brother to tell him about Richard at the fire station today. Maybe he'd call first and spare her the embarrassment of apologizing. They were adversaries by day but friends by night. Were they friends on the brink of becoming lovers? They'd come damn close less than twenty-four hours earlier. How could she be ready to trust a man so totally with her heart when, the truth was, she knew so little about him?

Her desk phone rang, interrupting her thoughts. "Hi Valerie, it's C.J. Kwin."

"Hey, C.J. What's up?"

"I'm sorry to bother you at work but Vince gave me your number and said I should call you. I received a strange e-mail this morning on my city account."

"What do you mean by strange? What's it say?"

"It says show Valerie the way."

She caught her breath. Snatching a pen from a coffee cup, she wrote the words on her desk calendar. "How is it written? What does it look like? Do you know what that means?"

It was written in large capital letters. "Vince says Inspector Mitchell thinks the e-mails are related to the arsons."

Her heart pounded. "Did you tell Inspector Mitchell about the e-mail?"

"Yeah, I did. He seemed pretty interested, especially when I told him that I think I know what it means. There is an old abandoned building on Springrove that used to be a clubhouse for the kids in that neighborhood. They called it The Way. In fact, I think the old sign still hangs there. Inspector Mitchell says that we should do what the note says, that I should drive you. He'll meet us there."

His words wrinkled her brow. Adam was allowing her in on the ground floor of a development regarding the arson investigations? He was going to let her be on the scene as it unfolded? He had to know it would be the lead story on the five o'clock news. Was he extending this olive branch to appease her tirade two nights ago? It sounded like a plan to trap the arsonist using her as bait but he must have thought it was safe or he wouldn't suggest she and C.J. follow the note. At least he planned to be there too.

"Okay. Do you want to give me directions and I'll meet you there?"

"No, I think I should take you there. The note says show Valerie."

"Well, all right, I guess. What time do you want me to meet you at the fire station?"

"That's not a good idea. You know the noise the city has been making about parking personal cars when not on duty."

She hadn't heard that and jotted a note on the desk calendar to check it out as a possible story. Maybe the city was having budget problems. C.J. continued speaking.

"I know you live in the same complex as Vince. Give me your address and I'll pick you up. Around four?"

She laughed to herself. No wonder Adam was willing to let her be part of this. He was setting it up to miss the evening newscast. There was no way she'd have a story ready by five. She acquiesced and recited her address. He said he'd beep for her from the driveway.

She stopped by her boss's office to update him and together they researched public property records for Springrove. None of the owner's names were familiar and without a specific address it was hard to know which parcel to focus on. Since Valerie didn't know how long it would take, they agreed to break the news story the next morning unless other news media arrived. She doubted it. She felt certain that C.J. wouldn't call anyone else.

Once she uncovered the details of the story, she'd return to work and record the news report. Her boss agreed to assign one of the college interns to assist her with whatever research she might need from official records. He was ecstatic that they'd have the exclusive story and another feather in WARJ's cap.

A dozen questions already were forming in Valerie's mind and she jotted them in her notebook. Did Favfan send the note to Kwin? She'd forgotten to ask him. Was the abandoned building a house or an old business? Springrove was practically outside the city limits, which deviated from all the other inner-city arson sites. Was that significant? If she called Adam now, would he trust her enough to divulge the address so she could be a little more prepared before her arrival? It would allow the intern to start researching the property history.

Disappointment put a pout on her face when the call went straight to Adam's voicemail. She'd eagerly anticipated hearing his voice. "Hi, it's Valerie. I had some questions I wanted to ask you, but I guess I'll wait until I see you there."

Her phone beeped and she peeked at the display screen. Damn. It was the low battery warning. She switched off the cell and connected it to the charger. She'd need a full battery for this field trip in case she ended up dictating the story over the phone.

Adam lifted his vibrating cell phone from his pocket and looked at the caller ID. V. Daniels. Was it Valerie or Vince calling? Jesus, he hoped it was Valerie. But her timing sucked. No matter which sibling it was, he couldn't take the call. He dropped the phone back into his coat pocket.

They were gathered around the same conference table that they'd sat at weeks earlier when Adam was first assigned to the fire investigation. Manuel Sanchez, the assistant director in charge of the agency, made a personal appearance to honcho this meeting. He was under pressure to make an arrest, especially in light of the homeless man's death.

All the evidence pointed to two men, Daniels and Kwin, but every bit of it was circumstantial. Sanchez thought that the notes to Valerie tipped the scales of suspicion toward Vince as a way to promote his sister's career. There was an element of notoriety attached to the Daniels name that seemed to appeal to Sanchez. He was looking to move up the ladder and Adam suspected he wanted to use this case to do it. Adam was adamant that he didn't think Vince was involved.

"Based on what?" Sanchez demanded to know.

"Call it street experience. Call it a gut feeling. I don't care what you call it." He spat his words. Call it the opinion of the agent in the field doing what I've been trained to do versus you, an empty suit. That's what he wished he could say.

Sanchez turned to Gina. "Gordi? You're as plugged in to this investigation as he is. What are your thoughts?" Gina was careful not to look at Adam so they wouldn't be accused of conspiring. They'd always had each other's backs and today wouldn't be any different.

"If you're looking for someone to bring in for questioning I think you start with C.J. Kwin. There are still too many unknowns attached to him."

"These are the agents in the field," their boss chimed in. "If they say look at Kwin first, I'm following that lead. I back them."

Sanchez smacked his hand on the table angrily. He had the authority to override them, but they would challenge him. Instead, he pointed his finger at Adam.

"You better be right. We'll send an agent this afternoon to pick up Kwin and bring him downtown, based solely on your hunch or whatever the hell it is. I hope the real arsonist doesn't get away. I don't want you there when our guy shows up. I don't want any connection between you and a federal agent. In fact, I want you and Gordi to stay out of sight today. It will look less suspicious if both of you are AWOL. Go get lost some place."

Gina and Adam walked out of the building holding hands. He reached into his coat pocket and retrieved his cell phone. There were three missed calls, one from another agent, and two from V. Daniels.

Once he and Gina were seated in his SUV, he listened to the messages. He didn't know the agent coming in but his message advised that he was en route to Benton Falls and wanted additional information about which fireman he was seeking. The agent said he wouldn't make a move before speaking with Adam.

The first V. Daniels message was from Vince. "He wants to talk to me about Valerie," he said when Gina inquired about the reason for the call. "He said he knows it is none of his business but he's concerned that I'm leading her on and not being fair to you."

Gina smiled. "I like both of them."

"Tell me about it." He punched the numbers to save the voicemail and keyed the phone to play the third message.

Gina arched her eyebrows at his reaction to the message. "Is it from Valerie?"

"Yes, but I don't understand it."

He switched the phone to speaker and replayed it.

"Hi, it's Valerie. I had some questions I wanted to ask but I guess I'll wait until I see you there."

"See you where?"

He shrugged. "I don't know. Maybe she set up another interview with Chief Cozza and she'll be at the fire station later."

"Do you think you should call her?"

A dozen different thoughts ran through his mind, reasons for and against calling Valerie. "I'll call her later. We should hit the road."

"What about the chief? Should you call him?"

"He did fine in her last interview. If Valerie scheduled another one, he'll hold his own." He shifted the SUV into gear.

"We are we going?"

Adam smiled. "You heard the chief. He wants us to go AWOL. Where would you like to go?"

She had a manicure and pedicure in mind and he was interested in the sports hall of fame. They headed across the state line.

23

V alerie stood in front of her clothes closet wondering what to wear for the field trip to Springrove and laughed at herself. She couldn't help remembering that Adam asked her to change her outfit before they went out the other night. Common sense told her to dress casually because, after all, she was going to an abandoned building. But she'd be seeing Adam and she wanted to look professional. And sexy. She decided on straight-legged blue jeans with blue high-heeled leather pumps and a blue-and-white checkered shirt with a navy blue blazer. She grinned as she tied a dark blue silk scarf around her neck, trying to imitate the knot Adam made when he added the red bandana to her attire. It didn't quite look the same but it worked. Hopefully, he'd appreciate her attempt to look country.

She checked that she had a fresh tape in her recorder and dropped it in her purse along with a new notebook. She switched her cell phone to vibrate mode and crammed it in her purse as well. When Kwin honked the horn, she was ready.

"You said that Inspector Mitchell will meet us there?"

Kwin backed his blue sedan out of her driveway. "Yeah, he said he would. But he said he'd stay out of sight, just in case whoever sent the e-mail is watching us when we get there. We're not supposed to look around for him. You know, act like it's just the two of us."

"Who sent you the e-mail?"

"I don't know."

"No, I mean who did it say it was from."

Kwin looked at her. "It didn't make sense to me. Something like fanfan. I didn't recognize it."

Springrove was in the northern part of the city where residents were older or out of work and couldn't afford to keep up their homes. It seemed to her there were two or three dilapidated homes on every street they drove down.

She read the road signs as Kwin executed a turn. "How do you know about this place?"

"I grew up in this neighborhood. It looked a lot different years ago when people cared about where they lived and could afford to keep up their properties. It's a shame that it's come to this."

He turned onto a gravel driveway that extended straight back then cut to the left and ended at the white garage door of a red brick ranch. A flagpole with a tattered American flag stood in the front yard. The house was set back on the property so that neighbors, if there were any, were far away. Most of the windows were cracked or broken and dead flowers hung limply over the sides of sagging window boxes. The grass was overgrown and an area that was once a fenced-in garden now caged an overgrowth of weeds.

Valerie crinkled her nose. "This used to be a clubhouse? It looks like somebody's home."

"It was once. You can't see it from this side but there is a screened-in porch around back that the kids used. C'mon, I'll show you." He opened the driver's door to exit.

"Shouldn't we wait for Inspector Mitchell?" The hairs on the back of her neck had jumped to attention.

Kwin looked around, then leaned inside the driver's door and whispered, "He said we shouldn't look for him."

"Do you see a car or something around?"

"No, but that doesn't mean anything. C'mon, let's go around back."

He closed the door and walked to the front of the car, stopping by the right headlight to wait for her. She zipped her purse closed and placed it on the floor against the front of her seat. There didn't seem to be a soul around so it was probably safe. When she climbed out of the car her heels immediately sunk into the pea gravel. Gingerly, she made her way to the front of the car, using it for balance. Kwin reached out and took her elbow to steady her.

"You always wear those shoes?"

She already was thinking she might not have planned well as far as her footwear was concerned, but she wasn't going to admit it to him. The driveway ended as they started along the side of the house and they walked on hard, packed earth, making it easier for her to step.

She tried to release her arm from Kwin's grasp but he held fast. When they rounded the corner and were at the back of the house, she spotted several junked cars, a pile of tires, and mounds of trash. The kids may have used this as a meeting place but they sure didn't respect it.

Kwin tugged her arm, urging her toward a set of dilapidated wooden steps that led to a screened-in porch. At one time, this must have been the perfect place to end a summer's day. But not now. What was left of the rusted screens hung loose like rotted tongues falling from gaping mouths. Old beer cans and empty gin and whiskey bottles cluttered the floor along with countless cigarette butts. She reached for the wobbly railing and carefully climbed the three steps onto the porch, wrinkling her nose as she did.

Kwin nudged her toward the door. "I checked the place out earlier. You have to go inside. I think it's what you're supposed to see." The hinges groaned when he opened the rotted wooden door and urged her inside. She blinked several times, adjusting her vision to the darkness. Dust filled her nose and cobwebs brushed her cheek. She jerked backward.

"Over there." Kwin's hand between her shoulder blades shoved her toward the northwest corner of the room. She could barely see in the dim light that filtered through the open door behind them. The soot-coated picture window didn't offer much light either.

Her heels made tapping sounds on the wooden floor when she stepped. She squinted and saw an old-fashioned cast iron steam radiator in the corner but not much else.

"Over here," he repeated. "Give me your hand." Kwin moved his hand from her back down her arm and snatched hers. A loud snap echoed in the room and cold metal pinched her wrist. He yanked her arm forward, throwing her off balance, and a second snap split the silence with a metallic ring.

She reached out with her free hand to steady herself on the radiator. "C.J.? What are you doing?"

She jiggled her hand and wrist but there was no release. What the hell? He'd handcuffed her to the radiator.

"C.J.!" she screamed, the first notes of terror creeping into her voice. "What the hell is this? What are you doing? Unlock these."

With her free arm, she grabbed for his shirt sleeve but he stepped out of her reach.

"C.J.!" Her voice an octave higher now, approaching a high-pitched squeal. "Please. What are you doing? Talk to me. What's this about?"

In the darkness, he stood silent, staring at her. His breath expelled in short bursts, like an angry bull. She changed her tone and demanded. "C.J. Let me go. Now. When Inspector Mitchell sees this he—"

"Inspector Mitchell?" He leaned close to her, his breath punching her face. "Do you call him that in bed?"

Her breath caught in her throat. "How dare you."

"No, Miss Daniels, how dare you. Who do you think you are, snooping into my background and nosing around in my past? You'll do anything for a story, won't you? Even sleep your way to one. Your brother is the finest man I know and you disgrace his name."

She tried to halt his exit. "If you're so concerned about my brother, how do you think he'll like what you're doing to me? Unlock these things and I won't tell him. I won't tell anyone." He was almost outside.

"C.J.!" She screamed her panic now. "Where are you going? You can't leave me here. C.J.!"

The door slammed behind him.

A dam dropped Gina off at the mall then, sitting behind the wheel in his SUV, he dialed Valerie, but it kicked into voicemail. Just like her to leave an obscure message and then not answer her damn phone.

"It's Adam. I was in a meeting earlier and couldn't take your call. I'm on my cell now. Call me back. I'll try again."

He returned the agent's call to discuss how to handle C.J. Kwin. Finally, he called Vince's back and had to leave a message. He couldn't blame Vince for his concern. He'd probably seen his vehicle parked in Valerie's driveway in the wee hours of the morning. Any brother would wonder what was going on. Adam smiled to himself. The hell if he knew himself.

He lost track of time wandering through the sports museum. He'd checked his cell phone periodically and left a second message for Valerie. A few hours later, he headed to the mall, wondering if Gina was finished with her pampering. Although their boss had said to get lost for the day, an uneasy feeling that something was wrong haunted him. He preferred to head back and he desperately wanted to hear from Valerie. He'd give her another thirty minutes and call her again. Maybe the third time would be the charm.

Valerie screamed until she was hoarse and her throat raw. She twisted and yanked on the handcuff trying to wrench it open and only succeeded in cutting and bruising her wrist. Then the tears came.

She sank back against the wall in defeat, dropped her head to her knees and sobbed. How could this have happened? How had she become a victim again? With her free hand, she wiped the droplets from her face and rubbed her runny nose on the shoulder of her blazer. Adam's baritone words echoed in her head, "That's not a word that suits you." It was as loud as if he were standing beside her, admonishing her.

She took a deep breath, lifted her head and sniffled. No, it wasn't a word that suited her. It wouldn't be a word that defined her. What good was sobbing and yelling when no one could hear? *Think Valerie! Think!*

Was Vince on his way to the fire station? He was scheduled to work this evening. They hadn't talked all day and that was unusual. But her phone was in her purse in C.J.'s front seat. Would Vince worry when he didn't reach her? Maybe.

Certainly he'd sense something was wrong. But how long would it take for him to realize she was in trouble? Her boss knew where she was, although not the exact address. But he didn't expect to hear from her for a couple of hours. He wouldn't think anything was amiss if it went longer than that.

Adam. She'd left a message for him. Too bad it was short and to the point. If she hadn't been so nervous when she'd called and, instead, been a little more specific about where she expected to meet him, he might know where to find her. But Kwin had said

Adam would meet them here, so she hadn't thought details were necessary.

Of course, never in her wildest dreams did she think she'd end up handcuffed to a radiator in an abandoned house in the middle of who knows where. Would Adam become suspicious when he couldn't reach her? She hadn't returned his phone calls, so why should he bother?

Because, her heart said, there is something between the two of you. He'll know something is wrong. She let herself hope he'd try to find her. The glimmer faded. How would he know where to look? She leaned against the wall, clutched her knees to her chest with her free arm, and closed her eyes, thinking about Adam whispering to her in the dark. Singing some song about standing tall.

How comforting it had been to have him wrap his arms around her and draw her close on all the nights she slept beside him with blankets between them. She'd looked forward to going to bed with him every night. It seemed so right. That was what he'd said to her the night they went dancing. "It does feel right. That's the problem."

He was Gina's partner, whatever that meant. But he wasn't her lover. Did that mean she had a chance? She recalled the warmth of Adam's lips on hers and the spark that ignited. If she allowed it, it could burn like the bonfire she hadn't wanted to leave. "We can come back," he'd whispered. Was that an invitation? She wanted another night out with him. She wanted to go to bed with him, this time without the blankets.

Adam was a man worth fighting to live for, a reason not to sit here helplessly until she died of thirst or starvation or who knows what. She had to get free. She raised her head, her eyes adjusted to the shadows now, and studied her surroundings. She was in a large room central to the layout of the house, like a family room, near a stone fireplace. When she stretched her arm as far as it could reach, a draft came from the chimney. The flue must be open. At least she'd have air.

A wrought iron fireplace set with a brush, shovel, poker, and tongs sat on the far side of the hearth. The poker might be sturdy enough to force apart the handcuffs. Or maybe she could use the tip to pry open the lock. She stretched as far as she could, hearing the underarm seam of her blazer rip. But the tools were beyond her reach.

She surveyed the remainder of the area. Aside from a pile of newspapers stacked in the middle of the floor and an overturned wooden folding chair, the room was barren. She needed something sharp. She considered the buttons on her blazer and her jewelry. Then she looked at her high heels.

She removed her shoe, staring at the stiletto heel. Last year her shoes set off the metal detector at the airport. The security checkpoint screener told her that women's stilettos have metal spikes in the heels. If she could figure out how to get to that spike, she might be able to pick the lock on the handcuffs.

Trying not to think about the dirt at the end of the heel, she inserted it between her teeth and jiggled and tugged at the rubber tip until her jaw hurt. Was it the tip that wiggled or was she loosening her teeth?

She couldn't give up. She laid the edge of the heel on the first pipe of the steam radiator and pressed the metal handcuff on top of it. She yanked, twisted, and turned the shoe. In this dark corner it was hard to see but she ran her fingertips to the end of the heel and felt a tiny gap. She tried once more, pulling with all her might, and the rubber tip popped off. But the exposed spike was too short to slide into the tiny hole on the lock. Using her fingers, she evaluated the ridge on top of the accordion-like pipes. Uneven. Rough enough, she hoped, to wear away the leather on the spike heel. She hated to ruin a good pair of shoes but this was, literally, a matter of life and death. With renewed determination, she sawed the heel back and forth on the pipe's edge.

Gina climbed into the SUV smiling and waved deep burgundy fingers at Adam. "Nothing like a fresh manicure to make a woman feel good.

"Have you checked with anyone back at Benton Falls?"

Her smile disappeared. "I called the bar about a half-hour ago to say I wouldn't be in until later. Happy hour is booming."

"You haven't heard from Valerie, have you?"

Gina looked surprised. She retrieved her phone from her purse and checked for messages "No. Didn't you call her back?"

"Three times. She hasn't returned any of my calls."

"Well that's odd. She can't still be mad. Maybe you should call the chief and see how the interview went."

He hadn't thought of that. He dialed the station's private line. "Fire district four-two. Daniels."

"Hey Vince. It's Adam. I couldn't answer the phone when you called earlier. Did you find my message?"

"Yeah. I wasn't scheduled until tonight but I came in early so Jimmy could take his wife to the doctor. I figured I'd be here whenever you rolled in. Listen, Adam, I'd like to talk to you about my sister."

"I know, Vince. I'll be there in a couple of hours. Right now, I need to know if anything is going on and if you've talked to Valerie."

Vince's voice changed. He sounded like the puppy the chief characterized him as. "Well, we are having a hot day here. No fires, though. Just some excitement with the cops."

"What do you mean?" He hoped he sounded clueless.

"There is an agent here looking for C.J. He has an arrest warrant. Only C.J. isn't here. He didn't show up for work. We tried to reach him at his apartment and on his cell, but we can't find him. The agent is still here. He's been in his car most of the day. Where are you?"

"I'm a couple hours away on business. Is your sister still at the station?" If Valerie had a nose for news she wouldn't ignore the arrival of a state agent with a warrant, not when she was already suspicious of Adam's authority. He imagined the grilling the poor guy got.

"Valerie? No, she's not here. I haven't heard from her all day. To be honest, I was wondering if she was with you. What's going on with you two, Adam? And what about Gina?"

Adam ran his hand through his hair. This wasn't the time to account for his conduct with Vince's sister or declare his intentions. "Vince, we'll talk about that when I come in. You haven't heard from her at all?"

"No, I left her a couple of messages. She didn't call me back. Why?"

"Did she have an interview with the chief at four?"

"Not that I know of. I've been here since three o'clock. What's going on?"

Adam repeated Valerie's cryptic message. "Do you know what her plans were for today?"

Vince was momentarily silent on the other end of the line. "I don't mean to be difficult, Adam, but are you asking officially or for personal reasons? Is it a coincidence that there is an arresting agent here and you're trying to find my sister? Is she in trouble?"

Twins. They would protect each other to the death. How should he answer this question? "I don't think the agent is interested in Valerie. I do think it's odd that she isn't answering her cell phone. And yes, Vince, some of it is for personal reasons, which I can't divulge right now."

Sitting beside him, Gina smiled and gave him a thumbs up.

"I'm sorry, Adam, but that's what concerns me. My sister has been through a lot. You know that. She's real vulnerable right now. It's not fair for you to take advantage of her. And what about Gina?"

Adam took a deep breath, trying to stay patient. "Vince. This.

Isn't. The. Time. Gina is sitting right here beside me, listening. I'll be on station later tonight and I swear we'll talk. But for now, we have to focus on finding Valerie."

"I don't know what's going on with you two. Valerie says I should trust her."

"You need to trust me, too."

There was a silent pause. "Yeah. But I'm holding you to that talk when you come in." He paused again. "Let me see if I can reach her. She doesn't usually call me when I'm working, but I'll try her cell. I'll call you right back."

Adam stared at the Call Ended. "She hasn't been at the fire station and he hasn't heard from her. I don't like this."

"I don't have a good feeling either," Gina said. "While you were talking to Vince I tried her cell phone and it went into voicemail."

Driving at speeds close to eighty miles an hour, Adam had them to the outskirts of Benton Falls in less than two hours. While in route, Vince called back to say he couldn't reach his sister. He tried her condo and he tried the radio station. Valerie was listed on the news budget to record a follow-up story on the Benton Falls arsons for tomorrow's first morning news broadcast. A co-worker had overheard her talking about going on a field trip but he didn't know any details. She was expected to return to the station sometime tonight.

Adam detected the edge in Vince's voice. "If she hasn't been here and she hasn't talked to you how is she doing a follow-up arson story? I'm starting to worry."

"Me, too. We're almost back in the city. I'm going to check Valerie's condo to see if everything is okay. Does she by any chance keep a key hidden outside somewhere?"

He dropped Gina off at her apartment and agreed to meet her at the bar. At Valerie's condo, he knocked first on the front door and when she didn't answer, he circled the unit, looking in the dining room and kitchen windows. It was apparent she wasn't on the first floor.

On her back patio, he reached for the third red clay pot from the right that contained a cluster of white silk daisies. He dumped the pot over and freed the door key taped to the inside.

Nothing inside the unit seemed out of order. He lingered in Valerie's bedroom, stopping in front of her dresser to lift a bottle of perfume and smell it. He closed his eyes and she filled his senses. Even absent, she was captivating. Back downstairs, he scanned the notes and papers on her desk and moved the computer mouse to wake up the sleeping laptop sitting open. But nothing offered a clue to her whereabouts. Standing in the middle of the kitchen, he dialed her cell number once again. He didn't hear it ringing in the house so, unless it was in silent mode, it had to be with her. He disconnected when it went into voice mail.

After returning the key to the pot of daisies, he drove to the fire station where her brother met him at the door.

"Anything?" Vince frowned when he shook his head and rubbed his left wrist. "Something's wrong Adam. I can feel it."

"I think so too. Is Bud here?"

"No."

"Find Bud. See if he knows where she is."

"Why would he know where she is?"

"He seems to know a lot about what she does. I think he might be following her. Maybe we'll get lucky and he bugged her car. Try to find him."

He ignored the surprised look on Vince's face and walked outside with his credentials in view to the agent sitting in a silver Ford parked in front of the fire station.

He leaned into the window. "Hey there, you know, you can hang inside if you want. These guys are okay. They'll probably give you a cup of coffee."

"Already had some of their coffee and used their facilities. I'm trying to monitor the radio in case we find this knucklehead. We went ahead with the warrant for his home and his car, but I haven't heard anything from that team yet."

Adam returned inside, hoping Vince had good news. No such luck.

"Keep trying. When you find him, call me. Or call Gina. I'm going to the bar."

Shots In The Dark was packed. The bartenders were hustling to fill all the drink orders. He didn't see Gina anywhere, but the younger bartender waved him over and reached for an envelope tucked beside the cash register.

"Not sure who left this," he yelled over the crowd noise and the jukebox. "It was on the bar."

Adam nodded and took the sealed envelope. "INSPECTOR ADAM MITCHELL" was printed on the front in capital letters. He ripped open the flap and removed a single sheet of paper. It likewise was printed in capital letters: 6134 SPRINGROVE — VALERIE.

25

Valerie scraped and sawed until about an inch of metal from her heel was exposed. Now she poked and prodded the tiny opening that latched the handcuff around her wrist. It had to be like picking a lock, although she'd never done that. She had a headache from squinting in the dim shadows. If she didn't unlatch it soon, she'd be working in total darkness.

She couldn't yell for help anymore and hadn't for at least an hour. Her throat felt like sandpaper each time she swallowed, which wasn't often. She was so thirsty she no longer produced saliva. It was hard to tell how much time had passed because the black face of her watch was unreadable in the darkness.

Suddenly, the softest click and the pressure released at her wrist. She was free. She lowered her arm and massaged her wrist, whispering a silent prayer of thanks. Vince always chastised her for not thinking things through or having a plan but her only thought was to escape this prison as fast as possible. Reluctantly, she kicked off her right shoe and slowly stood. Going barefoot probably was not a good idea but wearing one high heel would hinder her progress. But before she took her first step, the white shaft of headlights pierced the cracked picture window and bit into the darkness. She froze.

Even if her brother had missed her by now, he wouldn't know where to find her. She doubted anyone else would be coming to rescue her. Only C.J. Kwin knew where she was. The gravel crunched beneath the tires and then the lights disappeared. But the hum of the car engine continued until the sound came from the back of the house. She canted her head in that direction. The engine ceased and a car door slammed.

Quickly, she leaned back against the wall, slid down to the floor, and raised her hand to the edge of the radiator. She wedged the handcuff over her wrist to appear as if she was still a captive. She listened for his footsteps and at the first thud, she screamed.

"Help me please! Somebody help me!" Her strained vocal chords didn't provide much volume.

A wide flashlight beam cut through the midnight blackness of the room and blinded her. She shut her eyes and jerked her head out of the ray.

"Still screaming for help, Valerie? I would've thought you'd be in tears by now. Hanging out with a fire inspector must have given you some backbone. He was pretty brave running in to help your brother and Chester at the Rippey Street fire. I'm really glad he did, too. Kept me from having to play hero."

His words stunned her. "What do you mean?" The question sounded like the croak of a frog.

"Oh don't worry. I wouldn't have let anything happen to your brother. But, speaking of heroes, your knight in shining armor should be on his way."

Kwin threw his head back and burst into laughter, sounding much like a mad man.

"I don't know what you're talking about, C.J. Let me go, please."

"I don't know what you're talking about, C.J.," he mimicked in a high-pitched voice. "Oh please, pretty please let me go. Not so high and mighty now, are ya?"

He shined the flashlight along her body then aimed it onto her face again. She shifted her head out of the intense glare.

"Where is your shoe?" He found her face with the light beam. She'd dropped the shoe the minute the handcuff lock sprang open. It sat wedged between her hip and the radiator. She moved her face away from the direct light.

"I threw it at a rat."

Kwin's head dropped back and he laughed again. "Well, let's hope he has some friends." Abruptly, he turned and walked out.

Gina nearly shook her bartender after he recounted giving Adam the note.

"Did Adam say anything?"

"Nope. He just opened the letter and ran from the bar."

"Something's wrong. I can't stay tonight. You guys have to handle things." She glanced at the overflow crowd. "I'll give you both a bonus for this."

She held up her cell phone. Her rules were that employees could not have their cells with them while they worked. "Have your cell in your pocket," she instructed. "If I need help, I'll call you." They looked puzzled but nodded their understanding.

She drove first to the fire station. The men were in their living quarters but they came downstairs when the public bell rang. Gina rushed to Vince.

"Have you heard from Adam or Valerie?"

"Adam was here. He went to the bar. He told me to track down Bud, but I can't find him." He massaged his left wrist. "I can't find Valerie either. What's going on?"

"Do you know where Bud lives?"

"Yeah, just off Seventh. But I don't understand. What does Bud have to do with any of this?"

"I'll tell you in the car." She turned to the men on duty. "Can you boys cover for Vince? We have to find Bud. He's the only one who might know where Valerie is. And I think she's in trouble."

Both nodded yes. They ran to Gina's car and Vince rattled off directions to Bud's apartment. She reached into her purse for her phone and handed it to Vince, instructing him to dial Adam. There was no answer.

"Dammit. Of all times for him to not answer." She took a fortifying breath, reaching a decision that could end her career.

"Adam trusts you, and I trust Adam's judgment so I hope you'll keep this confidential. Adam is working undercover, looking for an arsonist within the fire department."

Vince started to laugh and shook his head. "Valerie suspected something like that. She even asked me if I thought Adam could be an undercover secret agent, as she phrased it."

Gina smiled. "Your sister is pretty close. We're missing a few pieces but all the buildings were saturated with an accelerant before they burned. We suspect Kwin used some sort of delayed igniter set off by an old-fashioned alarm clock to start the fires. We're not sure about his motive. We think he is sending Valerie the e-mails about the arsons but again, we don't know why. By now, we should have agents executing a search warrant at Kwin's home for his computer. We wanted to bring him in today for questioning but he disappeared. The fact that Valerie can't be found either isn't good. She was nosing around and she may have stumbled into the same information we discovered."

Vince stared at her wide-eyed. "We? Are you an undercover agent, too?"

He looked like a kid meeting the Easter bunny. "Yeah, but I'm here for different reasons. I—"

Vince interrupted. "So, you and Adam...?" His question hung in the air.

"Are partners. We're not romantically involved although I love the man to death. Like a brother. That was part of the cover. Adam is in love with Valerie. He just doesn't know it yet. If Valerie is in trouble, he'll die trying to save her. That's why I know if we find Valerie, we'll find him. I think Bud can help us out with that."

Vince pointed to a street where Gina should turn. "How does Bud fit into all of this?"

"It appears that Bud is monitoring Valerie, where she goes, what she does and who she sees. We don't think he is connected to the arsons only because he doesn't seem bright enough. But he is obsessed with her, so much so that he knows her every move, including the time she stayed with Adam at his hotel suite. Only the four of us knew where she was.

"If he's a kinky voyeur, hopefully we can embarrass him into telling us where she is. If he's directly connected to Kwin and the arsons, then I just may have to shove my gun down his throat to make him tell us where she is."

Vince held up his hand like a traffic cop. "Please, allow me the first move."

The second Bud partially opened the door Vince forced his way in, grabbed Bud's shirt between his fists and shoved him against the wall. They were nose to nose and Vince's voice was a menacing growl.

"Where's my sister, Bud?"

Bud immediately turned beet red and stuttered. "She—she's not here Vince."

He laughed a nervous laugh, snorted then smiled a crooked smile. "Why would you think she'd be here, alone, with me? I'm flattered."

Vince yanked him forward then slammed him against the wall a second time.

"I know she's not here." He spoke slowly and deliberately.

"Gina says you probably know where she is. Why is that Bud? Why have you been monitoring my sister?"

Gina, seeing that Vince had control of Bud, searched the other rooms. Bud didn't have dining room furniture and instead had the room filled with packing boxes. When she opened the door to a spare bedroom she stopped in her tracks. Pictures of Valerie covered the walls. There were posed publicity pictures, candid snapshots, and what any investigator would recognize as surveillance photos.

Some were black and white, others were in color. Newspaper blurbs that mentioned WARJ and included Valerie's name hung like patches over the walls, in between the pictures. Her name was highlighted in bright yellow on each clipping.

Gina called to Vince. "You're not going to believe this."

Vince shoved Bud ahead of him toward the bedroom. His jaw dropped when he saw the walls. "Holy Jesus."

Bud began to rock from side to side. "Vince, it's not what it looks like."

But he wasn't listening. He turned and punched him on the right side of the face, knocking off Bud's glasses and sending him backward to the wall. Vince was on him instantly, his hands knotting Bud's shirt so tight around his neck, Bud began to choke for air.

"What the hell is this? Where's Valerie, you son of a bitch?"

Gina grabbed his shoulders. "Back off, Vince. We need him to help us and to do that he has to be able to talk. Let him go."

He gave Bud one more shake then released his grip. Bud's head dropped to the floor and he shot a grateful look Gina's way. Gina smiled at him and spoke as if Bud were a six-year-old.

"You can understand why Vince is upset, Bud. We have to find her because we think she's in danger. I don't think you want to see Valerie harmed. If you know where she is, it's important that you help us."

Bud cast an uneasy glance toward his desktop computer then

immediately looked back at Gina. He stuttered and said he wasn't sure where Valerie might be. Gina hadn't missed the nervous glance toward the desk. She walked over to the computer and moved the mouse to reactivate the screen.

She clicked on one of the tabs on the home screen of a program she recognized. "This is a tracking program for her car, isn't it Bud?" She didn't wait for his answer. "But it indicates that her car is at home. What are these other monitoring tabs?"

Vince glared at Bud. "Get your ass in that chair now or so help me..."

Bud held up his hands defensively. "Okay, okay Vince. Take it easy." He rolled over onto all fours, stood tentatively to steady his balance, then sat at his desk.

Gina peered over his shoulder. "If you know where she is, find her now or you'll be facing charges of aiding and abetting in arson and murder."

Bud's hand trembled as it moved to the computer mouse. "I was out most of the day, Vince. I swear I don't know where she is. But give me some time. I can check a couple of programs and maybe locate her."

Vince snapped. "We don't have time, Bud, she's in trouble."

Tears rimmed Bud's eyes. "I'll help you, Vince. I'll do whatever I can. I don't want anything to happen to Valerie."

Gina studied the screen. "Isn't this a phone tracer? Open it."

Bud maneuvered the mouse to another tab. With a few clicks, he displayed an itemized log of the phone calls Valerie had made and received that day.

Adam had called seven times. She saw the one attempt she'd made and the phone call just hours earlier from Vince. A tiny envelope indicated that Vince left a message. She pointed to the one that showed an incoming call from C.J. Kwin.

"Does this program record the conversation, too?"

Bud nodded and, after two mouse clicks, they were listening

to Valerie's conversation with Kwin. The minute they heard Springrove she grabbed Vince's arm.

"How fast can you get us there?" They were already moving toward the door. She turned back to Bud and pointed. "Redeem yourself and dispatch the police and the fire trucks out there pronto. We don't know an address but if you can figure one out, call Vince immediately. Relay it to the emergency crews, otherwise give them the description of Adam's SUV. Send them out there fast. We'll deal with your espionage later."

She grabbed Vince's arm and they ran from the apartment, leaving Bud sitting at his computer desk with tears streaming down his cheeks.

26

Adam bolted from the bar, programmed his navigation system to the Springrove address and took off like a race car driver. The screen estimated travel time at twenty-three minutes. Twenty-three minutes to reach her. It seemed like an eternity.

If she was hurt he'd kill the bastard. He clutched the steering wheel with white-knuckled hands. With no idea about what waited for him, his priority had to be Valerie's safety and doing whatever that entailed. There were so many things he wanted to tell her, starting with a proposal that they spend a block of time together. He hadn't been able to sleep without her, let alone stop thinking about her. Now he wanted to sleep with her. If she wasn't ready for an intimate relationship yet, that was okay. Wrapped in his arms again beside him in bed would be enough. He'd wait for more. As long as she needed.

He'd accrued a lot of overtime working this case. He'd take time off and maybe convince her to go away with him.

He rehearsed how he'd begin the conversation. "My real name is Adam Michaels, and before you blow up about the deception let me explain." That temper of hers would flare up immediately. But he'd tell her everything, who he worked for, where he lived, what he hoped to build with her.

He owned a two-story log cabin on a lake. From the upstairs bedroom, you could see the water and enjoy the ceiling-high stone fireplace rooted in the first floor living room. That room opened out onto a wrap-around deck. Off to the side was an acre of trees that served as a natural habitat for a slew of different animals and birds. Adam had spotted deer, wild turkey, and even a coyote or two from the deck.

He pictured Valerie on the balcony beside him watching the sun set over the lake. He wanted to share it all with her. He glanced at the opened note lying on the front seat, typed in capital letters. Exactly like the e-mails sent to Valerie. She hadn't left him the note, Favfan had.

Was Favfan really C.J. Kwin? How had he lured her there? It must have been something very clever because Valerie wasn't stupid. She'd sensed something was not right with his so-called relationship with Gina. She'd been suspicious of his true identity. She'd been researching the arsons on her own and was smart enough to request the personnel files of the firemen, as if she, too, suspected someone on the inside. No, she wasn't stupid at all. Kwin must have been extremely deceptive.

Valerie's phone message. "I had some questions but I'll wait until I see you there" Where? Had Kwin somehow convinced her that he would be at this Springrove address? Kwin also had to be certain that Adam would come for her. Why was he so certain of that? Had he conspired with Bud, using Bud to spy on Valerie? Why would Bud go along with that if it meant subjecting Valerie to danger? That didn't jive with Bud's obsession over her.

If Kwin was acting alone, had he been following Valerie all the time? Was that his car that sped from the hotel parking lot the other night? They were all questions Adam couldn't answer. Kwin's actions and motives were an unknown. One thing he was certain of, however, was Kwin's underestimation of how hard he'd fight for Valerie. The bastard had no idea who he was dealing with.

His adrenaline rocketed. "You want her, buddy? Over my dead body."

He sped down Springrove cursing the dark country road for its lack of streetlights. He slowed when the navigation system indicated he was near the address and turned into a gravel driveway when it announced "Arrived."

In the dark, he barely made out the house sitting back on a wooded lot. His heart raced as he unlocked the glove box and retrieved his handgun. He tucked it in the back of his jeans and tugged his black leather jacket over it. Then he grabbed his flashlight and slowly stepped out of the car, surveying the area as he did. Total black. He shined the light over the front of the house and along the porch. It reflected off yellow caution tape stretched in crisscross fashion across the front steps. He raised the beam of light to the windows. The broken portals stared back at him like hollow eyes. If Valerie was here, where was her car? "Valerie?"

He heard a noise and strained to listen. The night din seemed amplified in the silence. He shined the flashlight beam toward the right side of the house, saw the worn path beside the building and slowly stepped toward it.

Valerie caught her breath and held it when headlights shined in the front window. Then a flashlight beamed danced around the ceiling. She hadn't heard a sound since Kwin left, including his car driving away. This was a second person arriving.

Where was Kwin? Was this a conspirator? Could Kwin see her? She'd remained sitting against the wall still faking the handcuffs just in case. Was he meeting someone here? Suddenly, Adam's voice rang out. "Valerie?"

She scrambled to crawl to the front window. "Adam, get out of here." But her raw vocal chords reduced her voice to barely a whisper. She yelled again without him hearing. She raised her head above the dust-covered windowsill and peered into the darkness.

Perched on her hands and knees in front of the picture window, she watched Adam approach the house. She called out again and then knocked a jagged chard of glass out of the frame. It shattered on the front porch. In the stillness, the noise was magnified a thousand times. He stopped in his tracks and aimed the flashlight in her direction. A shuffling sound startled her and she ducked and quickly crawled back to the radiator.

Adam shined the light on the porch again just in time to see a critter run along the wall and jump off. He turned his attention back to the path and followed it to the rear of the house. He wrinkled his nose at the heap of tires and trash in the back yard. Then his eyes widened and the flashlight illuminated the license plate on the blue car parked near the porch. Kwin's wife's car.

He shined the beam around the yard but didn't see anyone. Cautiously, as quietly as the creaky steps allowed, he climbed to the dilapidated porch. He called Valerie's name again.

Valerie felt around the floor for her other shoe and hurled it at the door hoping to alert Adam. It hit the wall with a bang and the backdoor swung open. "Valerie?"

Before she could answer, a loud thwack and a thud reverberated through the darkness. Adam fell face forward onto the floor, half in and half out of the door.

She stifled her scream when Kwin entered behind him, stepping over Adam's legs. He laid a flashlight on the floor with the beam shining toward the wall and grabbed Adam's left arm. She quickly and silently fumbled with the handcuff, wedging it around her wrist again.

Kwin grunted as he wrestled with Adam's size, trying to drag his lifeless body inside the door. He heaved and tugged and finally hauled Adam's feet over the threshold. The rickety door barely closed.

In the shadows, she clenched her teeth. *Think, Valerie. Think!*

She wanted to pummel Kwin to death. If Adam was dead, she just might. When Kwin finally shined the light on her, she was in the same position beside the radiator.

"I told you your knight in shining armor was coming. He's here." He swung his arm toward Adam, still panting from the effort to drag him inside.

"Here, take a better look." He rolled the beam over Adam's body. She gagged when it highlighted a wide gash along the left side of his head. Blood oozed over his ear and down his cheek. Dear Lord, was he breathing? His eyes were closed and he didn't move.

"You bastard." Kwin swung the beam of light around and shined it into her eyes. She squinted and jerked her head away from the blinding whiteness.

He sneered. "Since you're so hot for him, I'm going to make things good and hot for the two of you. It's what you both deserve."

He kicked Adam in the ribs, stepped over his body, and sauntered out the door. When his footfalls on the steps faded, she scrambled on her hands and knees to Adam. Leaning her face next to his she prayed to feel his breath. Nothing. She whispered his name. No response.

Kwin's footsteps pounded on the steps and she hustled back to her corner. Kicking Adam a second time, he strode to the overturned chair in the center of the room. With the flashlight tucked under his armpit, the light beam bounced around the floor and the walls like a crazy light saber. She couldn't tell what he was doing but he never turned his back on Adam's lifeless form.

She squinted, following the beam. It highlighted a Louisville slugger baseball bat on the floor near Adam's feet. Probably what Kwin used to hit him.

Now Kwin knelt on the floor, the flashlight wedged between his knees to shine on his hands. He twisted the key on the back of a white, wind-up alarm clock and tinkered with the knobs in the back. When he placed it on the hardwood floor, the ticking magnified tenfold.

Adjusting the light to shine on the clock, he attached first a red wire and then a blue wire to what looked like a cigarette lighter. Valerie watched horrified as he scattered the stack of newspapers across the warped floorboards, spreading out the pages, and drenched them with liquid from a red plastic gas container. The pungent fumes saturated the room, stinging her eyes and nose. She held her breath.

Gasoline? Kerosene? The fire chief had speculated that the arsonist used an accelerant to saturate all the fires. Oh God. Kwin was the arsonist. The sudden realization was as clear as day. And to her horror, he was setting another fire.

"Why, C.J?" she whispered. "Why did you set all those fires?"

Kwin turned on her in a rage. "Shut up. Don't you talk to me. You want to say something? Say goodbye to your lover."

On the floor, Adam groaned and he spun around. Thank God he was still alive. Kwin straightened, stomped toward Adam and delivered another kick to his side. Adam moaned and she felt his agony.

"Stop it." Her grating croak was less than threatening. "Stop it you son of a bitch."

He merely laughed at her weak outburst. He retrieved the gas can, and positioned the flashlight underneath his chin, giving himself a ghoulish appearance.

"Be right back, kids."

At the far end of the room, he disappeared down a stairwell she hadn't noticed earlier.

Immediately, she scampered over to Adam and leaned near his ear to whisper, "Adam, can you hear me?"

He mumbled something. It sounded like "run."

It didn't matter. She wasn't leaving without him. At least he was alive. She crawled over his legs and snatched up the baseball bat.

The room was dark enough that unless Kwin shined his flashlight in her corner as soon as he returned, he wouldn't notice she wasn't there. She crept toward the downstairs door on all fours, dragging the bat with her. Easing herself into an upright position, she leaned against the wall and waited for the monster's return.

Fumes permeated the room, gagging her. She shook off the accompanying dizziness, willing herself to fight the lightheadedness. She clutched the baseball bat in her two hands as if she were standing at home plate. Her brother's voice echoed in her head from when they were children playing wiffle ball in the street. "Swing level and swing hard," he used to coach her. Despite his help, she rarely hit the ball.

This would be the swing of her life.

Kwin's footsteps echoed from the basement. She took a deep breath and whispered a silent prayer. "Please God, help us." He came through the door with the flashlight focused on Adam. In the shadow, she aimed at the back of his head and swung. The sound of the bat smashing into his skull was sickening, like whacking a pumpkin. The force of the blow knocked the bat out of her hand but it also hit Kwin dead center. He screamed and went sprawling to the floor.

Valerie fell to the floor on her hands and knees and felt around feverishly for the bat. Kwin hadn't been knocked unconscious. He was moving and swearing up a storm. Just as she grabbed the handle of the bat and raised it he jarred it loose from her hands. Then he kicked her in the stomach sending pain shooting through her body and knocking the wind out of her. She screamed and fell against the wall at the same time as he stumbled backward.

He rubbed the back of his head and yelled, "You bitch." He swung at her with a blood-covered fist that connected with the side of her head, toppling her like an inflatable punching toy. He seized her arm and dragged her across the floor with much less trouble than he'd hauled Adam, given her smaller stature and lighter weight. She was too dazed to resist.

"You two belong together," he screamed, dropping her on top of Adam. "May you burn in hell."

He stifled sobs while he staggered on his feet, sending the flashlight beam around the room like a disco light. He made his way back to the alarm clock and shined the light on the contraption he'd rigged. Sprawled across Adam's back with her face close to his she felt the slightest movement from his head.

"Gun," he whispered.

What had he said? Her head was spinning and she thought she might vomit. Adam moved again, arching his hips up slightly against her and she felt the hard metal handle protrude into her stomach. She caught her breath.

"Gun," he repeated.

Kwin concentrated on the alarm clock, sniffling and muttering about inflicted pain he didn't deserve. His running dialogue was peppered with profanity directed toward her and Adam, but he wasn't paying attention to them.

She moved her left arm along her side and gently rolled toward Adam's shoulders just enough to raise her torso and block Kwin's view if he looked their way. She reached under his jacket and carefully removed the gun from his waistband. She had a healthy respect for guns. She didn't like hunting and agreed that guns in the wrong hands, like street gangs, were dangerous. But in the right hands, she conceded they were a necessary evil.

Three years ago, Vince had insisted she learn how to shoot

and he'd bought her a small handgun to keep in her home because she lived alone. She'd kept the weapon in the bottom of a sweater drawer for about a month before she begged her brother to take it back. Just having the thing in the house unnerved her. Now, feeling the cold metal in her hands, she knew what to do.

Kwin shined the light on them, swaying to keep his balance. She lay still with her eyes closed. Her face was buried in Adam's back but she could still feel tears filling her eyes. The ticking alarm clock echoed through her spinning head.

Kwin emitted a wild laugh, like a hyena. "You have fifteen minutes to kiss your lover goodbye. Don't worry. I'll fight the fire as hard as I can. Too bad it will be of no use." He stood, stumbled, swore at them and held his hand to the back of his head. As he passed alongside their bodies Adam swung his arm out and grabbed Kwin's ankle, stopping his progress and yanking him to the floor. Kwin screamed and kicked at Adam trying to free his foot.

Adam's sudden movement jarred Valerie as well. She rolled off him and sat back on her heels. The gun felt heavy in her hands as she raised it, squinted to make out the shape in the darkness and squeezed the trigger. Kwin shrieked and fell backward. Her hands trembled so violently, she almost dropped the weapon. Tears streamed down her face as she rose on her knees into a kneeling position. The smell of gunpowder singed her nose. She watched for movement in the dark.

"You bitch. I'll kill you." Kwin rolled over in an attempt to rise. With her arms extended straight out and both hands clutching the gun she aimed and fired a second and a third time. There was a thud. Kwin didn't move again.

27

S he was paralyzed. She couldn't move. She lowered the gun and sank back on her heels. Then she turned onto her hands and knees and threw up.

The ticking clock pierced her eardrums. Adam moaned and she shook her head to clear it. She leaned into his ear.

"Adam, can you hear me? Can you move?" He uttered something. It sounded like Michael. It made no sense.

She laid her cheek in front of his nose and mouth. His breathing was so shallow it scared her. She searched for a pulse but the gooey pool of blood on his neck prevented her from locating it.

She whispered to him, "Please, Adam, don't leave me. There's so much I want to say to you."

She yanked the blue silk scarf from her neck and wrapped it around his head. It wasn't the best bandage but it should slow the bleeding. She leaned forward again and placed a kiss on his cheek.

"Stay with me, Tex."

Fifteen minutes, Kwin had said. How much time had already passed? She ran her hands along Adam's chest and then across his waistband. He must have his cell phone with him. She felt along the back pockets of his jeans and finally found the slim phone tucked into his right rear pocket.

"This is the 9-1-1 operator. What is your emergency?"

She strained to speak. "Springrove. Send help."

The dispatcher couldn't hear her. "Hello? Can you speak up please? Do you have an emergency?"

Valerie tried again but her vocal chords were wrecked.

"Is someone there? Hello? Do you have an emergency?"

She laid the phone on the floor leaving the line connected. She was wasting valuable time trying to talk. Hopefully the operator would trace the call using the enhanced emergency service system. Valerie had reported a story on the new system months ago. It allowed police to capture the transmission from the satellite station and trace the origin of the call.

Meantime, the clock was ticking, echoing in her ears like a nagging insect. She grabbed Adam's shoulder, rolled the upper portion of his body onto his back, then reached for his pants leg and yanked the rest of his body over. He let out a low guttural moan.

"I'm sorry if that hurt," she whispered, not knowing if he could hear her. "Help me if you can."

She tucked Adam's gun in the front of his pants at the waist. Then she stood. The room started a slow rotation and a sharp pain shot through her side when she inhaled, doubling her over in agony. Clutching her left side she stumbled to Adam's feet. She bent over, pausing to stop the whirling, and grabbed his ankles.

But Adam's alligator boots prevented her from wrapping her hands completely around his ankles. She dropped to her knees. Wouldn't you think just once he could wear normal shoes? She yanked off first the right boot and then the left. Leaning backward her weight opened the rotted back door and she tossed the boots outside toward the path.

She rose again, closing her eyes against the stabbing pain.

She grabbed both of Adams' ankles and tugged. He barely budged. Every breath shot a pain to her side.

"Dammit Adam, help me." She grunted and dropped into a half squat to use her legs to drag him. She inhaled, ignored the jagged pain in her side and yanked. She almost fell over the threshold and Adam's feet were beyond the doorframe. That had to be a couple inches at least. He must be helping.

Now she shouted. "Again, Adam. We have to get out of here. Help me." She squatted and yanked again.

Gina cursed. "It's so damn dark, I can barely make out the driveways." She drove her car at a five-mile-an-hour crawl and aimed a flashlight out the driver's window, swinging it from side to side.

"You're doing fine," Vince said. "Just keep looking." He narrowed his eyes and followed the light shaft. He caught a glint of metal off to the left. "Wait, wait. Back up. What was that?"

Gina threw her car in reverse and backed up slowly, aiming the beam into the blackness. A battered black metal mailbox came into view and then Adam's black SUV.

Vince pointed excitedly. "Here! Here!"

Gina threw the car into park in the middle of the road and they jumped out. Vince came running around to her side of the car but he grabbed her before she could race up the driveway.

"Wait. Smell that?" His nose aimed into the air. She took a big whiff of the night air and coughed.

"Kerosene. Get your car out of here. Move Adam's if you can. I'll head inside." Sirens blared in the distance. Gina drove up the road a safe distance from the house then ran to Adam's vehicle, knowing his habit of leaving his keys under the floor mat. They were exactly where she expected to find them.

When she turned the key in the ignition, the headlights shined on Vince running along the right side of the house toward the rear, yelling for Valerie. She fumbled for the switch to move the seat closer to the pedals, backed out of the driveway, and parked the SUV behind her car. Then she raced toward the house.

~

Valerie was breathless, the pain in her side so strong she could barely move. She'd managed to drag Adam completely out the door and now he lay sprawled on the porch, his feet pointed toward the steps. What now? She couldn't possibly lift him, she could barely move herself. If she were able to drag him down the steps, surely his head would smack on each one, probably killing him. It was bad enough that her head was oscillating.

She actually thought she heard Vince calling her name. What she wouldn't give to have him here now. Suddenly, the alarm clock went off. She turned to look behind her into the house and watched in horror as the cigarette lighter emitted a spark onto a kerosene-soaked rag that immediately burst into flames.

She screamed a silent scream and turned back to Adam, prone and unresponsive. In her head, she heard Vince's childlike voice, "Stop, drop and roll, dummy, don't run."

She braced both her feet on Adam's side, one at his hips and one near his elbow, and shoved with all her might. Adam rolled over onto his stomach and she pushed again, rolling him over one more time and off the side of the porch. She stretched her legs out and rolled off the wooden porch after him just as the vapors inside the brick ranch met and married the flames and exploded into a balloon of fire.

~

The impact knocked Gina out of her shoes and onto her back on the gravel driveway. Stunned, she sat up and stared at the flames arcing up into the dark sky. She screamed Adam's name, jumped up and ran in the direction she last saw Vince.

She found him on all fours in the grass off to the side of the house, shaking. Gina reached him and screamed over the roar of the blaze, "Are you okay?"

Tears rolled down his face. She shook his arm forcefully. "They're not dead," she screamed, her own tears flowing. "I would know it. You would feel it. You'd know if she was dead."

Vince looked at her then turned his eyes to the house. The vapors had risen to the top of the rooms and the flames were burning high.

He wiped his nose on his sleeve and agreed. "Maybe they were in the basement. Let's go."

He grabbed Gina's hand and they ran toward the rear of the house. But when they rounded the corner they saw hot orange fingers of fire everywhere. They stopped short and stared helplessly.

Gina's entire body quaked. It couldn't be. They couldn't be dead. Not like this. She raised her right hand to her forehead to press away the thoughts. That's when she saw the black cowboy boot laying in the dirt. She tugged on Vince's arm and pointed.

Her eyes looked beyond where the boot lay to the collapsed porch that now was a heap of wooden debris. She took two tentative steps toward the mound of wood and wiped her eyes to focus. One white athletic sock stuck out between the slats. She turned and screamed to Vince, her words drowned out by the roaring furnace of fire. She pointed. She'd know that foot anywhere.

She rushed to the pile of broken wood and fell to her knees, frantically yanking pieces off the heap. Vince dropped down beside her. He dragged his shirt up over his head to protect his face and she did the same with her blouse. The heat was so intense she felt the skin on her exposed back burning and her eyelashes melting. Vince lifted a plank off Adam's back and revealed a small limp hand with a blue sapphire on the ring finger. Gina had admired the ring Valerie always wore. She'd said Vince had bought it for her last Christmas.

Furiously they began shoving the pieces of glass, plywood and plaster off of their bodies. She could hardly see or breathe. She thought she might pass out from the heat. Beside her Vince coughed and doubled over, then gritted his teeth and looked purposely at her. Neither of them stopped digging.

Suddenly, two gloved hands grabbed her shoulders and hauled her backward. She couldn't see who it was through the face mask but he motioned to his right and she saw a group of fully protected firemen running toward them, two of them aiming fire hoses at the flames. The cavalry had arrived.

A second pair of gloves grabbed Vince by the shoulders and dragged him backward, but he fought to keep digging for his sister.

Through the clear face shield, she recognized Bud imploring Vince with his eyes to let him lead Vince to safety. Behind Bud, two more of his counterparts motioned for him to let them do their job.

One of the men had uncovered Valerie and was lifting her into his arms. She was as limp as a rag doll. Two other men struggled with Adam, one grabbing his ankles and one lifting him up by the shoulders.

Vince nodded and leaned on Bud for support as they stumbled away from the fire.

The fireman holding her shoulders eyed her bare feet and lifted her into his arms as if she were a child. As he carried her away, she looked over his shoulder at Adam's lifeless body and burst into tears.

28

Valerie woke the next morning and wondered if there was any part of her body that didn't ache. Her brother was asleep in the chair by her bed. She smiled and reached for him, running her finger lightly along the stubble of his day-old beard. Vince sat up the minute her hand touched his face and grinned.

"Hi, you." He leaned in and kissed her on the cheek. "Don't you ever scare me like that again."

She smiled and tried to speak but she could only whisper. "Adam?"

He pointed to the ceiling. "He's one floor above us."

She croaked again. "Okay?"

"It's bad, Sis. He's in a coma. He hasn't regained consciousness."

She pursed her lips and tears sprang into her eyes. She sat up slowly and turned back the blanket.

Vince stopped her. "Whoa, what do you think you're doing?"

"Have to see him."

"He's unconscious, Val, he won't know you're there. You shouldn't be out of bed yet."

She raised her eyes to her brother. "Please."

"Don't look at me like that. You shouldn't...oh, all right. At least wait until I find a wheelchair, will ya?"

Vince knocked on the door to Adam's room and wheeled her in. Gina jumped from her chair and ran to embrace her, both of them wiping away tears.

She nudged Gina backward. "Adam?"

"We're not giving up. He has too much unfinished business here to leave us. That includes you."

A tremulous smile crossed her face and she nodded. Then she slowly dropped one foot to the floor followed by the other and raised out of the chair on her arms.

As if understanding her goal, Gina supported her and they walked to Adam's bedside. She squeezed Adam's hand and leaned to his ear to whisper an endearment.

She cast a glance to Vince and he jumped to assist her as she gingerly climbed onto the bed in a kneeling position and whispered to him again.

She shifted her weight and stretched out beside him, on top of the blankets as he had done all those nights when he'd climbed in bed with her. She propped herself up close to his chest. Taking his hand in hers she placed a kiss in his palm as he had done the night they danced. Then she clasped it to her heart and leaned to his ear again.

"I don't care who you are or what you do. I love you. Come back to me. We have so much to tell each other. We have a rodeo to ride, Tex. Don't leave me."

And just like that, his mouth moved. His lips turned up into the slightest smile. Gina and Vince closed in on the bed.

Valerie spoke louder this time, so everyone could hear. "Open your eyes, Adam." She caressed his cheek with a bandaged hand. There it was again. The slightest movement of his mouth.

Vince rang for the doctor and Valerie whispered to Adam. "I

want to dance with you again. I want your arms around me. I want to make love to you."

He didn't open his eyes but his lips definitely twitched. "It's a good sign," the doctor said after examining Adam. "It shows he can hear us. I'm more optimistic now, but there is no guarantee."

And so the vigil began. Gina, Vince, and others from the fire station decided they would sit with him in shifts, despite Valerie's declaration that she'd be there every minute until he woke up. Their goal was to keep constant sound around Adam, whether it was their voices talking to him, reading the newspaper or a magazine or playing his favorite country bands.

Even after Valerie's doctor discharged her, she refused to go home despite everyone's pleas. Her vocal chords remained damaged and she was restricted from talking unless it was absolutely necessary. But it didn't stop her from praying.

She sat alone with Adam on the fifth morning of his coma when he grew restless and began shifting in bed. He mumbled his name and her name. He gave orders.

She laid aside the book she was reading, lowered the volume on the CD player and limped to the bed. Caressing his forehead, she whispered, "C'mon, Tex. You should be mad at me. I threw your precious boots out the door. Wake up and scold me."

Although his eyelids remained closed, she detected movement beneath them. She squeezed his hand and rested her head on his arm. "Please Adam. Come back to me. I need to tell you I love you."

Her words made him smile. At least he thought he smiled. The fog in his head dissipated as she spoke, coaxing him out of the dark. His eyelids fluttered open and he blinked to clear his vision, his eyes darting around the room taking in his surroundings.

Beside him, a ragged plea. "Please, God, let him wake up."

He turned his head slightly and grimaced at the pain. Her head was between her arms, face down on the bed, praying for him. His arm felt like an anchor as he moved to touch her fingers. He swallowed and whispered, "You owe me a pair of boots."

Valerie's head snapped up and then she jumped to her feet. "Adam? Are you awake? For real? Say something else."

His gaze ran across her face and down to her bandaged hands. The wrap on her right side appeared to extend under the sleeve of her sweatshirt. A shiny salve coated the outside edge of her right ear and edged down her neck, lubricating scabbed skin. He wondered where else she was burned. Tears began to roll down her face even before he managed to smile at her.

"I love you too."

Through the waterworks, she grinned.

"It took you long enough to come back to me, Tex. I'm ringing for the doctor."

He knitted his eyebrows at her raspy voice, raised his hand and caressed her throat.

"Does it hurt?"

She shook her head. "I'm not allowed to talk until the vocal chords heal."

He rubbed his thumb along her jawbone. "Mmmm, I think I like that. Are you allowed to kiss?" Her eyebrows shot up and she grinned. Giggling like a schoolgirl she quickly leaned into his mouth to place a light kiss on the lips. Definitely worth waking up for.

She blushed when the door opened. "That will have to do for now."

Valerie adjusted his pillows then stepped aside for the doctor. "Welcome back, Agent Michaels." He patted Adam's arm. "I wouldn't move around too much if I were you. We'd rather keep you stable a little longer. How much pain do you have?"

Valerie resisted the urge to slap the doctor. Was that a rhetorical question? The color had drained from Adam's face and he winced when he tried to reposition himself, indicating the discomfort was high. At least the doctor didn't wait for an answer.

"I'll order a pain patch for you. That will help. I don't want you moving around. You have a hairline skull fracture that I'm worried about. That's the origin of the pain you feel radiating down your left side."

Adam raised his hand. "No pain meds. I can't be drugged up." The level of discomfort was reflected in his weakened voice.

The doctor nodded. "I understand that. This will be a topical relief patch, not something that will affect your whole system. But if I have to drug you to keep you still, I will."

Adam stared at him but when the doctor didn't back down, he offered a half smile and stopped moving. After the doctor left the room, Adam reached for her hand and said softly, "My head is pounding but it's important that we talk, sweetheart. I'll talk. You listen."

She smiled and nodded. He squeezed her hand. "I'm not Adam Mitchell. My real name is Adam Michaels..."

For the next hour he told her about his job, the racketeering case that brought Gina to Shots In The Dark, and the arson assignment he received that created the persona of Adam Mitchell.

"You and I actually met more than a year ago when you toured the agency. I don't know if you remember that."

How could she not recall meeting someone this handsome? She didn't.

"It's okay. I tried to get your phone number, but you blew me off."

Her eyes widened and her stomach dropped. She started to speak but he touched his finger to her lips.

"Ah, ah, no talking. It was just coincidence that I ran into you in the parking lot at Chez Cher's that night. By that time, my persona as Adam Mitchell already existed. I'm sorry for the deception but I hope you understand."

She'd listened to his recitation with trepidation, unsure how his story might end and afraid to hear how it involved her. She'd chewed the inside of her cheek nervously and folded and unfolded her hands in her lap. She removed a small notebook from her purse and, with a trembling hand, scrawled on the page. Tears rimmed her eyes as she turned the page for him to read. "Was it all fake? Everything you said and did?"

He squeezed her hand. "Not where you are concerned, darlin'. This is the hardest case I've ever had to work. I met a woman who stole my heart and I couldn't let her know. It tore me up that you didn't know my real name. Where you're concerned, it was the real thing. I hope you give me a chance to prove that to you. I don't know how else to apologize to you."

She knitted her brows in confusion and wrote again. "Do you think I'm mad at you?"

He looked deep into her eyes. "I wasn't truthful with you. It will be the last time, if you give me a chance to show you the real me. I hope to take you dancing again, to do all the things with you that I want to do. Can we start over?"

"Adam," she croaked. He raised his hand to silence her but she took it in both of hers and brought it toward her mouth. She kissed his fingertips and continued to speak. "I didn't kill a man and fight to keep you alive so I could be mad at you. I want to ask you for the chance to start over."

A grin split his face.

"Adam Michaels, huh?"

"Yes ma'am, at your service."

Gina walked in to find them laughing. She stopped short then realized her partner and best friend was alert and talking. She let out a small scream and ran to the side of the bed, trying hard not to cry. It didn't work. Adam embraced her and Gina gingerly hugged his neck. "You have no idea how scared I was."

He grinned sheepishly. "Sorry, Gina."

She straightened and looked from Adam to Valerie. "Are you two good?"

Adam looked tentatively at her and she smiled and shook her head enthusiastically.

He returned his attention to Gina. "Where ya been?"

She dropped into a nearby chair. "The coroner wants an inquest into Kwin's death."

Valerie gasped and he squeezed her hand reassuringly. "I don't remember anything beyond driving to that house. Can you tell me what happened?"

Gina reached for her briefcase and eased out a thick manila folder. "Valerie gave a complete and thorough statement to the police. She's incredible when it comes to details. Do you want me to read it to you? Does your head hurt?"

"Yes, my head hurts. But I can read it myself." He took the file of printed pages and began reading.

This had turned into an official briefing and she didn't belong. "Should I leave?"

Adam looked up from the page. "No ma'am. I don't want you out of my sight unless my eyes are closed to sleep. And then, I'd appreciate it if I could feel you beside me."

She blushed and Gina laughed. He continued to read. When he finished the final page, he laid it in his lap and turned to her. "Valerie. I don't know what to say. I read some of those paragraphs twice, feeling horror and unconditional love battle in my pounding head. Sweetheart, you're amazing."

She dropped her gaze, embarrassed, but couldn't suppress a smile.

He squeezed her hand and winked at Gina. "There's a lot of love in this room. I'm a pretty lucky guy."

EPILOGUE

Bud's obsession with Valerie turned out to be the key that unlocked both the arson case and the Sanchillio case. Kwin set up the computer monitoring programs for Bud, using his own cell phone to demonstrate the phone taps and tracking system.

Unbeknownst to Bud, Kwin already had Valerie under surveillance, in part because he found out she was checking the backgrounds of all the firemen but mainly because he had his own obsession with Vince. Bud was nosy by nature and never disconnected Kwin's number from the computer after Kwin's demonstration, which was how he knew Kwin monitored Valerie.

Jealousy made him record all of Kwin's conversations, including those with the Sanchillio brothers. When agents searched the Sanchillio home, they found evidence that they had paid Kwin to set the fires. Faced with arson and murder charges, the brothers agreed to cooperate and provided the evidence agents needed to close Gina's racketeering case.

Gina and Adam could return to their desks and resume their normal jobs. For Gina, it meant saying goodbye to Shots In The Dark and moving back in with her fiancé. In contrast, Adam expected a backload of case files on his desk that he'd ignored for weeks after being reassigned so hastily. He predicted the boss would complain about them not being completed. He was always in the dog house with that man.

Valerie strolled into his room the day he was discharged bearing a bouquet of pink roses and a shoebox with a bright red ribbon around it. Adam's heart skipped and he grinned. He reached for the roses, chuckling. "Hope you don't expect me to cry."

He opened the box and raised his eyebrows in surprise, admiring the black alligator boots. "Valerie, these are too expensive.

She smiled. "You said I owed you a pair. Try them on." Adam's doctor walked into the room. "Whoa, those are nice boots."

Slipping into them, he smiled at her. "They feel like they were made for my feet. Doc, are you gonna let me walk out of here in them?"

"Not exactly. Hospital policy is a wheelchair. I have some directions for you first. You're not out of the woods yet with this head injury. But you can lie around at home just as easily as in this hospital bed and probably be more comfortable. So I'll discharge you as long as you agree to keep the neck brace on at all times and take it easy. You are allowed very limited activity. Can someone stay with you?"

Before he could respond, Valerie cut in. "Don't worry doctor. He's coming home with me and I don't plan to let him out of my sight. If you need him to stay in bed, I'll keep him there."

"You will? I am?"

She looked at him defiantly. "I worked too hard keeping you alive to let you do something dumb on your own. Your recovery is in my hands."

"Aren't you going back to work?"

Ironically, the biggest news story of her career was the one she couldn't report herself. But the story made national headlines and Valerie received job offers from several larger radio stations and two major television stations.

"I plan to, once you're healed. Exactly where I work depends on whether or not we ride off into the sunset together." She giggled. "Remember, you have to teach me how to ride."

Adam laughed, unable to hide the mischievous grin on his face.

"You did make some pretty wild promises trying to wake me up. I may not remember everything that happened but I remember that." Heat crept up her cheeks.

He drew her into his arms and placed a light kiss on her forehead. "Ever had a cowboy?" he asked, moving his lips slowly toward her mouth.

Valerie grinned, wrapped her arms around him and raised her face to meet his. "Not yet."

The End —

If you enjoyed this book, please leave a review on Amazon.

More From This Author

BROKEN JUSTICE, BLIND LOVE

CHAPTER 1

S he lay dead at the bottom of the steps, contorted like a used bread tie. One tennis shoe had come off halfway through her descent and perched on the uncarpeted stair like an oil stain on an otherwise pristine driveway. Its mate remained on the woman's foot, which had rotated backward, pointing the toes inward instead of out.

The pale, translucent color of the woman's face made it obvious she was dead, but Patrolman Trish Kleerey checked anyway, careful to slip into latex gloves first. The woman's lifeless eyes remained opened in astonishment, as wide as bottle caps. Death surprised her.

Standing perfectly still, Trish scrutinized her surroundings, peering into the empty sunroom to her right and then the vacant living room on her left. The living room, its stone fireplace cold for months, spilled into an empty dining area. Visible sweeper runs ridged the beige pile carpet. No footprints left by a killer disturbed the straight lines.

All windows and doors appeared closed, at least from her present vantage point just inside the stained-glass door. The radio clipped to her shoulder epaulet pinged. "Officer Kleerey?

Homicide is on the way. They ask that you secure the scene and wait for their arrival."

She touched the transmit button. "10-4, Dispatch." There wasn't much to secure. A vacant house that had been on the market for months, one dead woman, and herself—both of them motionless. If she could explore the house, search the premises for clues, and employ her investigative skills, it might take the edge off her hunger for answers. She was the primary officer—earliest to arrive—on this murder scene. The murder was her first, a puzzle waiting to be solved. This was what Trish had trained for. She knew what to do and how to start, but homicide was on the way. Her job as a Recanturr patrolman was to do exactly what she'd done: report the incident and make sure nothing was disturbed.

Thirty minutes earlier as she contemplated her lunch break, she drove past the residence on routine patrol, and noticed the loose window screen on the side of the house flapping in the high winds. Spring in Northwestern Pennsylvania could be unpredictable, one day requiring overcoats and scarves and the next, teasing residents with a taste of summer. The weather forecast predicted this front would move through with two-days of storms, allowing March to exit like a lion.

Trish parked the cruiser in the driveway, struggled to yank the errant screen from its frame, and carried it to the front porch, intent on propping it up in the corner. She'd notify the real estate company listed on the sign in the front lawn when she returned to the station so they could replace it.

Was it curiosity or a sense of evil that edged up her spine, causing her to turn and peer through the oval glass window of the front door? One swift kick with her booted foot had freed the key from the lockbox and she'd stepped inside, caught off guard by the stench that assaulted her arrival. After checking for a pulse and contacting dispatch, Trish walked the outside perimeter of the house, noting all windows and doors were undisturbed. Then she returned to the woman, wondering how long she'd lain there and not wanting to leave her alone any longer.

Her career goal to make homicide detective could take its baby steps in this house, with this case, but she knew better than to tramp on her colleagues' toes. Some of the men already resented her. She'd graduated first in her class academically, received the expert marksmanship award on the firing range, and held her own on the department's obstacle course. She'd scaled a six-foot wall while wearing a thirteen-pound gun belt and dragged a one-hundred and fifty-pound dummy to safety. No easy task for her one-hundred-and-ten-pound frame.

No, better to make extensive notes regarding her observations of the victim and the scene and file her report. There would be other opportunities to lead an investigation. Besides, she had dinner plans with her best friend and she didn't want additional paperwork, which would force her to cancel again. Kandee complained the last time Trish postponed their pre-arranged dinner due to work. She didn't understand that crime didn't pay attention to a schedule and a cop couldn't always clock out at the end of an eight-hour shift. Kandee intimated that she'd made a special effort to carve out time for Trish, time that could have been spent with her new boyfriend, and Trish had wasted the evening by cancelling.

That conversation bordered on hurtful, but Trish dismissed it as bad moods on both their parts. This evening had been her idea and was meant to mend fences with her best friend. She didn't want to be accused of wasting any more of Kandee's precious time with Dwayne. Trish hadn't met this new boyfriend yet but that wasn't the issue. Kandee seemed different about this guy, guarded, close to defensive when Trish asked what she thought were normal girlfriend questions. He was in real estate, she knew that much, but Kandee hadn't offered much more information about how and where Dwayne made his living. Maybe she could learn more tonight. She'd have to gauge Kandee's mood first.

Tugging the door closed behind her, she strolled to the patrol car to retrieve her clipboard and await homicide. This wouldn't be the case to take her first-degree-murder virginity.

Kandee regarded her reflection in the mirror. It was just a simple slap. The impact against her tooth caused her lip to bleed, but only a tiny bit. No big deal. She'd endured much worse and she could argue that it was her fault. She shouldn't have mentioned his ex-wife's infidelity. Dwayne was so sensitive about it. Kandee had never given him any reason to distrust her and yet he was suspicious of her every move. Sometimes, it was difficult not to talk back.

She leaned in closer, canting her chin upward. Two fingerprints along her jaw line remained visible from where he'd squeezed her face last week, but those could easily be covered with makeup. The split lip and swelling presented more of a challenge. Especially since Trish Kleerey was already wary of Dwayne. Her cop's eagle eye spotted the fingerprints on Kandee's face the minute those two ran into each other at the grocery store last week and kissed hello. She'd raised a skeptical eyebrow when Kandee explained Dwayne had been overzealous with his love-making. He was an incredible lover when he wanted to be but the marks were from her hesitation to answer his question about a social media friend. At Dwayne's insistence, she unfriended the boy who spent four years sitting in the desk behind her in high school, despite her argument that he was married with kids and lived on the other side of the country.

Gently, Kandee dabbed beige concealer on her mouth and dug for her lip pencil. The combination of the outline and her darkest lip-gloss worked well. She'd have to remember to dab her mouth carefully with a napkin at dinner so as not to wipe it off.

Kandee smiled and waved when she spotted Trish sitting in the restaurant's back booth. Trish always kept her back to a wall in public venues. Ever the cop. Even as children, Trish strived to be aware of her surroundings, checking out the bleachers while she led the cheering squad on the football field and constantly scanning the room at high school dances, as if one of the pimpled teens would suddenly morph into a murderer. No one was surprised, especially not Kandee, when Trish graduated college first in her class with a degree in criminology and applied to various police departments. Recanturr Police snatched her up instantly, a no-brainer on their part, Kandee thought. The job pleased Kandee as well, since the City of Recanturr was eighty miles north of their hometown and they'd relocated together. Trish and Kandee grew up in Pittsburgh and loved the city, often making overnight trips back to the 'Burgh. Well, at least they used to, before Trish began working full-time.

Damn, Trish was still in uniform, which meant she'd worked later than planned. Kandee hated meeting her in cop mode. She'd chopped her short dark hair in an asymmetrical style with one side above her left ear and the right side to her jawbone. She supposed it fit neatly beneath Trish's police hat but Kandee thought the look was too severe. But then, Kandee had always been the girlie one of the two, using makeup and nail polish in middle school and devouring fashion magazines. Trish refused to pierce her ears, balked at Kandee's push-up bras, choosing instead to wear baggy clothes, and declined to put her five-foot-five frame into high heels. The rigid almost military Recanturr police dress code suited Trish–no jewelry, no nail polish and the barest of make-up. Kandee had always envied Trish's lush, naturally curly eyelashes and visualized even now how a touch of shadow and mascara would make her mahogany brown eyes pop.

She leaned over to plant a light kiss on her best friend's

cheek, careful to use the left side of her mouth. She plopped into the bench seat opposite Trish and immediately propped her chin in her hand, splaying her fingers out. "Sorry to keep you waiting. What's with the uniform? Are you in a time crunch?"

Trish's eyes narrowed. "No, I just got off duty and didn't take time to change because I didn't want to be late. I'm heading to the gym after dinner but I'm in no hurry. Tonight is just about us girls. It's good to see you."

"Oh, good. Do you know what you're going to order?" She opened the oversized menu and held it in front of her face. Seconds later, three fingers appeared at the top of the plastic-encased food list and nudged it down toward the table.

Trish stared at her. "What's wrong?"

She withered under Trish's stare. "Nothing. I'm starving, that's all. Why do you think something is wrong?"

Trish shrugged. "Well, you're acting oddly and," her eyes roamed Kandee's face slowly, studying it, "you look like something is off."

Kandee rolled her eyes. "Please turn off your cop radar and be my girlfriend for a change. I'm fine. Let's order."

Trish backed off, but only until after the waitress delivered steaming cups of tomato soup and gourmet grilled cheese sandwiches. "So how's Dwayne? When do I get to meet him?"

"He's fine. He's working a lot this week so I haven't seen him that much. He's been pretty busy. With your schedule and his, I've no idea when the two of you can meet."

"Oh? Well, busy is good, I guess. Has he sold some houses?"

"No, but he's had a number of showings. The housing market's in a slump right now."

"When was the last time he made a sale?"

She leveled her gaze on Trish. "Why?"

Trish's badge was polished to a high sheen and the light reflected off of it when she shrugged her shoulders. "Just curious."

"The housing market is very unpredictable. A realtor can close on multiple sales in one month and not have any in another. That's the nature of the business."

"So, he hasn't made any sales this month? And none last month either, as I recall. Does that upset him? Make him mad?"

This wasn't their first conversation about Dwayne and it wasn't the only time that Trish seemed hell-bent on putting him down. Trish hadn't even given him a chance, hadn't met him yet, but already she'd formed a negative opinion of him. She could be so unfair sometimes. Kandee shrugged and bit into her sandwich, wincing when the hot, gooey cheese touched her lip. She dropped the bread and grabbed her napkin.

"What happened to your lip?" Trish's right eyebrow arched with the question.

"I just now burned it with the cheese."

"No, it was swollen when you got here. What happened?"

Kandee faked a chuckle. "It was stupid, really. I dropped my earring and leaned over to pick it up and hit my face on the corner of the bureau."

"Which earring?"

"What do you mean which earring?"

Trish lowered her spoon and leaned back, crossing her arms beneath her chest. Kandee recognized this posture. She now sat across from Patrolman Kleerey, firmly planted in interrogation mode. "You are the master of minutia, my friend. You insert details into the simplest of sentences. Yet you can't tell me which earring you lost. You didn't say right or left, you didn't offer hoop or stud, you didn't provide any detail. So, what really happened to your lip? Did Dwayne hit you?"

A chill crept down Kandee's spine. Dammit. "The real question, Trish, is what happened to you? I don't even know you anymore. Ever since you put on that damned uniform, I've watched you change into something cold and calculating, constantly looking for the negative, always seeing the bad in people. People make mistakes. You should know that, you made a whopper years ago. No one is perfect and that goes for Dwayne. But you're so caught up in yourself, in your, your police presence, you can't see good in anyone. Do you even feel anymore? Are you capable of normal, human emotions?"

She rose, balling up her napkin and throwing it to the table, willing herself not to burst into tears. "I hit my face on the corner of the bureau, Officer Kleerey. If you want to turn that into a federal case, I don't think I have time for dinner." She pointed a shaky finger at Trish, already regretting her words. "The next time we meet, please bring my best friend instead of the cops. Or don't bother calling."

She pivoted and stormed out of the restaurant, her pulse racing. Hell's fire. Why did Trish always have to push so hard? It was an accident. He swung with his hand open. It was just a simple slap.

Trish's stomach dropped as she watched her lifelong friend bolt from the restaurant, her high heels clicking on the hardwood floor and her auburn ponytail swinging wildly as she hurried away. What just happened? It wasn't as if she was interrogating Kandee, she'd simply asked a question. A question she was certain she knew the answer to. She had this ability to sense things, like a psychic, although she didn't put much store in them. But it was true. It was as if she possessed a sixth sense, some kind of telepathy that warned her of trouble before it happened. It made her an outstanding police officer and had already saved her and her partner from life-threatening danger. She couldn't explain how she knew the door to the crack house was booby-trapped but she felt it and she'd begged her partner, Conner, to trust her. He hesitated, then acquiesced, and they backed off the front porch seconds before the device exploded. The force knocked them to the ground, flat on their backs, and they ached for days, but they survived. And, they snagged a solid arrest when the suspect tried to run out the back door.

Good cop, yes. Good friend? Apparently not. When had she forgotten how to be one of the girls?

Broken Justice, Blind Love is available on Amazon and through other eRetailers. Purchase your copy today on Amazon at
https://amzn.to/2rIut9I

Learn more about Rena Koontz — www.renakoontz.com